CORRUPT KNIGHT

KNIGHT'S RIDGE EMPIRE
BOOK 13

TRACY LORRAINE

1

BRIANNA

"I'm so sorry, Brianna. Things aren't usually this chaotic," my tutor says as she shuffles the paperwork before her, trying to find the one that relates to my new school placement.

To say I was relieved when I received my previous placement school and discovered that it wasn't Lovell Academy would be an understatement.

That place is the pits of hell, and the stories I heard from my previous school and the lucky teachers who had managed to escape only terrified me further.

But then, I made it three freaking days at the school I was allocated before my mentor was signed off sick with stress and no one was willing to take over.

So here I am again after a week of waiting for news, sitting in my tutor's office, praying the words 'Lovell Academy' don't roll off her tongue for my final student-teacher placement.

"It's fine. Everything happens for a reason, right? It obviously wasn't where I was meant to be."

"That's a great way of thinking. Fingers crossed this new school makes your last few weeks easier. Aha," she says, finally locating the piece of paper.

Her desk is a shitshow. How she manages to actually get any work done is a small miracle in itself.

"Okay, great." She scans the page and her brow wrinkles.

That one move makes butterflies erupt in my belly, and not the good kind.

Shit. It's Lovell, isn't it?

"I'm not sure we've ever had a student go here before," she says absentmindedly to herself.

"W-where is it?"

She looks up and the soft smile she gives me is anything but reassuring. It actually makes my stomach knot.

"Knight's Ridge College."

And I'm going to be sick.

"Brianna, are you okay?" my tutor asks, although I barely make out the words as my blood rushes past my ears and my head spins with this new reality.

Maybe Lovell wouldn't have been so bad.

I nod, although she doesn't look like she believes it.

"Knight's Ridge College is a fantastic school and sixth form. They are always rated outstanding and their results are second to none. It is a very exclusive school with above average fees to attend. It should be a very interesting few weeks, especially compared to where you've previously been."

You don't fucking say.

"I've heard of it," I force myself to say. "I-it should be interesting, for sure."

One single face pops into my mind before I even have a chance to shoot it down.

Nico fucking Cirillo.

I shake my head in the hope it'll force him out of it.

But it's pointless.

It has been since that fateful night Jodie and I met him and Toby in The Spot all those months ago.

His dark and dangerous eyes sucked me in the second I looked into them, and I was powerless but to allow him to sweep me under his spell. And then when he pulled me into his body and rolled his hips with mine in time to the music, I just knew.

I knew he was going to blow my mind and make me question life as I knew it.

Then Toby pulled out a baggie of Molly and I dived headfirst into the debauchery they could offer us.

I needed it. The previous few weeks at school had been hard going, and add everything Jodie had been going through with the loss of both her brother and her father, and life was tough.

I needed the release, she needed the release, and those two bad boys knew exactly how to deliver it.

If only I knew how thoroughly he was going to consume my life from that day on.

I thought they were going to be one-night stands. Hot, steamy, filthy-as-fuck one-night stands when Toby took us to Hades and let us all play out our wildest fantasies.

Even if I wanted to forget Nico, how was I meant to when he gave me the most memorable night of my life?

"Okay," my tutor says, studying me for a few more seconds as if she's scared I'm about to bolt. "They're expecting you first thing in the morning. Mrs. Hendrix, the Head of English, will be your mentor, and she will meet you in reception. Knight's Ridge College has high expectations of both their staff and their students, so make sure you go dressed to impress. They will take your appearance very seriously."

"Great," I mutter, glancing down at the leggings I'm wearing that are so overworn there's now a hole on my inner thigh, and the faded floral dress I threw over them before I left my flat this morning that I wore yesterday, and possibly the day before, without a second thought.

"You are a good teacher, Brianna," she assures me. "Your previous placements have loved you and your observations have been incredible. You have a way of engaging students of all backgrounds, and I have no doubt that extends to the type of students you will find at Knight's Ridge."

I just about smother my laugh at the polite way she describes the entitled, arrogant, pricks that I know attend there.

Okay, maybe that's a bit harsh. I've come to learn over the past few weeks that they're not all like that. Despite Nico's many, many flaws, his friends are pretty decent.

Toby, despite his initial... hiccup, shall we say, loves my best friend something fierce. He would die for her without even batting an eye, I know he would. Theo, Seb, and Alex are all... unique in their own ways, but their loyalty to their little family is unwavering. Daemon, well, I don't know all that much about that particular enigma, but I have it on good authority from Calli that he's pretty epic. I mean, she is secretly carrying his baby, after all...

And the girls... well, I've never met such loyal and supportive, empowered women in my life. From the second Jodie and I found ourselves in the middle of their group, I felt like I had found my home.

Other than Jodie, I've never really had any solid, ride-or-die girlfriends. Most of the ones I've had over the years have turned out to be nothing but shallow users who'd rather bring others down than help build them up. To say those experiences have made me wary of women's true intentions over the years would be an understatement, but those Cirillo girls... damn, they're fierce in a way I've only ever hoped to be over the years.

"Hold your head up high and walk into that place like you own it. They will appreciate your strength, resilience, and determination."

"I hope you're right," I mutter, feeling anything but confident about what I'm about to do.

"Now go and enjoy an extra day off. Get your head on straight, ready for tomorrow. I'll be at my computer all day, so if you have any questions or concerns, you know where I am."

It's on the tip of my tongue to confess that the guy I've been fucking on and off for the past few months is a year thirteen at Knight's Ridge College. That there is no way on this Earth I should be putting myself in the position to stand at the front of a classroom and have to put up with his stupidly handsome face. But my lips don't part and the words never see the light of day.

Instead, I take the piece of paper with all the information I need about my new placement and stand from the chair.

"Thank you for all your help with this. Let's hope we can get through to the summer without any more issues."

"I have every confidence in you, Brianna. There is a school out there that will be very lucky to have you as a member of their staff come September."

"Here's hoping," I mutter, making my way toward the

door. Every movement is hard with how tight my body is locked up.

With a grateful smile, I pull her door closed, but I don't allow myself to react to what has just happened until I'm a safe distance from the university building and then I let out the loudest, stress-releasing scream I can manage.

If only it actually helped.

By the time I've somewhat got my head around the situation, I'm in the middle of the park watching the ducks swim around in the small pond in the hope they bring me some calm.

My tutor is right, Knight's Ridge College is an incredible school. But is it the kind of school I want to be teaching in? Are the rich, entitled princes and princesses that attend going to be the kind of students I'm able to connect with?

While I might have been worried about the behaviour and violence in Lovell, I can't deny that that kind of secondary school is something I can understand.

Hell, I went to more than one, after all. Not as bad—nowhere is as bad—but I can talk to those kids. Many have hard lives, parents who either spend all their waking hours working to put food on the table or doing absolutely fuck all and taking every handout they can get while ignoring their child's existence.

But the uber wealthy?

How am I going to be able to relate? They're all driving around in cars I can only dream of, wearing jewellery I'd be too scared to even touch. They spend their summers holidaying in places like Bora Bora and the Seychelles. I'm lucky if I can afford to do a weekend in freaking Butlins.

I blow out a long breath as I lower my arse to a bench.

You've got this, Brianna.

A few little rich kids will not get the better of you.

Nico fucking Cirillo will not get the better of you.

"Fucking prick," I mutter to myself.

I know he's just been through something beyond traumatic, losing his dad the way he has, but he's been an even more unbearable prick than ever.

All any of his friends are trying to do is help, to support him through it, but he's shutting himself down, preferring to lose himself in a bottle of whatever alcohol he can get his hands on first.

They all thought I'd be the one to pull his head out of his arse, but just like I predicted, every time I've tried to reach out, to try and do... anything, it's been thrown back in my face. Or more so his door has been slammed in my face.

Pulling my phone from my bag, I ignore the notifications and find my best friend's number, hitting call the second I find her smiling face.

I silently pray that she's going to be able to answer. I need someone to tell me that I'm overreacting.

Nico has barely been at school since his dad died. He might have exams in a few weeks, but his education seems to have taken a back seat. Rightly so, I guess. I mean, I've never had a parent I give any kind of fucks about, so I wouldn't really know the right or wrong way to deal with one dying.

I helped Jodie through losing her old man, but then he turned out to be just as fucked up as every other parent figure—her mum aside—that I've had any real experience with.

Lifting my phone to my ear, it rings twice before it cuts out.

"Fuck," I hiss, slumping back on the bench.

It dings a second later.

> Best bitch: At work. Break in 30 if you wanna meet.

> Brianna: Getting an Uber right now. I have a situation…

> Best bitch: Hurry. kiss emoji

Thankfully, there's an Uber right around the corner, and in less than two minutes, I'm in the back of his car and we're heading across the city to where my bestie is now working… at a sex club. Coolest best friend ever.

The driver's eyes meet mine in the rear-view mirror after he pulls to a stop outside Hades, and I can easily read the curiosity within his dark stare.

"Have you had the opportunity to visit?" I ask, knowing full well that the chance is very slim.

Hades has a waiting list a mile long and the membership is astronomical—not something the everyday Londoner could ever even consider affording. But I don't like to judge; this guy could be a secret millionaire. Weirder things sure have happened.

"Unfortunately not. I'm sure intrigued, though. I've heard all kinds of stories."

"Well, do you want me to let you in on a secret?" I ask, leaning forward as if I have something really special to tell him.

"Always. You know us cabbies. We're experts at keeping secrets."

I can't help but bark a laugh at his teasing tone.

"Okay, well..." I pause, building the anticipation. "I can tell you without doubt that everything you've heard about this place is true. Ultimate adults playground. Now," I say, pushing the door open and stepping out, "enjoy the rest of your day. I know I will."

I'm still chuckling as I nod at the bouncer and head inside. I've been here to meet Jodie enough times now for almost all the staff to recognise me on sight—they don't even bother asking me for my membership card that I was happily gifted by my epic bestie. Like I said... Coolest best friend ever.

The lighting changes as I descend despite it still being morning and the place not actually being open yet, and the air turns heated, electric even. My skin prickles, memories threatening to pop up of the time I spent here with Nico.

Damn, that was a hot night I wouldn't mind repea— *No, Brianna. Do not go there.*

The bar is deserted, the stages, hanging platforms, and poles that are usually showcasing some of the city's hottest dancers empty. There is a part of me that wants to hop on up there and pretend I'm even half as seductive as they are every night of the week, turning patrons into nothing but puddles of need.

There's a bang on the other side of the bar that stops me from playing out the fantasy in my head before footsteps head my way.

"I can put some music on if you want to give me a one-woman show?" Jodie asks, amusement lacing her tone.

"I think we both know that I'm nowhere near good enough yet."

"Yet? So you're thinking of jacking in this teaching thing for a life of debauchery and sex?"

I blow out a long breath and turn away from the stage that held my attention.

"Right now, I'm seriously considering it, yeah," I mutter quietly.

"What happened?"

"Pour me a drink and I'll confess all my sins."

2

____

BRIANNA

"Oh shit," Jodie gasps when I pass her the piece of paper with my fate printed on it. "What the hell are you going to do?"

"There's nothing I can do. I can't tell them it's inappropriate because I've fucked one of the students."

Jodie's lips part to argue, but she quickly thinks better of it.

"And there isn't anywhere else?"

I shake my head.

I mean, I didn't exactly ask that question, but seeing as every other student teacher in the city will now be allocated a placement, I hardly doubt that there are schools out there just begging for one.

"This isn't something that is up for discussion, Jojo. I've got to complete this placement to pass." This is something she is more than aware of, after watching me freak out when my last placement went south last week.

"I know, I know. But Knight's Ridge?"

"I probably won't even see him," I reason. The reality of that is entirely possible.

Knight's Ridge College might have a relatively small student population compared to others in the city, but the grounds are colossal, from what I've heard. I've never actually stepped foot inside the gate. People like me just... don't.

"Probably not. But you might. You need to tell him."

I stare at her.

"What?" she asks. "He might open the door this time."

I shake my head, reaching for the glass of... I'm not entirely sure what it is.

"This had better be strong," I mutter before taking a sip of the almost neon liquid.

The second it hits my tongue, the alcohol burns and a satisfied moan rumbles in the back of my throat.

"If that desperate groan was anything to go by, you really should go and see him."

"Shut the fuck up. It's... it's been a while, I confess."

"Brad still away?"

"Yes," I hiss, feeling all kinds of frustrated about that fact. "It's not fucking funny," I snap when all she does is laugh at me.

"I know, I'm sorry," she says, doing a really shitty job of covering her amusement.

After draining my drink, I slump back in the booth Jodie directed us to.

"Tell me something good."

"The guys only have a couple of weeks of lessons left before exams start."

"I said something good," I groan. "Does my tutor seriously think I'm going to fit in there? I mean, look at me," I say, gesturing to the disaster that's staring back at my best friend.

"You're gorgeous and intelligent, and the kids of Knight's Ridge will be lucky to have you. It's only a few weeks, and before long you'll be looking forward to starting your first job and you'll realise that you're totally over-reacting."

"Am I, though?"

She glares at me, giving me her textbook Brianna's-being-an-idiot-again look.

"Yes. You are. But because I'm an awesome friend, tell me what you need to make this more bearable."

"I need to go shopping. I can't turn up tomorrow like this. I need... I need a fucking miracle. Or a lottery win."

"Well, seeing as you don't play, that's unlikely, but I have the next best thing." Something wicked sparkles in her eyes.

"Which is?"

"Wait here."

In a flash, she's gone and running across the bar.

I stare at my empty glass, wishing some other kind of miracle would happen and it would refill itself. Logically, I know that I haven't eaten and getting wasted is the worst kind of idea right now. But the temptation to drown all this bullshit is almost too much.

The second she's back, she slides something across the table before me beneath her palm.

"What?" I ask, waiting for her to reveal her trick.

"Ta-da," she squeals happily.

"Oh no. No. No. No. There is not fucking way that I'm—"

"You are. Toby has already approved it and agreed to take the shit for it."

I stare down at the Amex black card before me, my stomach knotting uncomfortably.

"You want to walk in there tomorrow with your head held high and feeling like you fit in?"

"Yes, but—"

"No, buts. He owes you."

"Orgasms, yes. Money, no."

"Babe, he probably won't even notice. You do know how loaded they are, right?"

"I try not to think about it." The kind of figures I've heard them talking about absolutely terrifies me.

I'm much more comfortable knowing that I have a twenty-pound note and a few coppers in my purse and have managed not to dip into my overdraft by the end of the month.

"Come on," she says, pocketing the credit card and reaching for my hand.

"We can't do this, Jojo."

"Of course we can, come on."

She physically drags me out of the booth and across the club.

"Don't you have to work?" I ask, looking back as if I'm expecting her fierce yet utterly terrifying boss to jump up and stop us.

"Nope. I'm free as a bird as of right now, and I want to go spend some Cirillo money."

"You know it's all drug and blood money, right?"

"And you're arguing about spending it, why?"

My lips part to argue, but I quickly discover I don't really have anything to come back with.

"Exactly. If it makes you feel any better, you can buy him something special for when you go and confess to being his new teacher," she teases. "Ow."

"It is not funny."

"It is a bit, though. Are you going to make him call you Miss Andrews? Or maybe it's ma'am there, because it's so posh."

"Shut your trap, bitch."

"Matron? Oh no, they're the ones who live in, aren't they?"

"I guess it could be worse, I could be expected to board," I mutter as we climb the stairs back up to reality.

"I bet all sorts goes on in those rooms."

"I don't want to think about it. We know how bad the boys are."

"Only two left to be wild. Well, until Nico sorts his shit out."

"Not gonna happen, Jojo. I'm not falling for a man like Nico." But even as I say the words, I can't help but wonder if it's already too late. If it was too late from that very first moment he touched me, kissed me, forced me to look into those wicked dark eyes.

"Sure, you're not. Brianna Cirillo does have a good ring to it, don't you think?"

I can't help but bark out a laugh.

"Even if I ever considered it, there is no way Nico will ever make that kind of commitment."

"Maybe he'll have to," she muses as she unlocks her fancy little car when we get close.

"What's that supposed to mean?"

"No one knows what's going to happen now. With Evan dead, there is every chance that Nico could take his job."

I wait until we're inside her car to respond.

"They can't actually think he's capable. He's barely emerging from his flat. He can hardly be second-in-command of the fucking mafia."

"He's grieving," she argues, making me feel like the shittiest person in the world.

"I know. I just... fuck."

"It'll take time. But there's nothing saying that when he comes out the other side he won't be capable. There's a lot to Nico we've yet to see."

"I'm only really interested in one part of him," I quip.

"That's not true, and you know it," she barks with a laugh. "You wouldn't be satisfied with just his cock, or his tongue. You need multiple parts."

"Yeah, his fingers too," I add quietly.

"You should have just taken me home," I argue when Jodie pulls her little car into the underground car park beneath the building she now lives in with Toby. It also happens to be the building where Nico is more than likely hiding in his flat.

"Brianna, what have you done with your lady balls?" she asks, making me rear back. "You are the strongest, most determined woman I know—and my life is now full of pretty fierce ones, so that is a huge fucking compliment. Yet one school placement has derailed you."

I let out a sigh. "I've been coming off the tracks for a while."

"Life's been hard," Jodie says. "With Joe's death and then..."

"You don't have to say it. I know. I know all of it. I could just do with a break from it all, you know?"

"We will. When you and the guys have finished school, we're all going to get away and just leave all this shit behind."

"I'm not sure."

"This isn't up for discussion, Bri. I want a break with my boy and my girl. No arguments."

"Fine," I concede because she's right. We do need it. And I am not myself right now.

Things haven't been right since... I'm not even sure when exactly, but I have every suspicion it coincides with a certain monster-cock-wielding male's arrival in my life.

Or maybe it was Valentine's.

Things definitely changed that night, and not just because I had a long time to think about everything after the prick left me handcuffed to a bed with nothing but my twitching muscles and his mouth-watering scent to remind me of how good it was for those few moments.

"Come on. You'll feel better when you've spoken to him."

Pushing the driver's door open, she climbs out, leaving me little choice but to follow.

My anxiety heightens as we climb through the building —not that Jodie notices. She's too busy messaging someone, Toby probably. And she only tucks her phone away when we finally spill out of the lift on the top floor.

Nico's floor.

With my bags in hand and the guilt I feel over spending his money sitting heavy in my stomach, I hold my head high and march toward his floor.

"He's in," Jodie confirms as we get closer.

"Great."

I suck in a deep breath as I come to a stop in front of the matte black door with a big, modern chrome number two in the middle. It sits right above the peephole, which is going to ensure he knows exactly who is standing on the other side. Again.

I have been talked into being here way too much recently.

Jodie and the others seem to think that I'm going to be the one to get through to him.

I think they're all delusional.

Nico is only interested in me when I'm on my back with my legs spread or on my knees with my lips wrapped around his cock.

Glancing back at Jodie, who is standing off to the side and out of view with her own bags hanging from her fingers, I lift my hand and press my finger to the buzzer.

Nothing but silence follows, but that's hardly a shock.

He's yet to willingly open the door to me.

The only time he has was when I started promising to do things I really shouldn't have while standing out in the hallway of an apartment building. Thank fuck it's mostly deserted and the only people who live on this floor wouldn't bat an eyelid at the levels I'd lowered myself to.

"Nico, it's Brianna," I shout like an idiot. "We need to talk."

Nothing.

"He's not going to let me in," I tell Jodie confidently.

"Promise what you did last time," she says teasingly.

"Umm..." I pause.

"Nico. Please. It'll be quick."

"That's what she said," Jodie deadpans.

"Seriously?" I bark, but all she does is give me an innocent face and shrug.

"Reinforcements will be here in a minute," she assures me, checking her phone once more.

"What is that meant to—" My words are cut off as the ding of the lift's arrival fills the air and voices float down to us.

"Oh look out, the cavalry has arrived," Jodie teases a

beat before Toby rushes around the corner and sweeps her up into his arms.

"Hey Bri," he says over her shoulder before slamming his lips down on my girl's and thoroughly distracting her as Theo and Emmie emerge from behind him.

"Ugh, put her down, man. "It's only been a few hours," Theo quips, forcing Toby to release Jodie for a bit so he can flip the leader of their group off.

Laughing at Toby, Theo turns his eyes on me.

This guy might only be eighteen, but he oozes power and danger like no one ever had the pleasure of meeting before. And I'm pretty sure he doesn't even try, it's just ingrained. Like it's in his DNA or something. Which it kind of is.

The heir to the entire Cirillo Family.

I guess really, I should be worried if he was anything less than the enigma he is.

"Not opening up?" he asks as if it's not obvious.

"Nope, are you sure he's even in there?"

Pulling his phone from his pocket, Theo turns the screen my way.

"He could have left his phone and fucked off out."

"Could have. But he hasn't."

"Right, well. He's ignoring me. Again. So I'm just going to go and—"

"No," Jodie cries, ripping her lips from Toby's, proving to me that she was listening despite having her face half sucked off. "You need to talk to him."

Suspicious eyes turn on me, and I feel about two feet tall as I stand there, wishing the ground would just swallow me up.

An image of me standing in front of all of them in a classroom at Knight's Ridge pops into my head and a shudder runs down my spine. Although, none of them are the scary ones. They'll all give me a free pass, maybe even be supportive during the time they have left there. But the guy on the other side of the door? He's an entirely different story.

Theo looks between the two of us, his brows knitted together.

"Is everything all right, Brianna?" he asks, sensing something bubbling up inside me.

"Yeah, she's just—"

"Jojo," I hiss, cutting her off. I'm not ready to tell everyone about this yet. At least, not until I've got my own head around it. "This was a bad idea. I'm just gonna go, and I'll catch up with him—" But as I step away, a beep fills the hallway before a door opens behind me.

"Go talk to him, Brianna," Theo says, his voice hard and allowing no space for argument.

He might not know what's going on, but clearly, he's read the seriousness of it.

"Umm..."

I meet Jodie's eyes, and they soften in encouragement.

"Go try and fix my boy, Bri," Toby begs, pain for his best friend showing on every inch of his face.

"Fuck. I—" I suck in a breath. "I don't think I hold that kind of power."

Without instruction from my brain, my legs take me closer to Nico's now open door.

A bolt of nerves shoots through me as I stare into the darkness within.

"You do, Bri," Toby assures me.

"Don't take his bullshit," Theo states. "Don't let him push you away."

Easier said than done.

Sucking in a huge breath, hoping I can drag some strength and confidence to go into battle with Nico, I step inside his flat and close the door behind me.

"N-Nico?" I shout, my voice cracked with nerves and anticipation for what I'm about to find. If the smell is anything to go by, it's not going to be pretty.

3

———

NICO

Something drags me from the dark depths of nothingness I've managed to sink into and I fight to stop it.

Down here, nothing can touch me, nothing can hurt me, and I can pretend that everything is okay.

That my world hasn't completely fallen apart.

The second reality comes back, so does the pain, the despair, the utter hopelessness I've found myself drowning in since the first explosion ripped through the country club that night.

It's like I'm stuck on a merry-go-round, only I'm not trapped living the best time of my life with happy music and brightly coloured horses and flashing lights. I'm trapped in the pits of hell, barely clinging on to a life I can hardly remember from before that night.

A life where everything had a place, where everything was as it should be. Where we ruled the city with an iron fist and took down anyone who got in our way.

But they beat us.

They fucking beat us, and they ripped us in two.

They ripped me in two, straight through my heart.

I care about very few things in my life, but the man they took from me that night was right up there at the fucking top of that list.

Squeezing my eyes closed, I offer up anything I have to stop the inevitable, but it's pointless. The crash of my slamming front door brings me fully back to, and soft footsteps close in on me.

Cracking my eyes open, I blink against the darkness that surrounds me.

I have no idea what time it is, whether it's actually still light outside or not. The blinds and curtains in this place haven't been open since I returned after that night.

I don't want to live in the light when I'm drowning in the darkness within me.

For a few seconds, I see nothing, no one.

But then, brightness sears into my eyeballs and I roar in frustration as my entire flat is bathed in sunlight.

Pushing from the sofa, I stand on unsteady legs, wincing as I fight to find the intruder who's decided to come torture me.

My eyes water as I stare at the brightness, everything blurred for long seconds until a vision appears in front of me.

"Siren?"

With the light streaming in from the windows, she looks like an angel.

Her light blue eyes find mine and a smile pulls at her lips as if she's pleased to see me.

Before I know what's happening, my legs are moving and I'm closing the space between us.

She gasps as she reads my intentions and takes a step back, but it's nowhere close to being enough to stop me.

Her back crashes against the windows behind her a beat before my fingers cup her face and I slam my lips down on hers.

Memories of the last time I caved and let her inside fill my mind.

Aside from being wasted or high, it was the only time I was able to get out of my head. The only time I've managed to lessen the pain.

Brianna Andrews.

The light my darkness craves.

My lips move against hers. I'm so lost in the promise of what she can give me that I don't notice that she's not returning my kiss, that her body is frozen against mine as I pin her against the window.

"Nico," she gasps when I kiss down her neck, biting down on her sensitive skin. I ignore the fact that it's not a demand to continue but a plea for me to stop.

I can't stop.

I don't want to stop.

I need her.

I need—

"FUCK," I bark, backing up the second she pushes harder against my chest, forcing me away from her.

Something that's already battered and broken inside of me cracks open wider at her rejection, and pain once again lashes at my inside.

"NO," I boom. "You're meant to make it better. You're meant to take it all away."

"Nico."

"Please, Siren." My voice cracks, but I'm powerless to stop it, or to even care. "I need y—"

She rushes forward, catching me before I confess that final word and collapse in a broken heap on the floor.

Her arms wrap around me and it feels so fucking good.

Too fucking good. But I don't have it in me to do anything about it.

My pain overrides my fear in this moment, and I'm more than happy to allow it.

We stand like that for the longest time, her holding me together, keeping all my jagged parts from falling away and stopping me from bleeding out all over the floor.

Since forcing myself to go back to school, putting a brave face on has been getting harder and harder.

I'm not ready to return to the world. I need time. I need... fuck knows what I really need. But sitting in a class prepping for my upcoming exams certainly isn't it.

But it's what's expected of me. What I have to do.

My future... my future is...

Some kind of pained sob rips from my throat and Brianna's soft voice meets my ear.

"It's okay. I've got you."

I suck in a shuddering breath as I continue to allow her to hold me.

It's not something I ever thought I'd let happen, but here we are.

I never thought I'd have to say goodbye to my dad, either. Well, not for a good few years at least.

I have no clue how much time passes with us locked in our embrace, but eventually, my alcohol-filled mind finally senses that we're moving.

Lifting my face from the crook of Brianna's neck, I find that we're standing in my en suite.

"Wha—"

"You need to shower, Nico. You fucking stink."

I watch her as she releases me as if she isn't even real,

just a vision my fucked-up head thinks it should taunt me with.

Sounds about fucking right.

And if she is nothing more than a figment of my imagination, I bet I won't even be allowed to lose myself in what she can really offer me. Her hug might have been nice—not that I'll tell her that—but pushing inside her tight cunt would be so much better.

The sensation of my school tie being pulled through my collar successfully drags me from that little fantasy and I look down, watching as her slender fingers make quick work of my shirt buttons.

A growl rumbles deep in my throat as her hot hands slide over my shoulders, pushing the fabric away.

"Just can't wait to get me naked, huh?"

Her eyes find mine, but unlike what I'm used to, I don't find the fire that usually burns within them when we're this close. All I find is pity, sympathy. It's almost enough to force me to put an end to this, to send her away like I should have done the second I found her in my space. But I don't, because after dragging my shirt from my arms, her knuckles brush down my abs as she reaches for my waistband, and I cave to that fantasy once more as she undoes my trousers and shoves both them and my boxers down my legs.

Her teeth sink into her bottom lip as she watches my cock bob between us.

I might be irreparably broken after the fallout of that night, but it seems my dick still wants to party despite the amount of alcohol I've tried to drown myself in.

Dropping to her knees, she rips her eyes from my dick in favour of my feet so she can free them from my remaining clothes until I'm standing before her, a naked, broken and empty shell of a man.

The ruthless soldier I always believed I was is long gone.

In his place is this... this...

"It'll get easier, Nico. I promise," she says, throwing my clothes aside and standing to her full height again, sadly not stopping to wrap those luscious lips around me. Although what she said when she pushed me in here is true, I'm more than aware of the fact that I can't remember the last time I showered. I'm not sure I could pay her enough to suck me off right now.

Planting one hand in the centre of my chest, she forces me back until we're standing inside my walk-in shower.

"Clean up," she instructs, reaching out to turn the shower on, probably more than aware I'm about to get blasted with ice-cold water. Sadist. "I'll be right ou— Argh, Nico," she screams when I don't let her jump away from the water and instead haul her against my body as it rains down.

"Let me go, dickhead."

"Later. Right now, I need help cleaning up."

Spinning her around, I push her up against the tiled wall and slam my lips down on hers once more as the water soaks her through.

She resists again, but she can't keep it up this time, and after a few seconds, her body relaxes against mine and her lips part, letting me in.

"Yes, Siren," I groan into her kiss. "You know the only real way to clean up my dick is with your sinful mouth."

She arches from the wall as a groan of need rumbles deep in her throat. Wrapping my hand around her thigh, I hitch her leg up around my waist, allowing me the space I need between her thighs to grind against her.

"More," I moan, gathering up the wet fabric of her dress and dragging it up her body.

Our kiss breaks for as long as it takes for me to pull it over her head, and long before it lands at our feet with a wet slap, we've collided once more.

It's been like this between us since that first night.

Addictive and never fucking enough.

Her bra hits the tray, my hands lifting to palm her breasts and pinch her nipples, making her moan with need.

"Tell me how badly you need my cock, Siren."

"Nico," she whimpers as I continue to grind against her, building her higher and higher without even really touching her.

Right before she's at the point of no return, I drop her leg and step back.

"What the— You fucking cock."

A smirk curls at my lips, and for the first time since I woke and found her here, I'm starting to feel like my old self.

"I thought you already knew, Siren," I warn, my voice low and raspy. "I'm worse than that." I drop to my knees before her, water bouncing off my back as I stare up at her.

Her chest heaves, her insane tits holding my attention for long seconds before I finally rip my eyes away in favour of capturing hers.

"The only place you're coming before I get my dick inside you is on my face."

A startled shriek rips from her throat as I suddenly drag her leggings and knickers down her legs. The flimsy fabric of her leggings rips long before I get to her knees and it turns me into a savage.

Pulling harder, I shred the rest of her clothing from her body, leaving her standing there in just a pair of socks.

"Fuck it," I mutter, lifting one of her soaked feet from the ground. I throw her leg over my shoulder and dive for her cunt.

The second her taste explodes on my tongue, I fully embrace that old part of myself that seems to come alive when we're like this.

"NICO," Bri screams above me as I suck hard on her clit. Her fingers sink into my wet hair and twist, trying to drag me closer. "Fuck. Yes. Make me come, baby," she demands like the desperate little whore she is.

Shifting a little, I push her leg up wider for better access and thrust three fingers inside her without any warning.

She screams for me as I set a brutal pace, sending her into a frenzy as I push her right to the edge of release and pull her back just as fast.

"Nico, you cunt. Let me come," she barks, her grip on my hair turning brutal. But I don't give a fuck. She can rip it all out, for all I care. All I want right now is for this to never, ever fucking end.

This is better than alcohol. Than drugs. Than fucking anything.

Just her, that's all I—

"NICO. Fuck. Fuck. FUCK," she screams as I rub against her G-spot just so and send her crashing over the edge.

I lap at her clit, let her ride out every second of her release. She deserves some kind of reward for being stupid enough to walk in here tonight. There's every chance she could have got a darker side of me that I've discovered in the past few weeks and ended up leaving with a very different kind of injury than what's filling my mind right now.

The second her grip loosens on my hair, I twist to the

side and sink my teeth into her thigh. Her skin breaks, the taste of copper filling my mouth, but it doesn't stop me.

"Argh, you fucking savage," she screams, trying to make me release her by pulling at my hair.

"Yeah, Siren," I mutter, looking up at her with a smirk.

Her eyes dip to my mouth, letting me know that her blood is coating my lips, and all the air rushes out of her lungs.

"My filthy little whore," I murmur before leaning forward and licking up the blood that's spilling down her thigh.

She hisses in pain, but it's going to take more than that to stop me.

Surging to my feet, I wrap my hand around her throat, pinning her back against the tiles. Her eyes are wild with desire, her own lip split from where she must have bitten it when she came.

"Whose whore are you, Siren?"

"Yours," she breathes, and I reward her with my lips.

She groans into our kiss as she tastes herself on my tongue and shamelessly grinds against me.

"You want my cock, Siren? Is that why you came here tonight? You can't find anyone else in the city who can make you scream like I can, huh?"

Wrapping my hands around the backs of her thighs, I lift her from the floor, my cock brushing against her sensitive cunt and finding her entrance.

"Nico, please," she whimpers.

"Not until you answer me."

I stare into her eyes, already knowing the answer but wanting to hear her say it.

Something I don't recognise flashes in her eyes, but it's gone before I get a chance to question it.

"Yes," she moans. "I came here so you could fuck me and remember the world is still turning outside your flat."

"I'm more than fucking aware," I growl, thrusting deep inside her, stealing her breath and hopefully any more talk about reality. I don't need to be thinking about anything outside of this shower right now, let alone the flat or the building.

None of that exists.

The only thing that does is her and this moment.

She screams as I thrust into her over and over, forcing her to slide up the wall and her nails to pierce my shoulders as she tries to hold on.

"You're not the only one," I grunt, mindlessly spilling words as I lose myself in the feeling of being inside her once again. "Best cunt in the city by far."

"NICO," she screams, her pussy clamping down as she comes for me, and I have no choice but to fall right along with her.

But just as pleasure rips through me, my eyes open and I find myself staring up at my bedroom ceiling as pain, grief, and loneliness crash into me once more, right alongside the pounding of my head from my never-ending hangover.

4

———————

BRIANNA

I'm awake long before my alarm goes off the next morning. My stomach is in knots, my heart is racing, and it's not entirely because of my new placement.

It's him.

It's always fucking him.

My phone dings on my nightstand, and stupid, naïve little butterflies erupt in my belly at the thought of finding his name lighting up my screen.

I hate myself even more when disappointment floods my veins when the inevitable happens.

> Best bitch: Stop stressing. You're going to kill it today. And if he has anything to say about it then… fuck him. Not literally— you'll be in a school, remember. *winky emoji*

"Sound advice there, Jojo," I mutter to myself.

> Brianna: Thank you. He was so wasted last night, I doubt he'll even show his face.

I squeeze my eyes closed and suck in a deep breath the second my thumb hits the send button.

> **Best bitch:** You sure you don't want Toby to tell everyone?

> **Brianna:** I've got this. I can handle the wannabe bad boys.

> **Best bitch:** Wannabe?

> **Brianna:** Yep. Wannabe.

But even as I type that message out, I know it's bullshit.

Those beautifully broken, corrupt boys rule that damn school. And if Nico doesn't want me there, then I have no doubt that he'll find a way to get me out very, very fast.

Hell, for all I know, I'm not even going to make it into reception to meet Mrs. Hendrix.

I step out of my building, the brand on my thigh stinging, a reminder of everything I'm trying to forget, and scan my eyes down the row of cars that line my street, wishing that one of them belonged to me.

It would make this morning a hell of a lot easier. But as it is, I can barely afford my rent right now, so for the foreseeable future, I'm going to have to make the most of the public transport our city has to offer. And unfortunately, that means I'm walking down my street to the nearest tube station over an hour before I need to meet Mrs. Hendrix. I guess the only bonus is that the city is already buzzing with life, and as I make my way down into the underground station, I find myself surrounded by the eclectic people who make up my hometown.

It takes no less than four tubes to get even slightly close to Knight's Ridge College, and as I emerge from the final station, there's still a pretty decent walk.

I'd planned on getting a bus, but seeing as the one I need sails straight past the stop a few seconds before I make it there, I hike my bags a little higher on my shoulder and keep moving.

"Holy Jesus," I puff out when I finally come to a stop beside the colossal gates that allow entry to the exclusive and elite private school. My skin is glistening with sweat, my bags heavier than I'm sure they were when I left my flat.

A car turns in as I stand there staring, questioning my life. It's a Bentley. Of course it freaking is.

Schooling my features and stuffing down my apprehension and nerves—okay, pure unfiltered fear—I hold my head high and walk through those gates like I own the place.

Jodie offered to pick me up. She offered for Toby to swing by on his way and bring me in. But I don't want to be piggybacking off them. And I also really didn't want to be seen getting out of a student's car on day one.

My connection with them is already going to make this placement harder than it needs to be, I'm sure. I really don't want my mentor, my colleagues, for the next few weeks knowing I'm friends with the elite of the elite here from day one.

I know what they'd think if they knew.

That I was here for a free and easy ride.

My stomach knots tighter as I consider once again that this placement might not be the huge coincidence I first thought it to be, and actually the meddling of one of them.

Would they, though? Jodie aside, do any of them care enough to try?

One face flashes in my mind, and I can't help but smile as I think about Calli.

She'd do this for me, but I'm not entirely sure she's been thinking about anyone outside of her own drama right now.

For a moment, my own fear is forgotten as I think about her, Daemon, and the secret they're hiding. Everything they've been through recently really helps to put my current situation into perspective.

Sucking in a deep breath, I force my legs to move faster and continue up the seemingly endless driveway.

More cars pass me, but I don't look over, I just focus on where I'm going. On what I'm about to embark on.

After what feels like the longest walk of my life, one that I'm sure not many staff nor students have done over the years, the colossal main school building appears before me.

"Wow," I breathe.

I might have spent all of last night studying the Knight's Ridge website to soak up everything I possibly could find about the school, but none of the pictures I looked at were able to express the sheer magnitude of this place.

It's... unbelievable. The architecture is beautiful, haunting, mesmerising.

It's still early, the only people making their way toward the main doors are staff, but I know that won't last long. With only an hour before school starts, there will be students getting ready for the final day of their week.

A fresh bolt of nerves shoots through me as I think of just a handful of those students.

Thankfully, they'll spend their days in the sixth form building. I just have to hope and pray that I never have to venture over there.

With my eyes locked on the biggest set of double doors I think I've ever seen, I keep moving. My feet hurt and my back aches with everything I'm carrying. It's something I'm going to have to get used to if I'm going to spend the rest of the school year here. That or I'm going to need to invest in a bike.

I almost snort a laugh as I picture myself cycling up the driveway amongst the expensive cars.

Really, it's hardly a surprise they never let student teachers in. I can only imagine that their members of staff are fully vetted to ensure they're the right calibre of person to teach the darling children of the city's—hell, the world's —elite.

I step through the doors with blood rushing past my ears and immediately focus on a woman sitting behind a small window to welcome visitors.

Her eyes find mine, a soft smile playing on her lips as I approach.

"Good morning," she says, thankfully without any judgement in her voice.

I don't belong in a place like this. I know this, and despite the new clothes Jodie insisted I buy yesterday, I'm pretty sure the receptionist knows it on first sight too.

"How can I help you?"

"Hi, I'm Brianna Andrews. I'm meeting Mrs. Hendrix."

"Perfect timing," a soft female voice says from behind me. "But please, call me Melissa."

Spinning around, I find a beautifully dressed woman clutching a laptop and a textbook to her chest.

The second I look into her eyes, I relax.

She's not the stuffy old matron I feared, but a kind, soft-looking mentor that I suspect I'm going to need during my time here.

"Hi," I squeak. "I'm Bri... Brianna."

"It's nice to meet you, Brianna. I have to say, I'm excited to have a student to work with. It's been a number of years since I've had the chance."

With a quick thank you to the woman sitting behind the reception, Melissa gestures for me to move toward another set of doors.

"I'll give you a very brief tour before we get started. I don't know about you, but I could do with a coffee before we dive into the serious stuff."

I release a huge breath I didn't realise I was holding at her mention of coffee.

"Yes, please."

"Brianna," she says softly. "There is no reason to be nervous. Knight's Ridge is going to be a fantastic place to spend the final weeks of your training."

I nod. If the situation were different, I'd agree in a heartbeat. Something tells me that the coming weeks are going to be an eye-opening experience and a serious learning curve in an entirely different way from my previous placements. But with Nico's presence looming over me, I fear it could be anything but fantastic and instead the exact thing nightmares are made of.

"I'm excited," I lie, forcing a smile onto my lips.

I spend the morning in Melissa's office talking through everything, planning observations, the tutor visits I'll need, and everything else that will ensure I complete the final few weeks of my teacher training successfully.

She tells me about her teaching career and how she found herself as Head of English here at Knight's Ridge and her hope that my placement here could be the first of many. As much as I want to burst her bubble and tell her that I might be a one-off, my reluctance to talk about my connection to this place stopped me from uttering a word.

All morning, she made sure I always had a coffee to hand, something that only ensured I liked her more. Everything seemed to be going great until she slid a copy of my timetable over her desk as the bell for breaktime rang out around the building both her office and the entire English department resided in.

It showcased the lessons she expected me to be in with both her and her colleagues, and those I was supposed to take over after a week of observations. But it was none of those which caught my attention. No—that was her final lesson of the day today. A year thirteen class.

"I've arranged for someone to give you the proper tour of the school next period. She's going to meet you outside my office when the next bell rings, so you've got fifteen minutes to visit the bathroom, get some fresh air, run," she jokes. "Or if you're hungry, there's always food in the staff room on a Friday. If we're fast, Mrs. Witcher might have a slice or two left of her famous coffee and walnut cake."

Almost before she's finished talking, she's escaping from her office without waiting to see if I'm going to follow. It must be some damn good cake. But no cake is going to make me brave enough to go walking outside while the kids are free.

The second the door clicks closed behind her, I slump down in the chair, let my head hang back and my eyes close.

I should be excited. The opportunities this place could open up to me... even having it on my CV could be huge. If I survive it.

I dig a cereal bar out of my bag and force it down, seeing

as my stomach is growling loudly, but I don't really want it, and I certainly don't taste it.

Checking my phone, I find a message from Jodie, checking in to see how my morning is going.

I send her a quick thumbs up because I don't have the energy or the mental capacity to really express how I feel right now.

I swear only three minutes have passed when the shrill ring of the bell cuts through me, making my heart jump into my throat.

Before long, voices ripple through from the hallway and the door swings open, revealing Melissa and a female student in her uniform. Although, I'm very quick to notice that she's not exactly wearing it as I would expect.

The sleeves of her blazer are rolled up around her elbows, her shirt is unbuttoned enough to tease the horny teenage boys I'm sure she's surrounded by, and her skirt is entirely too short—listen to me sounding like a judgemental adult.

When Melissa said she's organised for me to have a student tour, I was expecting to find myself standing beside their most loyal, well-behaved, and polite student. Something tells me that I might just have been gifted the opposite of that.

I can't help but smile as I continue to study her.

She's me, just a few years younger.

"Rhea, this is Miss Andrews," Melissa says, introducing us to each other. "I'm expecting you to take her to every corner of this school and tell her everything you know."

"Everything?" Rhea quips, a dark excitement glittering in her eyes.

"Anything that won't extend your time out of PE any longer than necessary," Melissa says with a smirk.

"She threw the ball at me first," Rhea states.

"Not the time, Miss Cirillo," Melissa warns as all the air rushes out of my lungs.

Cirillo.

Rhea Cirillo.

Theo's little sister.

While my heart rate picks up speed, I can't decide if this is a good thing or not.

From her 'I don't give a fuck' attitude and the state of her uniform. I'm thinking it's probably good. Something tells me she's not exactly a rule follower, and that she'll tell me anything I need to know should I ask the right questions.

"Fine. I just need you to know how unfair all this is. Katia is a bit—"

"Enough," Melissa booms, giving me my first glimpse at the hard-arse teacher she hides beneath her soft expression.

Rhea rolls her eyes, and I have to smother a laugh.

This girl must be hell to teach.

I love her already.

"Come on, Rhea. Before you get in any more trouble, huh?"

She smirks at me as I try to direct her toward the door.

"Sure, but I will have my say," she warns Melissa.

"I don't doubt that, Rhea. You just have more important things to do right now."

I don't see Rhea's reaction from behind, but something tells me there's another heavy eye roll.

"So where first?" I ask, hoping to distract her, but she says nothing.

I follow her silently, wondering what the hell she's playing at, but I find out the second we spill out of the hallway lined with offices and into what looks like an inside courtyard. It would look more at home in some fancy shopping centre with benches and potted plants than it does a school. This whole place is mind-boggling.

Finally, Rhea spins around and glares at me with her hands on her hips.

I steel myself to be dumped on the very first leg of their tour by what I'm sure is one of their most defiant students.

But when her mouth parts and words spill free, I realise I'm wrong.

So very wrong.

"You're the one who's fucking Nico," she blurts.

My chin drops in shock, firstly at how she even knows that, and secondly, at the volume with which she announces it.

"Rhea." It's meant to come out like a warning, but instead, it just sounds like a plea.

"Oh don't worry, I won't tell anyone, Miss Andrews." She smiles so sweetly at me that I have to fight my groan as I wait to hear what's next. But then she surprises me. "Not if you don't want me to. Us girls have to stick together against the men of the Family."

My eyes widen, a move she misses as she spins around, ready to take off again.

"So, gonna be his teacher as well as his fuck buddy?"

"Oh my God," I mutter.

"Don't worry, contrary to popular belief around these halls, you can trust me. It's the others you want to watch out for. Always out for themselves. Let that bit of gossip out and they'll all have a field day with it. Me, however..." She makes a show of zipping her lips and locking them. "Vault."

"I appreciate that, Rhea. But how about we focus on what we should be doing?" I suggest.

"Sure. So, as I'm sure you already figured, this is the

English department." She waves her hands around before pinning me with a judgemental look.

"What?" I ask hesitantly.

"English, really?" she asks, looking me up and down.

I might be wearing what I hoped would become my armour when I bought it yesterday, but I swear I might as well be standing here naked with the way she studies me.

"It's like, the most boring subject there is. Well, maybe aside from—"

"You're reading the wrong books," I state confidently.

Her brow quirks. "I'm reading the books I'm told to. Surely, they're not the wrong books, Miss?" she teases.

"For school, they are the right books. But for you to enjoy, not so much. You need to find something that captures your imagination and wraps you up in its world and refuses to let you go.

"Do you have a favourite TV show?" I ask.

"Umm... *Stranger Things*, I guess. I also..." She lowers her voice so no one can overhear her. "I love all those old US teen dramas. But don't tell anyone."

Ideas flicker through my mind.

"Leave it with me. Before the end of my time here," which arguably could be incredibly short, "I'll have you in love with English and reading."

"I'd like to see you try," she taunts.

"Challenge accepted, Cirillo. Now show me all the places I need to avoid to stop me from running into your cousin."

"Are you avoiding just that particular male or all of those connected with him?" she asks as we exit the building.

"Mostly just him. The others probably won't care that I'm here."

"But you think Nico will have a cow?"

"Something like that."

"You know, it's highly unlikely that he'll even show his face. He's not exactly been... present since Uncle Evan died."

Pain rips through my heart as the image of Nico's dark and haunted eyes from last night come back to me. The things he said, the way he broke right before me, ripped me in two.

It doesn't matter how crazy he makes me. When he drops his walls and shows me that kind of vulnerability, I'm like fucking putty for him.

I just have to pray that he's too lost in his own head to notice just how weak it makes me. Because the second he realises it, I'm fucked. Beyond fucked.

"I know," I mutter. "But he has exams, he'll be here eventually."

Rhea lets out a sad sigh, showing a little of how she's really feeling right now.

"It's okay to be sad, you know. It's okay to miss him."

"I know," she confesses. "I'm okay, I just hate that everyone I love is suffering. I've never seen Dad like he is right now. And Nico. The men in my family have always been larger than life, so to see them hurting..."

"Things will get better. The pain will lessen."

"But things are never going to be the same again. It blows my mind to think that my big brother will be the one in charge of all this one day."

"Theo will make a great boss, Rhea. I've no doubt."

"Oh totally, it's just a head fuck. He'll always be the annoying boy who used to hide my Barbies. Sometimes it's hard to separate that boy from the man, you know?"

"I don't have any siblings," I confess. "Hell, I hardly

have any family, so I'm not the person to be talking to about them."

"You get it though. No one else does."

"There must be other kids here who are a part of the Family."

"Yeah, but they're not the boss's daughter. Everyone is either threatened by me or jealous of me," she says sadly.

"Oh, but you come across so sweet and approachable," I deadpan.

"I'm the nicest person in the world. If you deserve it."

"I guess I should feel honoured then."

"You're different. You don't judge me. I don't think you see me as a little girl like the others do, either."

"You should talk to Calli. She's the one who'll really understand how you're feeling."

"Can you believe she's with Da— shit," she hisses, cutting herself off. When I glance over, I find guilt washing through her features. "I'm not meant to know about all that."

"So, how do you?" I ask, genuinely intrigued.

"May or may not have been eavesdropping on Mum and Dad."

"Rhea," I warn.

"I know, I know. But it's the only way I find out what's going on sometimes."

"As long as you keep what you hear to yourself."

"Of course. I'm not a moron."

"I wasn't suggesting you were. So," I say while looking around at the impressive buildings around us. "Where to next?"

5

———

NICO

"No," I groan, rolling over and shoving my face into the pillow, squeezing my eyes closed in the hope I can drift back off into my filthy dreams, which are much more preferable than my reality right now.

I force my brain to take me back to the shower as I railed Bri from behind, fucking her cunt like a savage, listening to her as she screamed out my name, begging me to let her fall for me.

My cock aches, pressing into my thick memory foam mattress, begging for the release I clearly didn't get in my slumber.

I lie there, letting the minutes pass by, focusing on the pounding of my head and the swirling of my stomach.

Both of them have been my constant friends since that night at the country club. The only things that have never left.

The same can't be said for everyone else.

And I know that's entirely my fault. I've been nothing but a cunt to everyone who's tried to come and help me. But I can't help it. Seeing them all getting on with their lives as if nothing has happened is painful. It's a reminder that someone can leave our lives and be forgotten about in the blink of an eye. I don't want that. He doesn't deserve to be forgotten. He was too good for that.

I want to remember everything.

Although saying that, while my head is swimming in vodka, that's not exactly an easy thing to do. And those happy memories, as nice as they might be, rip me in half when I consider that I won't get any more.

We had a plan. We always had a plan.

Dad was going to be there with me as I became a soldier, a capo, and then ultimately took over his position when he decided it was time, and not a second before.

But now, I don't have that. And not only am I not ready to take his place, but no one is going to want me to either.

I'm letting them down. All of them. I'm letting him down.

A pained sob rips from my throat as I consider what his opinion would be on how I'm dealing with all this and my stomach turns over once more.

"Oh shit," I bark, rolling out of bed and stumbling toward the bathroom.

I hit the tiles beneath the toilet hard, pain searing through my knees and up my thighs as I lean over, purging the poison still lingering in my stomach.

I heave until there's nothing left, my stomach empty and aching.

Falling back, I rest against the wall naked and wipe my forearm across my sweaty head.

Fuck, I'm a fucking mess.

It's almost been two weeks since the funeral, and here I am still drowning like it happened only yesterday.

Everyone says it's meant to get easier. But I call bullshit.

Nothing about my life is getting any easier right now.

But then, I lift my eyes from the dark tiles beneath me and they lock on my walk-in shower.

No, those moments in there with Brianna made things easier. Even if they were figments of my imagination.

Tipping my head back, I close my eyes once more, putting myself back in there with her. Running my tongue along my bottom lip, I can almost taste the sweetness of her blood as I sank my teeth into her thigh, branding her like the fucking cunt that I am. But fuck if it doesn't get my cock hard just thinking about her walking around, wearing the evidence of who she belongs to. I guess Seb wasn't entirely insane all those months ago when he carved up Stella's thigh with his initials.

Yeah, actually. I can totally see a nice deep NC on Brianna's inner thigh. The perfect mark to prove to anyone who might try it on with her that she's owned. And we both know that she likes to play with others.

Something toxic and bitter fills my empty stomach as I think about her being with another man.

It's never really bothered me before. She was just a hookup. One that was good enough to repeat, which is unusual, I'll admit. But neither of us made any promises, and we certainly never gave up getting our kicks elsewhere. I know for a fact I fucking didn't.

But now, the thought of being with anyone else, risking letting anyone else see my pain, is anything but appealing.

I might not want Bri to see it, but I fear that might just be too late. And even if she hasn't seen as much as I fear, she knows. She knows everything.

When I finally heave myself up from the floor and stand in front of the mirror, I'm horrified by what I find staring back at me in the mirror.

"Jesus, Cirillo."

It's a good job that my rendezvous with my Siren was only a figment of my imagination. There's no way in hell that she'd actually fuck me when I looked this pathetic.

I brush my teeth, shave and shower in the hope it somewhat brings me back to life. I have no idea what time it is, but if school is still happening then I at least need to make an effort to show my face.

Exams are starting... sometime soon, and as much as I might hate the world and everyone in it right now, I can't bail on them.

I remember the disappointment on Dad's face when I royally fucking up my first year in sixth form, forcing me to start over with Theo, Alex, and Seb. He'd be fucking livid if I fucked it up again and used him as an excuse.

He needs to be my motivation instead.

Pass these exams, boy. Prove your worth. One day you'll be standing beside Theo, ruling this fucking city. Prove the doubters wrong. Prove you've got what it takes.

I hear the words clear as day, as if he's standing right behind me as I walk into my bedroom and rip open my wardrobe to find a clean set of uniform.

My brows pinch as I stand there staring at the hanging clothes before me and my mind spins.

I don't remember getting undressed last night, and I certainly woke up naked.

Glancing over my shoulder, I find my clothes balled up in my laundry basket.

I do fucking weird shit when I'm drunk, because they hardly even end up there when I'm sober.

Shaking my head at my drunken antics, I finally reach for my shirt and trousers and drag them on before swiping my tie that's folded up on my dresser.

It's not until I find my phone out in the living room, the alarm that would have gone off hours ago ignored, that I even think about the time again.

Getting dressed could have been a totally pointless exercise.

"Lunchtime," I mutter to myself as I stare down at my screen, ignoring all the notifications. Most are from our group chat, but there are also tons of social media and banking ones too. Putting it back to sleep to deal with later, I stuff it into my pocket and try to forget about its existence.

As tempting as it is to strip back out of my clothes, I don't. The guilt that will hit me later for not even trying will be unbearable, so pocketing my phone, I grab my keys and my bag that I abandoned in the hallway when I got back yesterday.

I feel like death as I drive through the city. There's a little nagging voice at the back of my head which tells me that I shouldn't even be behind a wheel. But it's too late now.

Pulling up at the Starbucks closest to school, I order myself the biggest, strongest coffee they have and two paninis before continuing toward Knight's Ridge.

Despite being too hot, the coffee is long gone before I pull to a stop in the car park and stuff my face with both of the paninis.

It has little effect on the darkness and the pain that festers inside me, but at least my stomach is no longer growling to be filled with something other than vodka.

Students sit around the sixth form building before me, enjoying the sun. I watch them laughing with their friends, enjoying life. It's as if everything is right in the world. I guess it is with theirs.

But how? How can something so life changing happen

to me and yet it passes everyone else by? Why am I the only one who's suffering right now?

Calli is... fuck. I scrub my hand down my face. The less I think about what Calli is doing, the better. She's fucking Daemon. Daemon. Out of all of us, I never in a million years would have suspected that Daemon would have been the one to corrupt my little sister. Honestly, I thought it would have been Toby. But it turns out not even Alex, the life-long flirt, was the one to catch my sister's eye. Oh no, that was the darkest, most dangerous and twisted one of the lot of us. Daemon fucking Deimos.

I'm pretty sure Calli needs her head testing. Alex I could understand. He's a fucking puppy dog. I can actually picture them together. But his evil twin... nah. Honestly, I'm waiting for someone to tell me it's a joke. Although right now, I think that's about as likely as someone telling me that Dad isn't really dead.

I didn't have to be there that day to know it's true. I felt it, the bone-crushing loss of him. I felt it right down to my fucking toes.

When people start moving, I figure my hiding time is up.

I only have one lesson left of the day. English lit.

It's the subject I was most resistant to when I was forced to reconsider my options after I failed my first attempt at A levels quite spectacularly. Although, I don't really think it had much to do with the subjects, more the alcohol, weed and pussy I spent more time focusing on. Studying took a back seat, something which I'm now severely regretting.

If I didn't fuck that up, I'd have finished at this place last summer. I could have had a year working with Dad under my belt. I might have been in a better position for whatever is next for me.

Of course, it goes without saying that I want his job. I want to continue his legacy and fulfil the role that was allocated to me at birth.

But do I deserve it?

Fuck no. I'm far too young and inexperienced for the job, but right now, I'm anything but reliable. Damien would be a fucking idiot to trust me with anything other than keeping myself alive.

Everyone has disappeared by the time I finally summon myself to climb out of the car, the final lesson of the day having long started.

Ignoring the main entrance to the building, I walk around the side, toward the rear that will lead almost directly into my class. The fewer people I'm at risk of walking into the better right now. The bitches who walk these hallways would have a field day with the state of me.

I walk past the huge wall of windows that line the building, realising my mistake when more than a few heads from the classrooms inside turn my way.

Great plan, arsehole.

But it's not until I get to the final one, my English class, that I actually look up. And I have no idea why I do but something—someone—forces me to look through the windows.

And the second I do, my eyes lock onto a person that I shouldn't be seeing in this part of my life.

My legs stop dead on the spot as I stare at the woman sitting behind the teacher's desk, watching intently as Mrs. Hendrix goes over something ready for our exam in a few weeks. I have no idea what that might be, because my eyes never leave her.

Brianna Andrews.

The light in all my darkness.

The angel in all of my dreams who takes me away from all this bullshit is sitting in my classroom.

Why?

"Bri's a student teacher," a familiar voice says in my head, forcing me to squeeze my eyes shut and picture the moment Jodie told me that little nugget about her best friend.

"No," I say out loud as I stumble back, slipping behind a thick old oak tree while my heart beats out of rhythm.

My hands tremble as I remain frozen, my eyes on her dark blonde curls.

Disbelief washes through me. This can't be happening.

She can't be my teacher. She just can't.

I spent all night dreaming of being inside her, about sinking my teeth into her thigh so deep my mark will never ever leave her body.

Sh-she can't be—

"FUCK OFF," I bellow when the familiar beep of someone letting themselves into my flat hits my ears.

"Fuck you, prick." The deep rumble of my best friend's voice should probably be comforting, but the fact that he's managed to get access again after I shut them all out... Well, all but Theo. That motherfucker is impossible to lose.

"I'm going to fucking kill Theo," I sulk, knowing full well that he's granted Toby access despite me revoking it.

"I'd like to see you try," he teases as he emerges around the corner, still wearing his Knight's Ridge uniform. He dumps his bag beside the sofa and falls down onto it.

"What's this? You got dressed then changed your mind?" he asks, his eyes taking in my matching clothes.

"Something like that," I sulk, lifting my bottle to my lips.

"Ah, decided to spend your day with your new friend the Goose instead of us, huh?"

"Fuck off."

"Nope." He grins at me, and if I weren't so attached to the oblivion the bottle in my hand can offer me, I might throw it at his head. "You remember that it was Alex, Daemon, and your little sister's birthdays this week, right?"

"I gave them all cards," I grunt, remembering poking them all under their front doors and running away like a pussy earlier in the week.

"Oh yes, how could I forget the monumental effort you made with those."

I narrow my eyes at his sarcasm, seriously unimpressed by the fact he clearly only turned up to make my life worse.

Un-fucking-lucky for him, I'm pretty sure that's impossible right now.

My father is dead, my mother is a selfish cunt, and my... my... fuck... my no one is now what... my fucking teacher?

"Did you come here for a reason, or just to piss me off?"

"We're having a party at Theo's later. All of us." He pins me with a look that makes me want to curl up into the sofa and never come out again.

"No one wants me there," I point out.

"You're wrong," he states, sitting forward and holding my stare with his serious eyes. "We all want you there."

I can't help but scoff at that.

Before all of this, I'd have believed him. I was the life of the fucking party. But it seems that fun side of me died right alongside my dad.

"Nico, we're all worried about you. Locking yourself in here and only letting Brianna in when she offers sexual favours isn't going to make any of this better."

"You sure? You haven't felt the thing she can do with her—"

"I'm sure. Her skills might be out of this world, but they're still not good enough to fix any of this shit. To fix you."

"No? So what will?"

His eyes soften in a way I fucking hate.

"Nothing will, Nico. Nothing can erase what happened or how much it hurts. But as hard as it is to hear, life has to go on. You've got too much to live for to let it all pass you by."

"Oh yeah, like what?"

"Like all the women out there who don't know they need a piece of you. The Family who are yet to fully experience what a fucking epic underboss you're going to make one day. And..." He pauses to build the tension like an arsehole. His eyes darken, fire burning through them. "The fucking Italians. They need to know exactly what you, what we, are capable of as we unleash all kinds of hell on them for what they've done to us."

The need for vengeance runs red hot through my veins, turning my blood to poison. The bitter taste of retaliation, of retribution fills my mouth, making my muscles ache with the need to shed their blood and make them pay.

"That's better," Toby says, watching as his words fire me up in the way he was hoping.

"Do we have a plan yet?"

He shrugs, playing it cool. "I guess you'll need to drag your arse out of your flat and go and see the boss to find out."

"I have left my flat," I sulk.

"So where did you go today after dressing up like you might attempt to attend a class or two? To the shop for more vodka?"

"So what if I did?"

"Bro," he sighs, dropping his head into his hands as if he's running out of patience.

I get it. I ran out of that shit with myself days ago.

"Calli needs you, man. She needs her big brother now more than ever."

"She's got Daemon. She doesn't need me."

"That's bullshit and you know it. You're not the only one who's lost their dad, man. She has too. And her mother, from what I've heard."

"What's Mum done?"

"Nothing, that's the point. Calli moved out and she just... didn't care."

"She's a dick. I can't believe I didn't realise how big of one she was before all this."

"Your dad was too good for her," Toby muses. "She must have been a stellar lay."

"You fucking cunt," I bark launching a cushion at his head. "What?" I snap when a wide, shit-eating smile curls at his lips.

"I fucking miss you, man."

"Fuck's sake," I hiss, aware that he's never going to leave this flat until I've agreed to this fucking party.

It's the right thing to do, I know it is, but fuck. Spending a night partying like everything is okay is the last thing I want right now.

Closing my eyes, I fall back on the sofa, an image of a young, carefree Calli filling my head. She was always so sweet, so calm and kind. Fuck knows what Daemon has done to deserve her. Fuck, maybe he doesn't and I'm going to have to kill him sometime soon for breaking her heart.

But Toby is right. She needs me too. No matter how hard it might seem right now, I need to be there for her.

I'm not the only one suffering...

6

———

BRIANNA

"I think you're going to fit in really well here," Melissa says after the year thirteens have left the room, allowing me to breathe for what I'm pretty sure is the first time in the past two hours.

He was meant to be here. The second Melissa opened the register up, my eyes found his name and my stomach plummeted into my feet. My stomach knotted with anxiety and that mark on my thigh throbbed like he'd just done it.

Thankfully, I didn't recognise any of the other names on the short list. But that didn't really matter. The only one who did was him.

And he didn't show.

I shouldn't have been surprised. From what Jodie has said, he's barely shown his face in Knight's Ridge recently. But there's a part of me that hoped he would have just turned up and got the inevitable over with.

He'd have found me here, the truth would have been out, and I'd have already seen his reaction.

But as it is, I'm still sitting here fighting with the tight knot in my stomach that's threatening to make me vomit all over the ridiculously clean carpet beneath my feet. Seriously, since when did classrooms have floors that resembled hotel rooms? Since the little darlings' parents have more money than sense, I guess.

I can't help but wonder how much of the Cirillo blood money has paid for this place. I might not know all that much about the Family's businesses, but it's no secret they hold huge power over this place. And power means money, so...

"Is that okay?" Melissa asks, dragging me back to reality.

"Umm." I stare up at her with a wince.

"I'm sorry, I'm sure today has been more than overwhelming and here I am, throwing more at you. Forget about it." She shakes her head. Curiosity burns through me, but I keep my lips sealed in case I really don't like whatever her suggestion was. "Is there anything you need to prepare for next week?"

"N-no, I don't think so." Reaching for my folder, I flip it open to my new timetable.

"Okay, next week, you can meet the staff whose lessons you'll be in, and I'll ensure they'll get you up to speed with where they are."

"Thank you, I really appreciate everything you've done. I know I was kinda dropped on you last minute."

"It's really nothing. I'm excited to have you here. And not just because you can take over a few of my classes in the rundown to summer." She winks. "Do you think you'll be able to find your way back to the car park from here?"

"I'm sure I can manage," I say, gathering up my things, more than ready to escape for the weekend.

I all but run from the room, and the second I turn down the hallway, I collide with a brick wall—well, not literally.

"Oh my God, I'm so—"

"Anyone would think you're trying to escape, Miss Andrews," Toby says as he steadies me with his hands on my upper arms.

"Anyone would be right," I mutter under my breath. "What the hell are you doing?"

"Thought you might like a lift home. Must have been a hell of a journey this morning." His brow quirks knowingly.

"It was fine. Gave me time to think."

"Sounds dangerous," he mutters, gesturing for me to walk with him.

"You're telling me. But you really don't need to take me home. I'm more than capable of—"

"Brianna," he chastises. "The walk off the grounds is longer than necessary, let alone what, the bus and three tubes you need to get here."

"Four," I whisper.

"Fucking hell, come on." Taking my heavy bag from my shoulder, he throws it over his own and continues forward as if nothing just happened.

"Flirt like this with all the teachers, Tobes?" I tease. If I've learned anything about these boys, it's that one way or another they'll get what they want and really, it's just easier not to fight.

Unless it's Nico. Then I have full intentions of fighting until the bitter end, because I know the kind of benefits my defiance can be rewarded with.

Shit.

I shake my head.

I can't. I can't be thinking about that kind of shit while I'm working here. While he's still a student.

Jesus. He could lose me the only job I've wanted in my life before I've even started it.

The orgasms were good. But they weren't that fucking good.

"Nah, only the really hot ones."

"Careful, from what I've heard, your girl is having MMA lessons from the biggest bad-arse in town. I'd hate for her to ruin this pretty face."

He laughs at my response and the sound immediately relaxes me—that and we finally spill out of the building, allowing me to suck in some much needed fresh air.

No more words are said between us as we walk toward his BMW.

It doesn't matter how many times I might slide into one of their cars, disbelief always slams into me.

These annoyingly handsome and terrifyingly dangerous boys have the most insane cars. I don't want to think just how much it is to insure them, let alone how much they cost to buy. It's utterly mind-boggling.

"So, how was your first day at Knight's Ridge College, Miss Andrews?" he asks after dumping my bag in the boot and joining me.

"Do you have to call me that?"

"Why? Is it what Nico uses in the bedroom?" His brows wiggle and I groan. "Sorry, sorry. Bad joke. He'll be okay with this, you know," he assures me.

"No offence, Tobes, but I don't think any of us can predict how he's going to react to anything right now."

"You should have just told him last night."

"He was wasted. He never would have remembered."

"He's a prick."

"Something we can agree on."

Folding my arms over my chest, I let out a heavy sigh.

"Today was okay though, right? This place is going to give you everything you need to finish your training?"

I twist around to look at him, reality slamming into me.

"It was you."

He glances at me, his face a mask of innocence, which we both know is total bullshit. I've seen exactly what this boy is capable of, and there isn't an innocent bone in his body.

"Oh, don't give me that butter-wouldn't-melt look, Tobias Doukas. The reason I'm even here right now is down to you, isn't it?"

He clucks his tongue. "I just pulled in a few favours. I didn't know if it was even a possibility."

"Toby," I sigh.

"It was nothing, Bri. Just helping out a friend."

There are so many things I want to say to him, to chastise him for going out on a limb for me. It's not like anyone other than Jodie ever does it for me. But in the end, I swallow those words and go with the most important.

"Thank you," I whisper, my voice oddly choked.

"You're one of us now, Bri. We look after our own."

"I'm not though, am I? And now I'm here, I probably shouldn't even be spending time with you. Pretty sure that's against the rules."

"You knew us first," he argues.

"I'm not sure that's how it works," I counter.

"Fuck the rules, Bri. I'm sure you've figured out already that we run that school. Just do what you need to do while you're there. Maybe avoid things like fucking Nico in a storage cupboard or over your desk. And make the most of the reference that Mrs. Hendrix can give you from the experience. There aren't many student teachers out there who can claim to have spent time in Knight's Ridge."

"Lucky them," I quip.

He shakes his head at me as he takes a turn that's not in the direction of my flat.

"Toby," I warn.

"It's Friday night, and three of us celebrated becoming an adult this week. We're partying and you have zero chance of getting out of it."

"I can't get wasted with students."

"I guess it's a good thing that you don't teach me, and that the others are currently oblivious as to what's happening then, huh?"

"Nico isn't going to want me there."

"Is that what he told you last night? That he didn't want you?"

I swallow as memories come back to me.

"No, I didn't think so," Toby mutters, taking my silence for an answer.

Before I know it, I'm once again being driven into the underground garage beneath their building and walking toward the lift.

Thankfully, Toby and Jodie live on the floor beneath Nico, so at least I'm unlikely to run into him yet.

He keeps the conversation light as we make our way up, but my muscles remain locked tight the entire time from just being close to Nico.

Maybe I should just go up and attempt to confess all again.

And it would probably go something a little like last night did.

"Tomorrow," Toby says as if he can read my thoughts. "Tonight we're celebrating. Show my boy just how good life outside his flat can be and then talk to him tomorrow."

"Assuming he's sober."

"Give him a reason to be so."

"Are you suggesting I blackmail your best friend by withholding sex?"

"I miss him, Bri. At this point, I figure we need to do whatever it takes to drag him out.

"It's almost been two weeks since the funeral. He has got to find a way back to real life soon. He can't keep this up."

"I think you're barking up the wrong tree assuming I can be the one to do it."

"Nah, I'm not. I've heard the way he talks about your pussy, it's fucking golden."

"Gonna tell your girl you said that," I tease as we spill out of the lift.

"Go ahead. But you should know, hers is diamond-encrusted platinum."

"Of course it is," I mutter. "And don't you fucking forget it."

"No chance, Bri. No fucking chance."

Pressing his hand to the biometric scanner beside his door, he lets us both in but comes up short after placing my bag in the hallway.

"Jodie, delivery," he calls teasingly before footsteps head our way.

"Aw thanks, baby," she breathes, jumping into his arms and slamming her lips down on his.

"Ugh, I don't fucking need this," I mutter, turning my back on them and walking deeper into the flat.

I see the bottles of alcohol lining the kitchen counter long before I get to that part of Toby's flat. Kicking off my shoes, I dump my handbag onto the counter and set to work.

By the time Jodie returns with swollen lips and flushed cheeks, I have two mojitos ready to go.

"Your day went well then, I take it," she guesses as I drain the rest of my cocktail.

"It was good until…"

"Until?"

"Until the last lesson of the day. Year thirteen English lit revision class."

"Oh fuck."

"Yeah, oh fuck indeed."

"Was he in it?" she asks, ignoring her drink in favour of studying my reaction.

"He was meant to be. He never showed."

"What a relief."

"Oh yeah, because waiting for him to blow his lid when he finds out is so much better."

"Still think you're overreacting. That dress looks hot on you, by the way. Totally worth the price tag." She winks before sipping her drink and groaning appreciatively.

Yeah, my new wardrobe. Something else I need to confess to.

"Tell me Nico didn't pay for this one as well," I groan, looking down at the top Jodie holds up against me.

"Don't be silly, you've still got his card. I just saw this earlier after I visited Sara and it had your name written all over it."

Her words make my chest ache in the best way.

I love it. The sequin-covered loose tank with spaghetti straps is right up my street. And the fact Jodie stopped for it makes it all that special. Also makes me feel guilty as hell.

"Jojo, you shouldn't be spending your—"

"Stop," she demands, rolling her eyes as if we haven't had this argument a bazillion times. "The words you're looking for are 'thank you, Jodie. I love it and I can't wait to knock Nico on his ass while wearing it later.' I also grabbed these to go with it." My lips part to argue before realisation hits me. "Don't have a cow, you already own these. I stopped by your flat and got everything you could possibly need tonight."

"Thank you," I finally say, desperately trying to ignore all the other comments that are on the tip of my tongue.

"Good. Now throw that back and get dressed. I'm ready to party."

I watch my best friend as she pulls out a dress from her wardrobe and holds it up against herself, and I can't help but smile. Happiness literally pours from her. It's the best sight in the world after everything she's been through recently. It gives me hope that everything will work out, that Nico will find his way again, and that the guys will win this war with the Italians without any more loss. And I think about Daemon and Calli, about their little secret. About a future that no one else around us knows exists yet. The next generation of Cirillos. It makes me wonder who'll be next. Hell knows they're all at it enough to have made a million babies between them by now.

It's thoughts of Calli and Daemon that stop me from arguing about attending this party tonight.

I'm the only one out of the group who knows the truth—well, as far as I'm aware, I am. And that means Calli is going to need some backup tonight if she has any intention of continuing to keep her pregnancy a secret.

"Bathroom's all yours, bitch," Jodie teases. "Steal whatever you want in there."

She quickly begins stripping out of her clothes before pulling open her underwear drawer.

"The top wasn't the only thing I bought," she muses, forcing me to stop and turn around when I'm at the bathroom door.

"Oh shit, girl," I blurt, taking in the sheer black lace bodysuit she's holding up. "He's gonna blow his load when he sees you in that."

"Here's hoping he can hold it off a little," she teases. "I want the benefits too."

"You lucked out with Toby, Jojo. He's one kinky motherfucker who will always make sure you get yours before he does."

A wicked smile pulls at her lips and I can only imagine some of the filthy situations she's told me about in the past that are flickering through her head right now.

All of them make me jealous as fuck.

I might not want a man, or need a man—sex aside—but I can't deny that what she's found with Toby makes me wonder if it could all be worth it.

"Yeah," she says softly, thinking of her boy. "Every time."

"Lucky bitch," I hiss before finally stepping into the bathroom and swinging the door closed behind me.

"I'm pretty sure Nico is just as generous," she shouts after me.

"I'm sorry, who?" I call back, making her laugh.

7

BRIANNA

"He is going to kill you," Jodie muses as the two of us hang happy birthday banners around Emmie and Theo's living room while she and a pissed off Stella blow up balloons.

"Stel, wanna put a little more effort in there, love?" Emmie teases after waving off Jodie's concerns. "We all know you can blow better than that."

"Fuck you," Stella mutters, throwing the half-inflated balloon to the coffee table and crossing her arms over her chest in a huff.

"What did he do?" I ask, although I instantly regret it. I already know way too much about all their sex lives. Something that probably shouldn't be the case, seeing as I could be walking into one of their classes next week.

"Nothing. He did nothing."

"And he was meant to do something?" Jodie guesses.

"Yes. But instead... he just stood there. Just fucking stood there."

She gets to her feet and throws her hands up, storming

out of the room while everyone around me looks utterly bemused.

"So I'm guessing none of you knows what he did, then?"

"Didn't do," Jodie deadpans.

"Nope, no clue. Although, to be fair, it could be anything with them. He probably failed to catch a spider or something."

"She's probably way scarier to the spider," I mutter.

"You really think Seb is scared of spiders? He doesn't give me that vibe," Emmie says.

"Nah, he's probably one of those freaks who's scared of cotton wool or something," Jodie says thoughtfully, shooting me a look.

"What?" I ask with a shudder. "That shit should be illegal. Especially when it's wet. Ugh."

"What?" Emmie barks. "You're scared of cotton wool? What the actual fuck?"

"All right, biker bitch," I counter with a smirk. "What are you scared of?"

"Nothing?"

"Nothing. Seriously?" Jodie asks suspiciously as something dark flashes through Emmie's eyes.

"Well, I hate birds. They freak me the fuck out," Jodie announces.

"Oh my God," I laugh. "Remember that time I dared you to go to Trafalgar Square and a pigeon landed on your shoulder? I've never seen you move so fucking fast. It was the funniest thing I've ever seen."

"Fuck you. Aside from recent events, that was the worst day of my life, and all you did was laugh when that thing shat on me."

"I'm sorry," I say, holding my hands up in surrender. "I just wanted to push your boundaries a little. I wasn't expecting them to flock to you as if they could taste your fear."

"One of these days, I'm going to get you so drunk that you don't know what's happening and you're going to wake up the next morning in a bath of damp cotton wool."

"You wouldn't," I hiss, knowing full well that she would if she got the chance. Lucky for me, when we're drunk, we're usually at my flat and that doesn't have a bath. Not that waking up in a shallow shower tray filled with cotton wool would really be any better.

A door opens down the hallway and footsteps head our way.

Glancing over my shoulder, I find Stella looks almost as pissed off as she did when she stormed off, but her shoulders are a little looser.

"What about you, Stel? What are you scared of?"

"Fuck off, Stella isn't scared of anything either," Emmie barks. "You've seen her, she's a full-on bad-arse."

"I'm scared that I'll lose my mum before I've really got to know her. I'm scared that what she's had could be genetic and that it could affect Toby or me. Or our kids in the future."

Silence ripples through the room at her heavy confession.

"Shit, that's—"

"I'm scared I'll turn into my mother," Emmie blurts, cutting off what I was about to say.

"That's not going to fucking happen, Em," Stella says fiercely. "Even if there was a chance, we wouldn't let you."

Admittedly, I don't know all that much about Emmie's mum, but she's in rehab, so that pretty much tells me all I really need to know.

"She's right," I agree. "Your support network is too good for that to happen."

"Plus, you're too busy bouncing around on Theo's massive cock to have time for all that," Stella deadpans, the girl chat seeming to cheer her up at last.

"Massive, huh? How big are we actually talking here?"

Jodie snorts. "Says the dick expert."

"Pfft, nothing wrong with testing plenty out to find the one that fits the best."

"Whore," she scoffs.

"Takes one to know one." I cast my mind back to some of the wilder weekends we've had over the years.

"You corrupted me. All your fault."

"Probably. You told Toby about that weekend at Butlins yet when you had—"

"Can we not?"

"Oh no," Emmie says. "You don't get to drop a little nugget like that and then not tell us all the dirty details."

"Okay, so before Jodie found a rich boyfriend," I start, making her roll her eyes, "we used to do these singles only weekends. They were fucking epic. Full of every kind of willing man you could want."

"Most were total sleazeballs," Jodie adds.

"Okay fine, so you had to be a bit selective," I admit, dropping onto the sofa and replacing the Blu Tack in my hand with a cocktail.

"Anyway, there was this one night that we found this group of friends. They were a little older, hot as fuck. We... uh..."

"Bri," Jodie warns.

"What? I'm not going to tell them that we made our way around the whole group in one night."

Jodie groans, throwing her hands up in frustration before downing her own cocktail and wincing at the burn.

"Sounds like a good night. Don't worry, Stella has experience with multiple guys at once, ain't that right, Stel?" Emmie asks innocently while receiving a death stare from her best friend.

"If you're talking about that time in Nico's den of sin—that you weren't even at, I might add—then it's not exactly the same. I kissed them, and then... they watched as Seb..."

She trails off. "As Seb did what?" I ask, more than a little curious.

"Spread her legs and got her off in front of them all."

"Fuck," I breathe, disappointed not to have heard this story before. "In front of all the boys?" I ask, needing more details.

"Theo, Alex and Nico. Thankfully, Toby wasn't there. Daemon either. Although I did kiss him the night before," Stella admits with a wince.

"And you kissed the others too, I assume."

"Yep. I was hoping it would make Seb's head pop right off his body. Sadly, that never happened."

"Who's the best?" Jodie asks, totally unfazed by this story, so I can only assume she's heard it before.

"Theo obviously," Emmie says, standing up for her boy.

"Nah, I reckon it was Daemon. All that brooding darkness. Imagine it all channelled into passion."

"I'm not sure there was all that much passion. He was just willing to play my game. I think you're right, though. Have you seen him and Calli together? Pure fucking fire. Something tells me that she's never going to regret not testing out all the other sizes before settling with that one."

"Where the fuck is she anyway? She should be a part of this now she's got a dick to talk about."

"Probably busy with said dick," Stella muses. "Lucky bitch."

"You know," Jodie sighs, "if you let go of whatever Seb didn't do earlier, you could probably be making use of his right now. It's not like he'll ever turn you down."

"He's going to need to grovel first."

"As long as he's on his knees," I add, winking at Stella.

"Hell yes." She lifts her drink to faux clink with mine before she sinks it and announces, "More."

By the time we've finally decorated Theo's penthouse with all the banners and balloons, we're all three sheets to the wind thanks to the strength of the drinks I've been offering up.

It's partly selfish. If—when—Nico shows his face, I'm pretty sure I'm going to need the Dutch courage, but also, if the girls are half wasted, they might not notice when I start making virgins for our not-so-virgin Calli.

She confided her secret in me, and there is no fucking way I'm going to break her trust and let that little cat out of the bag before she and Daemon are ready.

"Oh, it sounds like the party is about to start," Emmie says when a door slams closed and heavy footsteps and deep voices head our way.

My heart jumps into my throat as they approach.

Sensing my unease, Jodie reaches over and squeezes my hand.

I glance over and regret it instantly, because her brow is furrowed and there's concern darkening her eyes.

I get it. I don't let anything or anyone usually affect me like this. But this is my fucking career. Literally the only thing I've ever really wanted since I was old enough to make a serious decision about the rest of my life. And if he fucks this up for me...

"What the fuck have you done?" Theo barks while Alex's face lights up in delight at all the multicoloured decorations.

Emmie hops up and launches herself at Theo, I assume hoping to distract him from all the tacky decorations with her lips. To be fair to her, it works a treat, because the second she's in his arms, his eyes slam shut and he loses himself in her.

"This is fucking epic," Alex announces while Seb's eyes are focused on his girl.

But, clearly still pissed, Stella ignores him and walks toward Alex instead.

"Happy birthday," she says. Wrapping her arms around his shoulders, she reaches up on her toes and plants her lips on his.

"What the fuck?" Seb baulks, staring at his girl kissing one of his best friends with wide eyes.

"What? Just wishing Alex a happy birthday," she says innocently, shooting Seb a scathing look.

"Baby," he sighs. "I'm sorry, okay?"

"Not good enough," she snaps, keeping herself tucked into Alex's side while he grins like a Cheshire cat.

"Your loss is my gain, Papatonis. I've heard she's killer in the sack."

"Yeah, you've fucking heard it from me. Now get your dirty hands off my girl."

Reaching out, Seb drags Stella away from a pouting Alex and backs her up against the wall. Pressing the length of his body to hers, he whispers something none of us can hear as he tries to make it up to her.

"Right, well," Alex says, ignoring them and rubbing his hands together. "Who's next to give the birthday boy some love?" He holds his arms out from his sides, offering himself up.

Toby walks farther into the room, rolling his eyes at his friend before pulling Jodie into his side, leaving me as the only one left.

"Looks like it's you and me then, babycakes," he teases, letting his eyes roam around my body. "And I must say you're looking mouth-watering."

Walking around the sofa, he jumps over the coffee table and wraps me up in his arms.

I laugh as he dips me low as if we're in an old movie. I just catch the sound of approaching footsteps before his lips find mine in a chaste and innocent kiss.

But as a deep, angry growl rips through the air, I'm not sure it looks like that to the man who's watching us.

"Oh fuck," Alex mutters against my lips before he pulls me back up. "At least I can say I'm going to go out with a bang."

The second I'm upright, he releases me and we both look at Nico.

His dark eyes hold a deadly warning as he glares at Alex before they turn on me.

There are so many emotions in his eyes that it's impossible to decipher how he's really feeling, but his anger comes across loud and clear. I just have no idea if that's because of what he just witnessed and the fact that Alex has his hands and lips on me, or if it would have been there regardless of what he walked in on.

"Where are Calli and Daemon?" I ask, in the hope of breaking through the tension that has settled around the room.

"I'll call them," Stella says, shoving Seb aside and pulling her phone out of her back pocket.

"Drinks," I announce, stepping around Alex and heading for the kitchen. Nico's eyes burn into me the entire time, but he never says a word. Instead, he stands there silently brooding, lost in his own head.

8

———

NICO

"Shit," I hiss under my breath as Brianna makes a show of walking around the living room before slipping into the kitchen, her arse and curvy hips encased in a skin-tight pair of black jeans. Her top half isn't much better. It's nothing more than a shiny scrap of fabric that I'm pretty sure I could shed from her body with nothing more than a sharp tug.

My mouth waters as I imagine stripping it all from her, leaving her bare for me. Bare and ready for the taking.

A heavy slap lands on my shoulder, startling me before a smug-as-fuck voice says, "See, I told you this was a good idea."

Toby takes off toward the kitchen where Bri is now making smooth work of knocking up the girls' cocktails, moving her arse right along with the shaker and ensuring she keeps my attention.

Miss fucking Andrews is in a whole world of trouble she's not expecting.

"Here," Toby says, shoving a beer into my chest.

"Nah, man," I say, pulling a bottle of vodka from my

back pocket. "I'm gonna need something harder than that for tonight."

"Just fuck her. Take the edge off. You know she'd be up for it."

Would she? Would Miss Andrews be a good little teacher for me and get on her knees and suck my dick like the pro that she is?

Heat tingles down my spine as that thought plays out in my mind, and when I look up, I find the cocktail shaker unmoving in her hands and her eyes boring into me.

My lips twitch before a dark smirk curls at one side of my mouth before my eyes drop down her body again, letting her know exactly what I'm thinking about.

When I finally focus on her face once more, she swallows harshly, my attention clearly affecting her as potently as her proximity does to me.

"Nah, she's not worth it," I say, ensuring she can read my lips, possibly even hear the words as they roll off my tongue.

She startles, letting me know that she heard me loud and clear.

I allow myself to take a trip around her body once more before I turn my back on her and stalk toward the others in the living room.

"Here," Emmie says, shoving a couple of party poppers at me.

"Ugh."

"Oh don't be such a miserable fuck. We're celebrating."

"Yeah, so we are," I mutter, taking the things from her and falling onto the sofa with a grunt of annoyance.

I might have agreed to be here, but I said fuck all about enjoying myself. Even less about faking it.

If they want me here, then they're going to have to take me as they find me.

"They're still not answering," Stella announces, lowering her phone from her ear.

"Already told you," Bri shouts over. "She's too busy making the most of Daemon's cock."

All the air rushes out of my lungs at her suggestion, my teeth grinding and my grip on the bottle in my hand becoming so tight I wonder how the glass doesn't shatter.

"I bet he's fucking dirty," she deadpans. "Stella's already told us how good a kisser he is."

"Oh, has she now?" Seb sneers, his arm whipping out so quick that Stella has no chance of dodging him as he wraps his fingers around her throat and pins her back against the wall. Pressing the length of his body against hers, he growls something in her ear and she sags in his hold, a whimper falling from her lips.

I might be watching them, but in my head she's Brianna. It's her big blue eyes staring up at me, it's her pulse thundering beneath my fingers as I fight the thin line between hate and desire and try to decide if I should fuck her or throttle her.

Suddenly, all eyes turn on me and I quickly realise that the growl that just ripped through the room wasn't from the couple who are about three seconds away from fucking right here in front of us but me, courtesy of my imagination.

"Fuck this," I mutter, fed up of their concerned, sympathetic eyes.

Abandoning my vodka on the coffee table, I storm through Theo's apartment just as Ant and Isla appear to join the party. Ignoring the fact that a fucking Italian has been invited, I continue forward, slamming the bathroom door so hard the floor beneath me vibrates.

"Fuck," I breathe, curling my fingers around one of the basins and hanging my head. My heart pounds, my blood roaring between my ears as I battle with my demons and my need to drag Brianna out of this flat and force the truth out of her.

Fuck it, maybe I should do it right here so everyone can hear what she's been doing today.

It was good enough for Seb, and I already know that Bri would be up for it. Dirty bitch.

But you don't want to claim her, a little voice says in the back of my head.

You want to do the opposite.

As I stand there arguing with myself over a woman I both don't want and can't have, the heavy bass of the music out in the living room gets louder as the party gets started without me.

Just about sums up my fucking life right now.

I want to be out there. I want to be laughing with my friends, enjoying my life. But it feels wrong. All of it.

Something broke in me that night. It shattered the second of that first explosion, and then it totally fucking ruptured the moment I laid my eyes on my dad, lifeless in the rubble.

It's an image I can't get out of my head, and one I equally want to forget but forever remember.

Headfuck doesn't even begin to cover it.

I have no idea how long I stand there lost inside my own head, but no one comes to check on me, and I'm not entirely sure how I feel about that.

I take a piss, and then after washing my hands, I finally risk looking up in the mirror before me.

Sucking in a long, slow breath, I force myself to

continue staring into my eyes, seeing the pain, the grief, the desperation.

I give myself ten seconds.

Ten seconds to get my shit together before I head out there and make an effort to celebrate my friends' and my sister's birthday.

It's just one night.

One night. And if I'm really lucky, it will end with an intense one-to-one with Brianna as I force the truth from her lips.

I walk out of that bathroom with my head held high and determination filling my veins.

The second I round the corner, a very familiar voice hits my ears and I can't help but wince. I've totally checked out on her these past couple of weeks. I know it's wrong—I knew it was wrong—but I couldn't help it.

"Where's Nic—"

I continue forward, my sudden appearance cutting Calli off as her eyes find mine.

"Nico," she cries, rushing toward me as if everything is okay between us.

Guilt floods me at the way I've treated her, the way I reacted to discovering her relationship with Daemon.

I freaked out. I know I did. But she's my little sister. My sweet and innocent little sister.

I've spent my entire life trying to protect her from the horrors of the life we've been born into, and yet despite all of that, she's managed to end up fucking the most dangerous and fucked-up one of us.

Her arms wrap around me, the warmth of her body

seeping into mine, and it settles something inside me that I wasn't expecting.

She doesn't hate me.

She should.

But she doesn't.

She's too good for all of us, not just Daemon.

Tucking her face into the crook of my neck, I can't help but wonder if she's soaking just as much strength up from me as I am her right now.

The thought is something akin to a baseball bat in the chest.

But, unable to dive into the painful shit, especially when we're meant to be celebrating, I fall back on my safety net. Sarcasm.

"And you couldn't wait another minute so I could take a piss," I mutter, returning her embrace and holding her tighter than I'm sure is really necessary.

"It's good to see you, Bro," she whispers in my ear, her words wrapping around my heart and squeezing tight.

"You too, Sis. He still treating you right?" I ask, unable to drop the big brother act. All the while, Bri's comments from earlier float around my head and cause a shudder to race down my spine.

"You know it," she agrees without missing a beat, and my eyes lock on Daemon's over her shoulder. "Come on, let's party."

Unsurprisingly, Daemon doesn't react at all to my warning glare. If anything, I'm sure his dark eyes twinkle with accomplishment before the fuck shoots a look over at Bri.

"Just go over there. Enjoy yourself," Calli says, startling me and letting me know that she didn't miss that look her new boyfriend and I shared.

Ugh, my stomach knots. My baby sister has an actual boyfriend.

"I... I can't, Cal," I say, finally releasing her before taking off across the room to find my discarded bottle of vodka. If all these couples are about to start grinding up against each other like they usually do, then the best way to get through this night is to be so wasted that I forget one of them is my sister. I just need to pray they're not into PDA quite like Seb and Stella, who seem to have made up at last—or at least Seb is putting in maximum effort to make it happen as he kisses her like she's the air he needs to breathe.

I fall onto the sofa, lifting the bottle to my lips and chugging a more-than-generous amount as Brianna emerges from the kitchen and delivers each of the girls a cocktail.

From the state of them all, it's more than obvious that they've already had plenty, but it doesn't stop any of them throwing this one back like it's a shot. Well, Stella and Emmie do, preferring to be distracted by their boys to wasting time drinking. Calli and Jodie take it a little slower, thank fuck.

When Brianna gets back to the kitchen, I watch her throw a row of three shots back, clearly deciding that the potent cocktails are still too weak if she has to be here tonight before she saunters through the room.

But before she gets to wherever she was going, Jodie intercepts her, catching her hand and pulling her toward her to dance.

Brianna shakes her head at whatever Jodie says as I tip the bottle to my lips once more.

My head is beginning my spin nicely, my perception blurring, allowing me the escape from reality that I crave so badly.

At some point, I know it's not going to be enough. It's

why I've got a little baggie of Molly in my pocket. Sometime tonight, I'm going to need more, and something tells me that she's going to be the reason.

A wide smile lights up her face as she dances with her friend. Alex joins them, but I'm too enthralled in the way her body moves in time with the music to pay any attention to him.

Her movements are hypnotising and as her hips roll, I can't help but let my imagination run away with me, imagining that she's beautifully naked and moving like that against me.

Fuck.

Reaching out, I tug at my trousers, giving myself a little space.

Thankfully, everyone is too lost in what they're doing to notice me suffering from just watching Bri dance.

I have no idea what it is about her. She's like fucking kryptonite. Has been since I first saw her that night.

I only went to be a good friend. I never would have imagined that Toby would have led me to such a spitfire.

I had no idea back then that he'd set the whole thing up. And to be honest, I'd have been too lost in her large blue eyes and sinful curves to even care anyway.

Letting myself remember the events of that night, of our little trip to Hades does little to stop the semi I'm rocking.

How many girls would allow their one-night stands take them to a fucking sex club and screw them every which way while others looked on?

Your siren, that's fucking who.

It is like she was made for you.

Shaking my own thoughts from my head, my eyes follow Brianna's movements as Alex steps in front of her, immediately moving with her.

My teeth grind, the bottle that was halfway to my lips for another swig pausing.

Motherfucker.

All my breath comes out in a rush as he spins her around, forcing her to face me, and skims his hands down her body.

Not needing any more invitation than that, Brianna leans back against him, resting her head on his shoulder and moving in time with the music.

My eyes lock on his hands possessively wrapped around her hips as if she's his, and my temperature spikes.

Rolling my eyes up his arm, I pause at the bandage over his bicep but give it little thought. It'll be the least of what he's got to deal with if he gets too fucking handsy.

Alex is off his face, that much is more than obvious when I get to his eyes. They're blown wide, telling me that he hasn't just stuck to the potent cocktails Brianna has been delivering to everyone since way before I got here, if their levels of intoxication were anything to go by. Not that I can really comment. I started way earlier than I should have done today. And if it weren't for me trying to do right by my sister, then I'd already be blacked out and locked in my flat alone in the hope another bottle of vodka might just be the key to making everything stop hurting so fucking much.

As if he can feel my burning stare, Alex's eyes find mine over Brianna's shoulder. But if he senses the warning, then he completely misreads it because he smiles wide at me. Motherfucker knows exactly what he's doing.

Not in the mood to be tormented by one of my best friends, I push to my feet and storm toward the kitchen. I need more vodka after all. And that Molly in my pocket is calling my name.

I pull the baggie from my trousers, but movement across the room catches my eye before I can even take one out.

A flash of dark blonde hair and a mouth-watering arse have my legs moving before I know what I'm doing.

Anger surges through me, the bitter taste of betrayal right behind it.

Alex has barely noticed his dance partner has left. He's already turned around and started dancing with Ant and Isla.

Fuck knows why we're partying with a fucking Italian, but I figure I don't have a lot of say in anything right now. I just need to turn up, plaster a fake smile on my face, and pretend I'm not falling apart one painful crack at a time.

Ant moves slowly, the beating he took at the hands of his leaders still causing him issues, but he doesn't seem all that bothered by the pain as Isla wraps herself around him like a snake, Alex pressed in right behind her as the three of them laugh and enjoy themselves as if he belongs here.

With no one paying me any attention, I follow my deceitful siren toward Theo's bathroom and slam my hand on the door a beat before it closes.

She shrieks in shock but quickly jumps back before the door hits her in the face.

But she doesn't cower.

She never does.

No matter how much I might want her to get on her knees for me, she never will. Not in the submissive way I want, anyway. She always holds too much power for that.

Just like today, when she swiped the world from beneath me with just her mere presence.

No one should have that kind of power over me.

Ever.

If it were anyone else, I'd have stormed in there and

dragged their lying, deceiving arse out by their hair. But this isn't just anyone. It's Brianna. My siren. And she fucking disarms me in a way that terrifies me. She makes me react to things in ways I never expect, ways I never have with anyone else.

"What do you want, Nico?" she sneers, her eyes sparkling with intoxication, making her a million times hotter than usual. Which really is saying something, because she's smoking on her worst days.

Ignoring the fact that I'm standing here, and that the door is now wide open, she hooks her top up and undoes the button on her jeans as if she's going to continue like I never stormed in.

"What the fuck is wrong with you?" I bark, my anger boiling over.

Reaching out, I collar her throat before she has a chance to shove her jeans down and get right in her face.

It's a fucking mistake, because her sweet mango scent fills my nose, and fuck if my mouth doesn't water.

Lingering, hazy images from my dream last night come back to me and my cock presses against the confines of my jeans.

"Me? What is wrong with me?" she asks incredulously. "The only one of us with an issue here is you, you arrogant twat. Now, will you get out of my fucking way? You can watch if you want," she offers, clawing at my forearm in the hope I might release her.

"Oh yeah. Shall I take a photo too?" I offer, making her brows pinch in confusion. She knows I can be all kinds of kinky, but taking a photo while she pees is a new one, even for me. "I could take it to your new boss so he has a better understanding of who he's just employed," I threaten.

Her eyes narrow, her jaw ticking in irritation.

"Fuck you, Nico. I'm not scared of you and your empty threats," she growls.

Goddamn it, her fire gets my cock rock hard.

She's the only one who has since that night in The Spot. And I fucking hate her for ruining me like that.

It makes me need her.

And I don't need anyone.

Ever.

"Empty?" I taunt. "None of my threats are empty, Brianna. I thought you knew who I was. What I'm capable of."

She snarls at me, and my cock jerks in response, wishing those full lips were being put to better use.

"You need to get yourself out of my life, Brianna Andrews, or you can bet your fucking arse I'm going to shatter everything you've spent years working toward faster than you can get on your knees to suck my fucking cock."

At my threat, something I'm not used to seeing flashes in her eyes as her brave façade begins to slip. But she quickly steels herself once more to go toe-to-toe with me.

"Cunt," she hisses.

"Takes one to know one. *Miss Andrews.*"

9

———————

BRIANNA

All the air rushes out of my lungs as my name rolls off his tongue.

No. Not just my name.

My teacher name.

He knows.

He—

Fuck.

"N-Nico," I stutter like a fucking idiot.

No man has ever made me question myself like he does.

I've always been strong, independent, and I've never given a fuck as to what any man might think of me and my decisions. But since the first moment I met him, it's like he's wiggled his way right inside my head, because I find myself wondering what he'd think, if he'd approve.

It's bullshit. All of it.

But it's only got worse since he lost his dad and dived into the endless dark pit of grief.

Now, I just want to do something to make it all better. Like I did last night.

And I really don't want to make any of it worse, which is exactly what I think my presence at Knight's Ridge is going to do.

"No," he sneers, getting so close to me that his nose almost brushes mine. His harsh, angry breaths fan over my lips and down my neck, and I can't help my skin prickling with desire. "You don't get to Nico me, you lying fucking—"

"I tried to tell you," I hiss, my own anger hitting all new heights at the audacity of this wanker. "If you dragged your head out of your own miserable life for two seconds, then you might see that other shit is going on around you."

"Fuck off. I'm more than allowed to hide right now."

"Yeah, there's no need to be a cunt though, is there?" If it's possible, his hate-filled eyes darken even more than before.

"What else?" he demands.

"What do you mean, what else?" I parrot.

"What else are you lying to me about?"

"I'm not lying to you about anything, you entitled prick. Now let me go. I don't want to be in here with you."

I claw at his forearm, my nails cutting into his skin. But despite how much it must hurt, his grip on my throat never loosens.

In fact, I'm pretty sure it gets fucking tighter.

"If you're gonna strangle me, at least put your hand in my knickers at the same time," I taunt, the amount of alcohol I've consumed tonight making my lips looser than they should be.

"Fucking whore," he hisses.

"Hasn't bothered you in the past," I taunt, jutting my chin out in defiance.

Fuck this man for trying to make me think less of myself

or question my promiscuity. I fucking love my life, my sex life even more. At least I did until I met him.

"You're right, it hasn't. I seem to have forgotten what you're useful for."

His free hand threads into my hair, and before I know what's happening, my knees hit the tiled floor beneath me and I'm eye level with the massive bulge in Nico's jeans.

"You really aren't put off, are you?" I taunt, my traitorous body reacting to the fact I've turned him on despite his vicious words.

"Your mouth and your cunt are the best parts about you, Siren. I thought you knew that."

Ripping his jeans open, he awkwardly shoves them down over his hips, letting his aching cock spring free.

My mouth waters for a taste of him, and it only gets worse as he wraps his hand around his thick shaft and starts working himself.

"You really look like you hate me right now," I tease, ripping my eyes from his dick to find his.

He glares down at me, his eyes completely blown with anger and desire.

It's a heady feeling, knowing that I can bring this powerful man to his knees. Maybe not literally, seeing as I'm the one down here, but metaphorically, I have all the fucking power, and I'm about to prove it.

He leans forward and rubs the head of his cock against my lips, but I keep them pressed tight together, sinking my teeth into my own flesh to stop the temptation to suck him deep and watch him lose his mind from winning out.

"Siren," he growls, trying to force himself into my mouth.

But all I do is stare up at him with my brow quirked.

You don't get to talk to me like that and think I'm going to bend to your will, Nico Cirillo.

"Fuck. You drive me fucking crazy," he booms, his fingers tightening in my hair until my eyes water and I begin to think he's going to come away with handfuls.

He fists his cock almost violently, his face twisting as if he's in pain, but if he is, then he doesn't stop.

No more vicious words spill from his lips and he stops trying to get inside my mouth. As much as I might want to taste his desperation, his desire for me right now, even if it's clouded in hate, I still keep my lips sealed shut, breathing heavily through my nose instead as I watch this evil god of a man come undone before me.

He might not realise it, but he's showing me almost as much of his vulnerability as he did last night, and that knowledge makes my chest ache for this lost, broken, hurting man.

"Fuck, Siren. Fuck."

Swallowing thickly, his Adam's apple bobs as his eyes darken.

Desire tightens in my lower stomach as I watch him race toward the end.

Fuck, he really shouldn't look this goddamn sexy falling apart for me.

"Siren," he groans, his body stilling for a beat, giving me a warning of what's about to come.

But I don't shy away, and possibly stupidly, I don't shut my eyes either.

Instead, I hold his hard stare as his cock jerks in his hand and he comes all over my face.

The second he's done, a smirk curls at his lips, his whole body relaxing as the endorphins from his release rush through him.

"Fuck, you look good like that," he mutters. And fuck if that praise doesn't give me bloody butterflies.

I shouldn't want to please this infuriating brute of a man, but fuck...

I've always known that I'm a little bit wrong in the head. Meeting Nico has only confirmed that.

Without releasing my hair or looking away from his cum that's dripping down my cheek, he tucks himself away.

The need to fight him, to force him to let me up, to do anything burns through me, but I lock it down and instead just wait to see what he's going to do next.

Reaching out, he runs his finger through the sticky residue on my skin, sweeping it up.

"Come on, Siren. You're wasting it."

His words make me gasp and my lips part before I fully predict his next move and his cum-covered digit pushes inside my mouth.

"That's better."

He does it again, cleaning me up and letting his taste coat my tongue as I continue to stare up at him like a shameless whore.

"Look at you, such a great role model down there with one of your student's cum all over your face. I hope Knight's Ridge knows how lucky they are to have such a whore of a teacher inside their classrooms."

Unable to say anything with his finger deep in my mouth, I do the next best thing and sink my teeth into him.

"Motherfucker," he hisses, pulling his injured digit free just as the coppery taste of blood fills my mouth.

His hand finds my throat once again and I'm hauled to my feet.

"What are you going to do now then, big man? You

gonna punish me some more?" I taunt, probably a little bit too excited about that prospect.

Jesus, I really am a whore.

His sneer turns vicious as he stares down at me with his eyes blown and his chest heaving.

"You think that was punishment, you haven't seen anything yet."

"Nico," I squeal as my feet leave the ground and I'm thrown over his shoulder like a rag doll.

"Quit fucking complaining," he barks, the crack of his palm colliding with my arse ripping through the silent room. "We both know you love it. I don't need to spread your thighs to know that your cunt is dripping wet for me right now."

I huff in irritation.

"Come on, Miss Andrews. Talk to me. Tell me just how badly you want to be railed by one of your students."

"Fuck you. I don't want you anywhere near me." It's a bare-faced lie and we both know it.

It doesn't matter how savage, how brutal he is, I'll always come crawling back for more—possibly even literally if he asks in the right way. It is just that good when we collide and give in to this barely restrained hate that crackles between us.

In only a few short seconds, he's marching us through Theo's flat. The music is still pumping, and there are couples still dancing as if we never left. Although...

As a familiar moan rips through the air, I lift my head, dragging my eyes from Nico's impressive arse to find Seb fucking Stella on Theo's sofa.

"Shit," I breathe, shamelessly watching as he thrusts into her without abandon, giving zero shit that their friends, Stella's brother, is in the room.

Ripping my eyes away from them is harder than it probably should be, but somehow, I manage it, and I quickly find that Toby is being more than distracted by Jodie, and not too far away from them, Calli and Daemon are lost in their own little bubble of happiness. I can't help but smile as he kisses her with such reverence, such love that it makes my heart ache in the best kind of way. Both of them deserve it. So much.

As Nico continues through the room, I find that Alex, Ant, and Isla are no longer anywhere to be seen.

Interesting...

But before I get a chance to really consider what that might mean, I'm carried straight out of Theo's penthouse and practically thrown into the open lift.

"Nico, what the—"

"You're leaving. Right the fuck now."

He stares at me with a fierce hatred burning in his eyes, and despite feeling the same after the way he's treated me tonight, I can't deny the disappointment that settles heavily in my stomach.

I wanted more. So much fucking more.

A bitter laugh that makes his brows pinch rumbles up my throat.

"You're a coward, Nico Cirillo," I hiss. But it's not enough, and before I know it, the lowest blow I can think of comes tumbling from my mouth. "Your father would be ashamed of you right now," I sneer, my top lip peeling back in disgust.

Disbelief floods his face a beat before it gives way to nothing but anguish.

I take a step forward, pain slicing through me that I just caused that look on his face, but I'm too slow, and the doors close, cutting us off.

Guilt floods me, and my stomach turns over, threatening to bring up the concoction of alcohol I've consumed tonight.

"Fuck," I breathe, stumbling back against the wall and dropping my head into my hands.

I probably shouldn't care.

But then, there are a lot of things I probably shouldn't do when it comes to Nico Cirillo.

He seems to be the exception to all my rules.

My heart pounds, ensuring I feel its beat in every inch of my body as a massive lump climbs up my throat.

I'm the worst person in the world.

Tears burn my eyes as the car makes its way through the building, and by the time it comes to a stop, they're barely clinging to my lashes.

The doors part, and with my gaze locked on the floor beneath me, I step forward, ready to make my escape.

But I come up short when a pair of familiar trainers fills my vision.

My heart plummets into my feet as my eyes lift, climbing up his body.

His chest heaves with exertion. How the fuck he got down here so fast, fuck only knows, but he has.

My breath catches when my eyes collide with his wretched ones, and before I know what's happening, his body collides with mine, and I'm forced back into the lift.

10

NICO

The second the doors close, I know I can't let her walk out of this building.

My legs move faster than I thought possible as I fly toward the stairwell and practically jump entire floors at a time, not pausing until I'm racing through the doors and coming to a grinding halt in front of the lift as the light above lets me know that I made it just in time.

My chest heaves and my muscles burn as I wait for the ding that will let me know she's about to be revealed.

What she said upstairs, it fucking hurt. More than it probably would if it had come from anyone else's lips.

I swear the slowest two seconds of my life drag past as I wait, but finally, that familiar ding rings out and the doors part, making my heart pound even harder and my anger and desire for her to surge once more.

I step forward, my body colliding with hers, forcing her back into the lift as she tries to make her escape.

My fingers grip her jaw as her back hits the wall, her eyes wide as she stares up at me in shock.

"I don't fucking think so, Siren," I growl, slamming my

hand down on the button for the top floor of the building before crashing my lips to hers.

But as we ascend through the building, she refuses to kiss me back, her defiant and stubborn streak as strong as ever.

"Give in, Siren. I know you want it."

"Fuck you."

"Yeah," I muse. "That's my fucking plan too."

Wrapping my hand around her thigh, I hike it up around my waist, allowing me to press my erection against her.

"Nico," she gasps when I hit the right spot. The second her lips part, I make the most of them, plunging my tongue inside her mouth.

She fights me. I wouldn't expect any less from my little spitfire.

But as my hand slips to her throat, my grip tightening in warning and allowing me to feel the thundering of her heart, she caves.

A deep growl rumbles in the back of my throat when she finally submits to me.

The ding of the lift's arrival on the top floor almost passes me by as I lose myself in her.

It's dangerous.

She's fucking dangerous.

One touch. One kiss and the grief, the anger, the confusion of everything that is happening around me right now just drifts away. She becomes my entire world, the only thing I can think about, focus on. She is the only thing I want.

A violent shudder rips down my spine and I manage to drag myself away.

The doors behind me open, but I don't move. I just stare

down at her with my chest heaving and desire coursing through my veins.

She stares right back at me without a flicker of hesitation in her eyes. And I know that if I were to send her away again now, she'd go without another word.

It's what I should do.

I need to figure out a way to stop being so fucking weak around this woman. But also... I can't.

Twisting my fingers in the sequined top she's wearing, I drag her forward, crashing her body against mine.

"One chance," I growl down at her. "This is your one chance to walk away."

A smirk curls at one side of her mouth.

"Have I given you any indication that I'm scared of you yet?" she asks.

Now it's my turn to smirk.

Prior to Brianna, I became somewhat used to seeing that flicker of fear in a girl's eyes. Almost all the girls I fucked knew who I was and what I was capable of. I used to thrive on that power.

But Brianna has never shown it. She's matched my brutality with a brand of her own and she has never revealed any kind of weakness.

There is a part of me that craves it. I want to see that flicker of hesitation, of fear in her eyes. I want to push her right to the edge until she has no choice to look at me like the girls of my past.

But there is another part that loves that it's not there. That she's willing to go up against me, no matter what I throw at her. She stands there and willingly takes it all before throwing most of it back.

If anything, I think I'm more scared of her than she is of me.

"Fuck you, Brianna Andrews," I growl, wrapping my fingers around her throat and forcing her backward out of the lift.

A feral grin spreads across her lips as her eyes continue to darken with need.

"No, Nico. Fuck you," she spits.

"We'll see."

All the air leaves her lungs as I slam her back against my front door. Pressing my hand to the scanner, I push the handle down and let her fall for a few seconds before I sweep her into my arms and carry her through my flat and launch her onto the bed.

She lands with a squeal as I drag my shirt over my head and reach for the abandoned bottle of vodka on my bedside table.

"No," Bri booms, making my movements pause.

"Excuse me?"

"I said no." She pushes to her feet and places her hands on her hips. "You want me, you say good night to that. I'm not putting up with a wasted, limp-dicked subpar fuck tonight. You can forget it."

I can't help but laugh. "Baby, even off my head you know I can deliver the goods." My eyes drop down her sinful body. Why is she still clothed?

"I'm not willing to risk it. Either I'm your main focus, or that bottle is. Choose."

Silence fills the room. Only the sound of our rapid breathing can be heard as I stand there frozen in the middle of an ultimatum.

I'm not sure anyone has offered me one before.

Especially one that involved sex.

Ripping my eyes from hers, I stare down at the bottle in

my hand, my mouth watering for that burn, that promise of nothing it offers me.

But then I look back at her.

Alcohol might promise me nothing, but she promises me oblivion.

The bottle hits the floor with a solid thud and I rush for her.

"Don't read too much into this," I mutter a beat before we collide once more.

I have no idea if she was able to hear it, or make it out, but fuck, I feel better for saying it.

"Never. You never need to worry about tomorrow morning with me," she confesses, letting me know she heard every word the second I drag my lips from hers in favour of her neck. "Yes," she breathes, her head falling to the side to give me more space.

I suck and bite the sensitive skin, ensuring I leave enough marks behind that when she does wake up without me tomorrow, she knows exactly who was here. Why her blood is buzzing with the rush of endorphins and her muscles ache in the way that only comes from mind-blowing sex.

Wrapping my fingers around the hem of her top, I drag it over her head and discard it on the floor before I go for her strapless bra, allowing that to fall at our feet in favour of sucking her nipples into my mouth greedily.

"Nico," she cries, her fingers sinking into my hair as I lave at one of her breasts while squeezing the other in my hand, pinching her nipples until it has to hurt. "Oh shit. Please."

"Keep begging like a filthy little whore, Miss Andrews, and you might just get what you want."

"Don't," she chastises, although it's seriously lacking the fire I'm sure she was hoping for. "N-not here."

My eyes hold hers as I continue. They're dark and hold the promise of all the things I want.

Standing tall once more, I step closer, letting her breasts brush against my chest.

"Ni—"

"Shut the fuck up, Siren."

I crash my lips to hers once more, licking into her mouth as if I'll die without her.

To be fair, with how these past few weeks have been, there is a chance I might.

Her hands roam around my body, making my skin prickle with desire, my need for her escalating to the point I wonder if I'm gonna blow in my pants.

She might have taken the edge off this all-consuming, toxic thing we've got going on in Theo's bathroom, but I'm pretty sure my cock has forgotten all about it.

A violent shudder rips through me as her fingers brush my lower stomach, and she tugs at my fly.

"Desperate for my cock again?" I murmur into our kiss.

"Don't read too much into it," she says, stealing my previous line. "It's the only part of you I like," she confesses, sinking to her knees and dragging my trousers and boxers down my legs.

My cock springs free, rock hard with precum leaking from the tip as if I haven't been touched in a month.

Abandoning my jeans around my knees, she wraps her fingers around my shaft and leans forward, licking up the precum. Her eyes close as she savours it, and fuck if my chest doesn't inflate at the sight.

"Filthy whore," I groan a beat before she sinks down on my length, taking all of me right to the back of her throat.

Something no other girl I've ever been with has done before. It makes my head fucking spin.

My hips thrust forward the second she pulls back and my grip on her hair tightens, holding her on me.

"You're not going anywhere until I've come down your throat, Siren."

Her watery eyes stare up at me, and despite being unable to talk with her lips straining against my width, I can almost hear her agreement.

I fuck her throat like a savage. Every thrust of my hips banishes the demons that keep dragging me back down into the darkness of despair.

Tears stream down her face, dark make-up staining her cheeks as she takes my cock like a pro.

My grip on her hair must be unbearable, but I'm powerless to release it as I race toward the end.

"Fuck. Siren. Fuck," I bark, my booming voice echoing around my silent flat. "Fucking addicted to having you on your knees," I confess without any thought. "Fucking love it. Fuck. Fuck. FUUUUCK."

My cock jerks as I shoot ropes of cum down her throat, and she doesn't disappoint, swallowing it all down.

I don't release her until I'm spent, and even then, all she does is pull back and lave the head of my dick with attention, lapping up anything that's left and cleaning me up.

In another lifetime, Brianna Andrews is my perfect woman.

As obsessed as I am watching her worship my dick, I finally kick off my jeans and boxers, my erection quickly coming back to life when she doesn't stop playing with me.

That is until I reach down and tuck my hands under her arms, hauling her from the floor and throwing her on the bed once more.

Reaching out, I return the favour and rip open her skin-tight jeans, peeling the teasing things down her legs.

"Such a shame," I mutter, trailing a finger over the delicate lace of her thong.

She stares down at me, her chest heaving, her make-up utterly ruined, and her eyes sparkling with desire.

"Hoping for commando?"

"Nah." Twisting my fingers in the lace, I tug them harshly from her body. They practically disintegrate, leaving her beautifully bare before me. "Not quite pretty enough not to ruin. Try harder next time."

"I didn't dress for you, dick."

"I know," I say with a smirk. "Because if you did, you'd have turned up at my door naked."

Pressing my hands to her knees, I spread her wide before me.

"And just look how much you like that idea. Waiting outside in the hallway, risking being caught. Waiting to see if I'm going to let you in and give you what you need."

"Nico," she whimpers when I blow a stream of cool air across her heated, glistening skin.

"You'd be standing out there with your own juices dripping down your thighs, wouldn't you, Siren? So desperate for my dick, you'd stand there like the shameless, filthy little whore that you are. You'd fucking beg too, wouldn't you?"

"Please," she moans as I skim my hands down the inside of her thighs, not getting close to where she really wants me.

"I've got what I've needed from you tonight, Siren. Twice, actually. You shouldn't even be here. You should be heading home to spend your night wondering why you were alone. Why I sent you away."

"But you didn't," she pants, her body trembling with

need. "And you want my pussy too much to even consider trying to do it again."

Goddamn it, she's right on the fucking money with that one.

Because as much of a stubborn motherfucker as I might be, there is no fucking way that she's walking out of my front door until her legs are barely holding her up and my cum is dripping from her body.

"Just like last night."

Her words give me pause for a beat before my fingers glide over a mark that I'd missed on her inner thigh.

All the air in my lungs comes out in a rush as I stare down at that mark. My fucking mark.

L-last night...

Last night was a drunken dream. A figment of my imagination.

Shattering in her arms. Letting her both hold me up and attempt to put me back together.

It never really happened.

I'd never allow her to see me that vulnerable, that weak.

But...

"Nico?" she whispers, sensing that I'm having something akin to a meltdown when I should be eating her like she's the most delicious thing in the world. I mean, she is, but that really is not the point right now.

I swallow down the anxiety that that realisation drags up, because if I allow myself to think about last night being real for too long, then there's every chance that I'll be the one to get up and walk away.

You're a Cirillo soldier, Nico. The future underboss. There are certain things expected of you. And the most important is to never lose face. You want to be respected. You need to show those motherfuckers that you are worthy, strong, un-fucking-breakable.

I squeeze my eyes closed as Dad's voice echoes through my head.

Do not show fucking weakness.

Ever.

Gritting my teeth, I rip my eyes open and stare down the woman who stupidly tried to hold me up last night.

Stupid, stupid girl.

"I fucking hate you, Brianna," I growl before dropping to my front and sucking on her clit so hard she screams like a banshee, her legs kicking out as she tries to deal with the sensations I suddenly force on her.

"Put your feet on the bed or I'll stop," I demand fiercely when her heel collides with my kidney.

"You wouldn't fucking dare."

"Fucking try me, Siren. I thought you knew me better than to dare me to do anything."

Our eyes hold for a beat as I stare at her over her body, fire crackling between us. But in her eyes, I now see an understanding, a compassion, fucking pity that I'm sure wasn't there only moments ago, and it makes my stomach knot painfully.

That is, until her fingers twist in my hair and she shoves me back down between her legs.

"Make yourself fucking useful or I might as well be alone and doing it myself."

"You fucking should be," I mutter before I bury myself between her thighs and lick and suck her until she's coming all over my face and screaming my name as if I'm fucking God.

I mean, I'm pretty sure I am. In terms of oral sex, anyway.

11

BRIANNA

Why the hell does he have to be so fucking good?

Why?

It's not fair.

Why couldn't one of the nice boys I've gone out with possess these kinds of skills? The ones who hold the door open, pull your seat out and talk about a nice and peaceful future with a white picket fence and two point five kids.

A shudder of disgust races down my spine at the thought of that being my destiny. But the fact I don't want that isn't the point.

Why does the man who makes my body fly like no other have to be such a dangerous, broken, miserable cunt?

"Nico," I gasp as he throws my legs over his shoulder and impales me on his impressive dick.

My breath catches as he slams into me so hard he hits my cervix.

"Fuck, your cunt is as mind-blowing as your mouth."

He grinds his hips, hitting both that place deep inside

me and my clit with his pelvis, and I almost go flying over the edge again despite having only just come on his face.

There have been very few men over the years who've managed to drag multiples out of me alone. Usually if I put in a helping hand and, you know, actually locate my clit, then I can have a couple.

But Nico far from needs a hand to send me flying over that edge over and over.

It makes me want to hate him all the more.

Personality aside, he's the perfect man. Gorgeous and unbelievably skilled in the bedroom. It's just a shame he uses his mouth for anything other than licking my pussy.

With one hand gripping my hip to stop me shooting up the bed with his powerful thrusts, he skims the other up my stomach and grabs my breast, squeezing it with the perfect pressure.

"Fuck yes, clamp down on my dick, just like that. Fuck. Siren."

Should I have let him drag me back here after he descended through the building like freaking Spiderman? No, probably not. I should have stood my ground and—

"Oh fuck, NICO," I scream, every single thought apart from what he's doing to my body right now falling from my head.

His thumb circles my clit so perfectly, I see fucking stars as he continues to thrust into me with steady, measured movements that make me climb higher and higher.

Sweat covers both our bodies as we move together in perfect sync.

In these moments, it's like we were made to be together. Like we were meant to find each other, sent to set each other's worlds on fire with this insane passion and desire to consume one another.

"Come for me, my filthy little whore," he demands, his voice deep and raspy with desire, his eyes eating me up, taking me in as if this isn't real.

Hell, it'll be easier tomorrow if it's not.

One more thrust and roll of his hips sends me crashing over the edge. Pleasure like only Nico is able to deliver races through my body, eradicating all my doubts, stress, and stupid fucking decisions. And it doesn't fucking stop.

"Oh fuck, Siren. FUUUCK," Nico growls, his cock jerking deep inside me before he spills his seed in my pussy and collapses on top of me.

We stay there in a heap of sweaty and panting bodies as our highs fade and reality begins to trickle back in.

"Stop it," Nico demands, startling me.

"I'm not doing anything," I argue with a delirious laugh.

"You are. You're thinking. Stop it or leave."

"I'm not allowed to think?"

"No, not unless you're considering just how much you want to get on top and ride me."

Another laugh tumbles free. I blame the orgasms for shattering the tension between us. "You just came."

"And you're just lying naked beneath me. But if you're done and want to think, you know where the door is."

"You're a cunt," I snap, forcing myself from beneath him and swinging my legs from the bed.

"Where are you going?"

"Fuck you, Nico. Fuck you."

In a rush, I escape to the bathroom. In hindsight, I probably should have scooped up my clothes and ran for the front door. Fuck my nakedness or his cum that's running down my thighs. Most of the people who might stumble across me have already seen it all.

Fucking hell, I really am a filthy whore.

Oh well. Shit could be worse.

I could be celibate and frustrated. Or stuck with one boring motherfucker with a tiny penis that he can't even get up.

I swing the bathroom door closed behind me with a dramatic roar of anger, just in case Nico hadn't already got the memo that he drives me fucking crazy any minute of the day that his cock isn't inside me.

I ignore the toilet for a second in favour of the glass that's sitting beside the sink, my desperation for a drink bigger than my need to clean up.

I fill it with cold water and just lift it to my lips when the door crashes back against the wall and the entire fucking thing slips from my grip, smashing around my feet.

"What the fuck are you—"

"Don't move," Nico barks like the bossy fuck he is.

Glancing at the shards of glass, I figure it's probably a good call to listen to him.

He fucking doesn't, though, and strides right over.

"Hands on the basin, Siren." When I don't follow orders, his fingers twist in my hair and he directs my face so I have no choice but to stare into the mirror before me and directly into his eyes. "Do as you are fucking told."

"B-but the glass."

A shriek peels from my lips as I'm suddenly bent forward. My hands fly out to catch me before I crash into the basin.

"Could have just done as I suggested," Nico mutters behind me before his fingers slide up my thighs, through the mess he left me in, and he tuts in disapproval. "Wasteful," he chastises before his fingers spear me, pushing his spunk back inside.

"Fuck," I bark, my muscles clamping down on his fingers as he curls them just so.

He pushes me lower, my cheek pressing against the cool porcelain of the basin.

"Nico, what are you— Shit," I hiss when the head of his cock presses against my entrance.

"Last night," he growls, teasing me with just the tip. "I need you to forget everything that happened."

"Why?" I gasp as he suddenly thrusts forward, filling me to the hilt.

He yanks on my hair and I'm dragged from the basin and forced to face the mirror once more.

His eyes are feral over my shoulder and his muscles are pulled tight as he holds back from fucking me like a savage.

"Because I fucking said so, and my filthy little whore likes doing what she's told." He pulls out and thrusts forward once more. "Don't you?" Thrust. "Siren."

"Nico," I cry, unable to do anything but stand there, looking deep into his eyes as he tries to fuck the memory of last night out of me. "It doesn't— Fine. Whatever you want."

His eyes alight with accomplishment and his nostrils flare as he continues trying to restrain himself.

"What I want—" He cuts himself off suddenly, his grip on both my hair and my hip tightening. "I want you screaming my name, again, and again, and a-fucking-gain. And then when you can't possibly go again, or take any more of my cum? Then you can leave."

"Sounds like a great fucking deal to me," I confess, silently challenging him with nothing more than my eyes.

"And the second you walk out, we're done, *Miss Andrews.*"

My teeth grind at his use of my teacher name again, but

as much as I might want to argue, I know he's right. I'm just too dick drunk right now to really appreciate how walking away, how never doing this again, is the only way to handle this whole situation.

***

Just as he promised, Nico fucked me every which way after carrying me from the bathroom, ensuring at least one of us didn't stand on the glass. He, on the other hand, bled all over his carpet and I'm sure the bed, but with the dark sheets it was impossible to see and easy to push aside as he continued to work me over so thoroughly that when he finally passed out, I wasn't entirely sure I still had control of my limbs.

"Oh fuck," I hiss, immediately reaching for the bedside table when I attempt to stand.

What exactly did that motherfucker do to my knees?

I glance down to make sure they're still there and am relieved to find that they are. What I'm not so thrilled with are all the bite marks and hickeys that litter almost every inch of my body.

A quick glance over my shoulder lets me know that Nico is still out for the count, and I finally find the strength to get to my feet and collect up my abandoned clothes.

I find the scrap of lace that used to be my knickers and I almost stuff them in my jeans pocket, ready to go in the bin. But at the last minute, I change my mind and instead leave them as a reminder of my visit, placing them on the pillow I just lifted my head from.

With my clothes bundled in my arms and my shoes swinging from my fingers, I pad toward the door. Really, I need to use the bathroom. What is going on between my thighs is beyond gross. But mostly, I just need to get out of here.

Walk of shame from Nico Cirillo's flat two nights in a row, you hussy.

I shake my head at my own thoughts.

Walking away now when he's asleep is easier. I can only imagine how he'd react if I were curled up beside him when he woke in the morning, or more likely tomorrow lunchtime after the amount of alcohol he drank and how we went at it.

Exhaustion pulls at every muscle in my body as I move toward the door.

At the last minute, I pause and look back.

I regret it instantly.

Nico is passed out naked with one arm thrown over his head and the other resting across his stomach. One of his legs is twisted up in the sheets while the other is free, giving me full view of everything.

"Damn you for being so fucking beautiful," I mutter quietly before ripping my eyes away and leaving him to sleep.

Dragging on my clothes, I try not to think about my overused pussy rubbing against the roughness of my jeans as I push my feet into my shoes. After sucking in a deep, calming breath, I pull the front door open and step out, letting it close quietly behind me.

Thankfully, and as expected, seeing as it's the middle of the night, the building is silent and deserted.

I pull my phone from my bag as I descend in the lift, and unlike last time, I open up the Uber app and set about ordering myself a car.

Only, the bloody thing refuses to confirm my journey because my bank card gets declined.

"Fuck," I hiss, trying Apple Pay and discovering the exact same thing. "No, no, no."

The lift dings and the doors open. I spill out into the entrance with my head spinning.

I can't walk home from here. Even if it weren't the dead of night and I were wearing knickers, it's still too far. Especially in these shoes.

I step out into the darkness, hoping that some fresh air might provide me with clarity.

It doesn't.

Looking up at the imposing building before me, I consider going back up and waking Jodie and Toby. I could crash in their spare room and they'd even give me a lift back in the morning.

But the thought of that, of having no choice but to confess the reason I'm still here fills me with dread.

I didn't actually leave, I spent the night fucking one of my students.

My stomach turns over and I have no choice but to twist around and heave into the bush beside me.

But it's while I'm barfing up what's left of tonight's alcohol that an idea hits me.

Flipping open my purse, I pull out Nico's credit card.

I hated using it yesterday. It's something I'm probably always going to regret, and never be able to forget, seeing as I need to wear the clothes I bought with it to school. Unless I want to turn up looking like a Primark model. Anywhere else, it wouldn't bother me in the slightest. But there, where I know people, where I'm going to need all the armour I can find to deal with Nico? Yeah, it was necessary.

And right now, unfortunately for me, he's my only option.

I update my Uber app with his card details. Thankfully,

it doesn't need any kind of approval from him, and it books my car.

I push any unease about what I've just done aside and walk toward the car park entrance so I can hop into the back of the car the second it arrives to get me the hell out of here.

12

———

NICO

A bang wakes me. But it's not enough to make me open my eyes or even consider moving.

Something tickles my nose, and when I reach up to move it and my fingers brush the soft lace, memories from the night before hit me.

Now, I know they're real.

I can feel them. Feel her. Smell her.

My fingers tighten on her knickers and instead of shoving them aside, I find myself bringing them closer.

Her scent floods my senses, making my mouth water and my cock hard.

After the number of times I took her last night, it would be easy to think my dick would want a day off, but it's insatiable when it comes to my siren.

No. Not my siren.

Just... Siren.

Brianna.

Miss fucking Andrews.

A smirk twitches at my lips as I consider what we did last night.

I fucked my teacher.

The thought sends fire raging through me.

Over the years, there have been plenty of members of staff that the guys and I have lusted after. But as far as I know, none of us have put those little fantasies into action. Until now...

Okay, so I guess it could be seen as an entirely different situation.

I knew Brianna—had fucked Brianna—long before she turned up sporting a staff name badge at Knight's Ridge. But still, the fact stands. In a couple of days, she's going to be standing at the front of a classroom and I will be her student.

I roll onto my back, taking her knickers with me as I imagine fucking her over the teacher's desk after class.

Fuck, yeah. The next few weeks could well be better than the previous few.

"Nico, you lazy motherfucker," a familiar voice booms through my apartment, letting me know what the bang was.

"Fuck off, I'm sleeping."

"Alone, or are you balls deep in—" The door flies open before Toby finishes that sentence, obviously deciding that he wanted to find out for himself. "Huh, well, that's boring. Is that blood?" He gawks.

"Fuck off, Tobes," I groan, not bothering to cover up in any way. It isn't like he hasn't seen it all a million times before. Hell, before he hooked up with Jodie, there was a time or two when we double-teamed a girl that—

"It smells like sex in here," he points out before striding across the room, dodging the blood splatters, ripping the curtains apart and throwing a window open.

"Hey," I complain as the warm morning—is it even morning?—air washes over my heated skin.

"The fucking sun will be going down soon," Toby points out as he strides back across the room and pokes his head into the bathroom.

"Do I look like I give a shit about the sun? Close them," I demand.

"No."

"Why are we friends again?" I shout when he stalks through my bedroom and disappears. I stretch as my body finally wakes up while he crashes about.

"Will you fucking cover up?" Toby barks when he walks back in with a dustpan and brush. Where he found that from, fuck only knows.

"What? I didn't invite you in here. But don't worry, because of your unwanted presence, it'll go down in a minute."

"Because that will make it better. I'm sure it just winked at me."

"Fuck you," I groan, scrubbing my hand down my face.

"What happened last night, Nic?"

For a second, just a second, I let my mind wander back.

When my cock starts to stir again from memories alone, I finally reach for the duvet and pull it over my bottom half.

"You said it when you walked in. Had sex. Just like all you motherfuckers probably did, from the way you were all going at it when I left."

"When *you* left?" he asks, quirking a brow.

"What? I'm not in the mood for riddles and games. If you have a question, fucking ask it."

"Fine. What happened with Brianna?"

"I fucked her. A lot."

Silence follows my statement.

"What?" I finally snap, unable to bear the tension.

"There's something you need to know."

My eyes widen and my curiosity gets the better of me. I drag myself up so I'm sitting against the headboard. My body pulls and aches in the best possible way, but when Toby's eyes drop to my feet, I realise how much they sting.

"Do you have any glass in them?" he asks, looking concerned.

I shrug, not willing to talk about my feet right now when he clearly has something to say.

"Go on, don't let me stop you from confessing your sins."

My heart rate increases as I stare at my best friend, wondering what the hell he could need to tell me.

We don't keep secrets. We never have. Nothing is worth risking the friendship we share. But something tells me that might just have changed as his expression darkens.

"Brianna is going to be a student teacher at Knight's Ridge."

Breathe in.

Breathe out.

Breathe in.

"You knew?" I fight to keep my expression blank, but it's a fucking feat.

Clearly reading something on my face, he dips his head and rubs his hand over the back of his neck.

"I set it up," he confesses.

All the air rushes out of my lungs as I stare at him.

It takes him a few seconds, but his eyes eventually lift from the floor in favour of mine once more.

"When?" I demand.

"After her other placement fell apart last week."

"And you didn't think to tell me?"

"She wanted to herself. She came over Thursday night to tell you but—"

"But what?" I bark, my heart beginning to beat out of control as I think about what happened Thursday night instead. Not that her turning up and telling me that she was about to be my teacher would have been any better. Worse, maybe. If that's even possible.

"I don't know, you tell me what distracted her." His eyes dart down to my covered dick, a smirk pulling at his lips.

"She was in my English lit lesson yesterday," I confess, making all the blood drain from Toby's face. "Yeah, see. You should have told me."

"What happened? I mean, it can't have been that bad if you spent the night fucking her."

"Nothing happened. I didn't walk inside the classroom."

"It's just a couple of weeks," Toby assures me. "Just stay out of her way, let her do what she needs to do and focus on your exams. Anyway, it's not like you've even been at school. Something tells me that you're not suddenly going to turn into a conscientious student."

"I might." If my teacher has anything to do with it.

"Nico," Toby warns, hearing my unspoken words loud and clear.

"What? I think we can both agree that I've spent enough time moping in here. Maybe it's time to rejoin the world and figure out how to pass these exams."

"Well, you can't fail them. Your dad would be so disappointed," Toby says while his eyes hold mine steady.

"You're a cunt," I hiss, hating just how much those few words hurt.

"I'm not wrong though, am I?"

I glare at him, the air between us turning dark, but if Toby senses it, then he blatantly ignores it.

"Get your arse up. We're hitting the gym and then we're working."

"Working?" I still. The thought of putting my suit on and heading out on a job fucking terrifies me.

"Revising," he corrects. "Everything is still quiet on the real work front. Damien is still working with Stefanos and Galen."

Guilt surges through me that I'm not there. That I'm not a part of the plans to bring those motherfuckers down.

"It's okay, Nic," Toby assures me. "They understand. Take your time."

"It's not fucking good enough though, is it," I hiss, finally rolling from the bed, swiping the dustpan and brush from Toby and storming toward the bathroom, swinging the door angrily behind me. The bottoms of my feet burn, reminding me of the events of the night before and I cure myself when my dick twitches.

"ARGH," I bellow, my anger, grief, and utter uselessness colliding again.

I clean up quickly, then take a piss, brush my teeth, and reluctantly step into the shower.

As much as that infuriating woman might piss me off, I also don't really want to wash her sweet scent from my skin.

As the warm water hits my shoulders and races down my body, I try to force the memories from my previous two nights with her down the drain with it.

After a few deep, steeling breaths, I turn the water off, grab a towel, and head back to my bedroom.

Toby is nowhere to be seen, but I can hear him moving around out in my living area, so after dragging on some gym clothes, I head out to find him... tidying up.

"What the fuck are you doing?"

"What the fuck does it look like?" he spits, transferring

dirty glasses and plates from the kitchen counter into the dishwasher. "You haven't been letting Carolina in, have you?" he asks, referring to the cleaner who works between all our flats in this building.

"I haven't been letting anyone in. I thought that was obvious enough when I changed the permissions on security. Which you seem to have ignored."

"You can't keep me out, bro. You should know that by now."

Being the cunt I am, I hop up onto my barstool and let him continue.

"This place is a shithole. I'm amazed Bri was willing to stay here."

"She didn't have any interest in my flat, Tobes," I quip. "Her eyes were solely on the prize."

"Pig."

"Pot calling the kettle black."

"Hey, I take offence to that. I treat Jodie exactly as she deserves," he argues.

"Now you do. It wasn't always that way."

"Yeah, well. I fucked up. And I'll spend every day of the rest of my life making up for it if she lets me."

"See right there, that's the difference. I don't want the rest-of-my-life bullshit. So fuck what she thinks of my messy flat. As long as she's sucking my dick well, nothing else matters."

"Jesus. Have you heard yourself? No wonder Bri hates you."

I shrug, refusing to allow his words to cut into me any more than they already have.

"She's a bit of fun, and she's under no illusion that it's anything more than that."

"So you're going to let her do her job?" he asks, pinning me with a deadly look.

"Sure. I'll let her teach me a few lessons. If she's lucky, I'll be a really, really bad boy."

"Fuck my life. Come on, you're a mess."

Kicking my dishwasher closed, he marches over, wrapping his fingers around my upper arm and practically dragging me off the stool.

"Fucking hell, Tobes."

"You're out of shape and we all need you on top form. It might be quiet now, but war is coming and we need to be ready."

His words make my heart sink, but I can't exactly argue. As soon as Damien gets the intel he needs, we'll make a move, I have no doubt. It's just the when that's in question.

***

Just like he promised, Toby pushed me as hard as he possibly could in the gym. By the time he let up, I was a sweaty, trembling wreck. But I can't deny that it didn't feel good.

The gym used to be my safe place. The place I could escape to when life got too much. I could put my headphones in and forget about the bullshit that was happening outside that room.

I've lost that since Dad died. Everything I used to enjoy, everything I used to know feels like it's been ripped away from me.

But if being down in the basement with Toby taught me anything, it's that I need to find a way to rediscover the person I was before that building started falling on our heads.

Brianna and Toby are right with what they've said recently. Dad would be ashamed of me right now. Losing myself in drink, drugs, and Brianna's pussy.

It's not how he'd have dealt with all this.

He'd have been focused, determined, and burning the motherfucking city down to get answers, to find the men responsible for causing such devastation on our Family.

After stumbling back into my flat, with a sweaty Toby right on my heels, he shoved me into my room to shower again while making use of my main bathroom. Then, he proceeded to order us dinner and placed a whole bunch of textbooks in front of me.

It was like old times, just with the addition of the vast black pit of pain and grief that seems to have taken up residence in my chest.

He took great delight in telling me that Jodie was busy hanging out with the girls but refrained from telling me if that included Bri or not. Prick.

He also stole my phone the second we returned from the gym to stop me from even trying to reach out should I have wanted to. Which of course, I didn't.

And the next morning, I'm once again woken by someone banging on my door.

"Go away," I bellow, nowhere near ready to restart the study session Toby has already warned me is happening today.

I pointed out that really, he should just go next door and study with someone on his own intellectual level, but he insisted that I was a better study partner than Theo. I mean, I get it. I'm way more fun. But some of that IT shit he was studying yesterday was well beyond anything I'm capable of.

The knocking continues despite my refusal to let whoever it is in.

"For fuck's sake," I mutter, rolling out of bed and pulling on a pair of boxers. That's all the fucking effort whoever is at the other side of my front door is getting.

The knocking continues as I walk through my living area.

"All-fucking-right," I bellow before twisting the lock and ripping the door open. "What do you—" My vicious words die the second my eyes land on a concerned pair of familiar blue ones. "Calli?"

"Hey, Bro," she says with a wide, genuine smile. "How's it going?"

"Uh…"

I look behind her, half expecting to find Daemon loitering, and I breathe a sigh of relief when I don't find him. That feeling is quickly followed by a fuck load of guilt.

"Can I come in? I have breakfast," she says, holding up a paper bag and takeout coffees.

"Uh…"

"Jesus. I'm coming in," she decides, pushing past me and marching down toward my living room. "No one is following me," she calls back when I don't instantly close the door and trail after her.

"Right," I mutter to myself as I finally swing the door closed.

By the time I get to her, she's ripped open the paper bag and she's got a chocolate croissant half stuffed in her mouth.

"What?" she asks around her mouthful of croissant.

"Just wondering what the hell he saw in you. You've got crumbs… everywhere."

She glares at me, but there's no real fire in it. There

never is with Calli. She might want to be a bad-arse like Stella and Emmie, but deep down, she's just too nice, too sweet. She can hookup with the baddest motherfucker in the world and she'll still be my little sister. Just maybe a little less innocent.

"Fuck you, Bro. I'm a catch and you know it. You, on the other hand..." Her eyes drop down my body, lingering on each bite, scratch and hickey. "Look like you've been ravaged by a bear. Have fun Friday night?"

"You really want details?" I ask, stalking over and stealing one of the croissants.

"Sure. If you can handle hearing mine in return."

A shudder rips down my spine at the thought.

"Nah, you're all good. I'll let you use your imagination. Check this one out on my arse, though."

I turn around and tuck my thumb under the waistband of my boxers as if I'm actually going to show her.

"God, no," she cries, covering her eyes with her hand. "Go and put clothes on. I came here to work, not be traumatised."

"Work?"

"Yep, Toby said—"

"Fucking Toby," I mutter, combing my fingers through my hair as I back up toward my bedroom.

"It's time to pull your head out of your arse, big brother. I know it hurts, trust me, I do. But he wouldn't want this," she says, gesturing to my flat.

Fuck. Why do those words hit so much harder when they're said by my little sister?

"I know," I mutter quietly. "Don't eat all the croissants," I warn before heading back to my room to find some clothes.

"I can't promise anything."

I walk into my bedroom with the weight of the world pressing down on my shoulders.

How I've treated Calli over the past couple of weeks has been unforgivable. The way I spoke to her after discovering what has been going on with her and Daemon... well, she has every right to never speak to me again.

But here she is. Okay, under Toby's intrusion, but still, she was well within her right to tell him to fuck off.

I drag on a pair of sweats and hoodie, aware that I will have to go out there and figure out a way to make it up to her.

If that's even possible.

With a heavy sigh, I head back in the hope she hasn't already demolished the pastries.

Her eyes track me as I make my way over and fall onto the sofa beside her.

"I'm sorry, Calli."

Her eyes soften as she studies me.

"If he's it for you, you know I'll support you all the way."

It fucking pains me to say it, because all I've ever wanted for her is a nice, danger-free, somewhat boring man for her. Pretty much the opposite of Daemon. But I'm pretty sure it's a bit late for all those hopes and dreams now. She's fucking moved in with him.

Her eyes get a little glassy and her bottom lip trembles before she launches herself at me, throwing her arms around my neck and holding me tight.

I return her embrace as she sniffles against my neck.

"Dude, don't cry on me. You know how uncomfortable that makes me."

"Suck it up," she whimpers, her grip tightening. "I've missed you."

"Fuck. Me too, Cal. Me too."

"Everything is going to be okay, you know," she murmurs after long silent seconds. "We've just got to stick together."

"Yeah," I breathe, thinking of the woman who's been left behind in all this. "You spoken to Mum?"

"Nope. Not since I moved out. You?"

I shake my head.

"You think she's forgotten we exist?"

"Cal, if I hadn't seen photographs of her pregnant with both of us then I wouldn't believe she was our mother."

"What did he see in her?"

"I don't know. But I suspect it was hiding between her thighs."

"Ugh, Nico," she complains, finally sitting back, but not before she slaps my shoulder.

"What? It's probably true and you know it."

"Yes, but it doesn't need discussing," she mutters. "I just wish I could ask him. He was so..."

"And she's a raving bitch," I finish when she trails off.

"I miss him."

Reaching for her hand, I squeeze it, hating the way her voice cracks with emotion.

"I know, Cal. Everyone keeps saying that it'll get better but..."

"Everyone can't be wrong."

We let out simultaneous pained sighs before Calli reaches for her coffee and I grab another croissant.

"So..." I start and she groans, guessing what's coming. "Talk to me about Daemon. All I know is that you're fucking and you've moved in with him without telling me so..."

"I love him, Nico. We're not *just* fucking."

"Thanks for confirming that you are fucking," I say around a mouthful of buttery pastry.

"I thought I'd lost both of them. Having him back is... it's everything."

"How's he doing?"

"He's good. Will be left with a few more scars than before, but he's going to be fine. Even better when he's allowed out to go and kill someone."

I can't help but laugh at the look of confusion on my sister's face as she explains what her boyfriend wants to go and do.

"Now that is something I can understand. We're going to ensure every one of those motherfuckers who hurt us pays, Cal. We won't let them get away with it."

"I know. I don't doubt any of you. I just pray they don't take any more from us. That we're ready."

Unease ripples through me, because after the past couple of weeks, I'm anything but ready. My session in the gym yesterday with Toby only confirmed that.

"We'll be ready. Those cunts won't get away with hurting us."

"We should probably do something productive," Calli says, grabbing one of the textbooks I left out after my study session with Toby.

"Great. I can't wait."

"A few weeks and it's all done. No more studying or exams," Calli says, glancing over at me nervously.

"Cal?"

"I-I'm not going to uni, Nic. It's not right."

My chin drops, my lips opening and closing like a fish for a few seconds before I finally find some words.

"Okay. If that's what you want."

"It is," she agrees, but despite her words, she barely relaxes.

"What is it?" I ask, searching her eyes for the answer.

"N-nothing. It's just all this. It's been... a lot."

Reaching out, I squeeze her knee in support. "We've got this. We're gonna do Dad proud. Keep his legacy alive and take this world by storm," I say, although I feel much less confident about that statement than how it sounds.

"I hope so. I want to make him proud."

"Cal, he was so fucking proud of you."

"I wish he knew about Daemon."

"He does," I assure her. "And he'll be happy you've got him by your side."

We study and talk about everything and nothing for hours. It's... nice. Easy. A throwback to times gone by. It's been a while since we've hung out just the two of us like this, and it makes me realise just how much we need it.

But eventually, reality comes calling in the form of Calli's phone ringing.

"Ah, time's up, big bro," she says, staring down at the screen before swiping it and lifting it to her ear. "Hey, devil boy," she says, her words making me equally as happy as I am horrified. "Yep, he'll be right there."

I get up and take our empty cans to the kitchen when she starts telling him that she loves him. I might be able to get on board with them being together, but I have limits.

"You need to go to Theo's," she says after hanging up.

"Why?"

"Damien, Stefanos and Galen are there for a catch up."

"Do they know something?" I ask hopefully.

"You're looking at the wrong person. I have no clue what's going on."

"You know they're meeting," I point out.

"Two very different things. Ant's up there with Daemon, too."

"Ant?" I ask, my body automatically locking up at the thought of the Italian who seems to have moved in with us. Literally.

"You can trust him. He almost died getting Daemon back to me. He's also got information and contacts that you all need."

"And he's willing to just tell us all?"

"I don't know the details, but he hates his uncle almost as much as you all do, so yes. I think he's all in."

Unable to argue, I help Calli pack up her stuff and together we head out of my flat and let ourselves into Theo's.

As promised, everyone is sitting around Theo's sofas, looking beyond tense.

"About time. I can't deal with all this alpha, big dick energy any longer," Emmie announces, hopping up from beside Theo.

Damien watches her with curious eyes as she smacks a kiss on his son's cheek and bounces over in her black shorts, fishnets and biker boots. Emmie is... well, fucking epic to be fair, but I don't think she's what any of us pictured for the future boss of the Family.

"Emmie," Theo warns.

"What? We're not going to cause trouble. Well, not too much," she teases, throwing her arm around Calli's shoulders and grinning widely.

"Sure you're not. Just... make sure you take someone if you go out."

"Pfft, please. I have a gun and a knife. We can hold our own."

"Angel," Daemon begs, looking horrified at the thought of Calli having to fight anyone.

"We're not leaving the building. Ignore her. Have fun. And if you need any suggestions for your next book club, just let me know," she teases, letting me see a whole new side to my sister before the two of them disappear from sight.

"Okay, Anthony, is your boy ready?" Damien asks the second the door slams closed.

"Sure is." Ant wakes up the laptop sitting on his knees and his best friend, Enzo, appears before us.

"Great. Now there's two of them," I mutter, earning myself some serious side eye from everyone in the room.

13

BRIANNA

I don't get a wink of sleep. I spend all night tossing and turning, coming up with all kinds of crazy scenarios for how today is going to go.

I checked the timetable that Mrs. Hendrix gave me about a million times, praying that I read it wrong all the times before when it said that I was in her double English lit year thirteen class before lunch today. But each time I looked at that piece of paper, the truth stared back at me, unyielding and unmoving, my fate taunting me with a million possibilities. One where Nico ignores me and pretends we've never met before, not one of them.

Even if he does by some miracle do that, then I'm going to know every time he looks at me that he spent most of Friday night eating my pussy.

Fuck. My. Life.

The sun hasn't risen when I eventually give up on trying to sleep and roll out of bed.

I have the world's longest shower in the hope of washing all my doubts down the drain, but when I step out, nothing has changed. My stomach is still knotted up in dread, and my heart is racing with my anxiety.

I do my make-up in the hope it'll cover up my unease and curl my hair. I waste enough time that after triple checking I've got everything, it's about the time I need to leave anyway.

Thoughts of the four tube changes, the bus, and the long walk up Knight's Ridge's grand entrance don't fill me with any kind of excitement.

But knowing my future depends on the next few weeks, I throw my shoulders back, hold my head high and step out of my flat.

My phone dings as I walk down the stairs—no fancy lifts here—and my brows pinch when I find a name I wasn't expecting staring back at me.

> Toby: Arranged a little surprise to make your life easier…

> Toby: Check your post box.

> Brianna: WHAT HAVE YOU DONE?

My heart pounds as I race down the final few stairs and fly toward my post box.

My hand trembles as I unlock it, because I already know this is something big.

It's Toby and the freaking Cirillos. He hasn't just left a good luck card for me.

"Holy fuck."

> Brianna: You are in so much shit, Doukas.

Toby: I take payment in the form of blowies from your best friend. Please discuss with her. *winky face*

"Fucking hell."

With the small black key fob locked in my hand, I push out of the main door of our building and scan the row of cars before me.

A black Audi A1 catches my attention because it stands out like a sore thumb amidst the other cars, and when I press the unlock button on the key in my hand, its lights flash, welcoming me toward it.

A laugh full of pure disbelief falls from my lips as I pull the driver's door open and drop into the seat.

Brianna: I might not even have a licence…

Toby: Don't insult me like that. I know you have a licence. You passed on a Thursday at eleven twenty-five. Your examiner was called Mark. And I bet you wore a short skirt and he checked out your legs.

Brianna: It's a good job my best friend loves you.

Toby: Yep, I'm a lucky motherfucker. Enjoy your ride… I know I will. See you later.

Toby: And don't worry about Nico. I'll handle him.

"If only that were fucking possible," I mutter as I look around at my surroundings and a little squeal of excitement falls from my lips.

I shouldn't accept it. I should drive it straight to their building and refuse it.

But the thought of those tubes, all the sweaty commuters, and the long-arse walk up to those imposing buildings while the elite kids of London drive past me in their Aston Martins and Maseratis...

Yeah, or I could just use it for a few weeks. Take advantage of my connections and make my life easier. Something tells me that Nico is going to owe me over the coming days.

More so than what you've already spent on his credit card...

"Fuck it," I say to myself, pressing my finger against the start button. In only a few minutes, I have my phone synced, my music playing, and I'm pulling out of the space. All I can hope is that my day continues to be better than I was expecting.

The drive to Knight's Ridge is smooth with barely any traffic, and before I know it, I'm heading up the insane driveway that leads to the ominous buildings which hold the fate of my future teaching career.

The car park is practically empty with other staff members' cars littered around. It means I thankfully don't have to park next to something that costs more than I'm likely to earn in a lifetime and worry about opening the door on it.

I kill the engine, plunging myself into silence before grabbing my phone once more and opening our previous conversation.

> Brianna: Thank you. You have no idea how much easier you have made my life. If Jodie doesn't get on her knees to thank you, I will.

I hit send without thought and the second it shows as read, I panic that it might have been a little much.

> Toby: Save your skills for my boy.

"Been there, done that," I mutter to myself as I find my conversation with Jodie.

> Brianna: FYI you owe your boyfriend a bazillion blow jobs. Might want to stock up on lip balm.

> Best bitch: So I've heard. Can't say I'm complaining. He always reciprocates.

> Brianna: Lucky bitch.

> Best bitch: No midnight visitors last night, I take it?

> Brianna: Thankfully not. My vag needed a rest.

> Best bitch: Like that's ever stopped you before.

> Best bitch: Good luck today. Not that you need it. x

I blow out a breath as I close down my messages. I wish I had her optimism.

Straightening my spine, I push the car door open, grab my stuff, and head in the direction of Mrs. Hendrix's office almost an hour before I was expecting to arrive.

The beginning of the day was great. I got to meet Mrs. Hendrix's year ten tutor group, which of course included Rhea, who was surprisingly polite and well behaved. Melissa tried to tell me that they were a handful, that she'd been given the more challenging students to mentor, but they were all posh little teddy bears compared to the students of my past.

And then I spent two hours with different members of the English department in a year seven and then a year ten class. The behaviour of the students in both were exemplary, the teaching fantastic and inspiring. I found myself drawn into the lessons more than once in both of them.

Not having to worry about what the students are doing every five seconds sure frees up time to dive deeper into subjects than I've previously been able to.

I'm so lost helping the year tens write sonnets that the bell ringing through the ancient hallways outside the room startles me.

The girl I'm sitting next to laughs before she begins packing away her books and the teacher brings the lesson to a close.

"Are you ready for a coffee, Miss Andrews?" he asks as the students begin to file out of the room and he powers down his computer for break.

"So ready."

"Monday is chocolate biscuit day if we're fast enough."

With a smile playing on my lips, I follow Mr. Atworth out of the room and then the English building.

The second I step out into the burning sun, the sixth form building fills my vision.

Students and teachers are moving around everywhere.

It should be impossible to make out a single person in the sea of bodies.

But it isn't.

My steps falter the second my eyes land on his.

He's stopped dead in the middle of the main entrance to the building, forcing the other sixth formers to move around him.

His face is hard, his jaw set and his eyes dark. His Knight's Ridge uniform fits him like a second skin. No school uniform should look that good on anyone. It should be fucking illegal.

The deep, rumbling voice of Mr. Atworth hits my ears, but I don't register his words or know if he's even talking to me as my attention is swallowed up by the enigma of a man before me. Even if I didn't know who he was, what his future holds, it would be impossible to miss the danger, the power that emanates from him. The only thing more terrifying would be if Theo were to step up beside him.

A shudder rips down my spine as a second later, that exact thing happens. And it's not just Theo, but all of them.

I swear, as the five of them stand there holding court over the school, a wave of unease, of fear, goes through every other single person out here.

It's bizarre. It's... a serious eye-opener.

Obviously, I knew they had power, were respected, but I'm not sure I ever could have prepared myself for the true level of it.

Even the staff seem to be slightly terrified by the boys staring out over their land.

His eyes continue to hold mine captive as a sneer pulls at his lips that has dread flooding my veins.

You're not scared of him, Brianna. He's just trying to mess with your head.

Unlike everyone else, I don't cower, I don't avoid their gazes, I don't run. Instead, I rip my eyes from Nico's and stare each of them dead in the eyes. Alex and Seb are the only ones who look at all shocked to see me.

"Brianna?" a hesitant voice says from a few feet away, and when I finally drag my eyes from the baby mafia standing before me, I find Mr. Atworth looking between me and them with concern in his eyes. "Are you coming?"

"Yes, of course," I say confidently, offering him a sure smile. My actions are totally at odds with how I'm really feeling, but I can't start my first week at Knight's Ridge outwardly showing everyone who so much as glances my way that I spent both Thursday and Friday nights with one of their most high profile students between my thighs.

Christ. I'm so fucked.

When he starts moving again, I follow behind as Nico's glare continues burning into my back.

"I assume you know who they are?" Mr. Atworth asks once we're in the safety of the building that holds not only the staff room but all the admin offices.

"I'm aware, yes."

"Okay, so you don't really need me to tell you that you'd be best to avoid them at all costs?"

"Not really, no." But something tells me it's not going to be a possibility.

"Thankfully, they'll be leaving soon."

"There must be others though?" I ask. I might know more than any teacher needs to about those five boys and the girls who belong by their sides, but I've never really been party to any talk about younger members of the Family. Rhea aside, of course.

"Of course, there are members of the Family in most

year groups. But I think it will be a few years yet until we have a year group which is quite as formidable as those five."

Six, I think, my mind shooting to Daemon, who's still locked up in his flat like a prisoner while the others try to figure out a way to deal with the Italians.

"Enough about them," he says, pushing through the door and allowing the strong scent of decent coffee to fill my senses.

But as much as my mouth might water for the pick-me-up, it does little to help me forget the people we just left behind. The dread that's sitting heavy in the pit of my stomach for the approaching lessons gets heavier every second.

I barely taste the chocolate biscuit I manage to snag, and by the time people start leaving to get ready for their next lessons, I'm a bag of nerves.

"Thanks for this morning. I really enjoyed your lesson," I say honestly to Mr. Atworth.

"You're welcome any time, Brianna."

With a smile, I take my empty mug to the ladies who run the small kitchen before heading out to find Melissa.

"Hey," I say, finding her sitting in her office, pulling some revision sheets from a folder.

"How was your morning?" she asks.

"Fantastic."

"I'm glad to hear it. Ready for what's next?"

My stomach plummets.

No. I'm really fucking not.

"Yes. Bring it on." I force a smile on my face.

"Okay, let's go then. They've only got eight lessons left before their first exam, so every second counts now."

Eight lessons.

Eight hours.

Surely, we can do eight hours without fucking this up for either of us... right?

We slip into the sixth form building without running into anyone, and in only a few minutes, Melissa has her lesson set up and ready to go.

"Perfect timing," she says as the bell rings. "Are you okay with getting the register up?" she asks, nodding to her laptop.

"Of course."

I open it up and stare at the students' attendance in this class. I already know Nico is here—I've seen it with my own two eyes. But still, that little tick for his previous lessons taunts me from the screen, making my stomach turn over and bile burn up my throat.

The first couple of students that walk into the room barely even spare me a second glance, nor do those who follow them. Just like Friday, all of them are the picture of the perfect student.

I keep my eyes locked on the door, hating that I'm unable to appear unfazed by what is about to happen but equally unable to avert my eyes.

I need him to see that I'm owning this situation, that I won't cower to him and his stupid threats and brutal touches. Hell, we both know I crave them.

Something which really needs to stop.

A couple of minutes tick by, but he doesn't appear.

"Okay, let's get started then," Melissa says before launching into the revision topic for this class while I fall into my own head, my eyes drifting to the window when a shiver of awareness runs down my spine.

My breath catches when I spot a dark figure leaning against the thick trunk of an old oak tree.

His eyes are glued to mine, a dark warning swimming in

them.

You should have talked to him properly about this, a little unhelpful voice says.

I don't notice him move until he holds his phone in front of him, making a show of doing something.

Not a second later, the sound of my own phone vibrating in my bag hits my ears and my heart jumps into my throat.

Fuck.

Nico stares back at me, his brows lifting, silently demanding me to look.

Ripping my eyes from his, I take in what's happening around me, aware that pulling my phone out in class isn't what I should be doing right now, but my need to know what he's playing at is too much to deny.

Once I'm happy that Melissa and everyone is distracted, I pull my bag closer and slide my phone out.

I've got a few notifications and emails, but I ignore them in favour of Nico's message.

Although I quickly find that it's not just a message. It's a fucking video. And I don't need to play it to know what it is —the still image staring back at me says it all.

"Fucking arsehole," I mutter to myself.

Suddenly, dots start bouncing, the movement of the screen startling me as he types.

Nico: I wonder what Mrs. Hendrix would think of you having it off with one of your students in a lift, Miss Andrews?

His words have my stomach plummeting into my feet.

It's wrong, oh so fucking wrong, but after ensuring my phone is on silent, I hit play.

"Oh my God," I gasp quietly as I watch Nico slam me

against the back wall of the lift before he almost engulfs my smaller body with his, playing me until I cave and fall so deep under his spell that I forget the rest of the world exists.

It's mesmerising watching us together—so much so that I miss Melissa asking me to put her presentation up.

"Miss Andrews?" she asks for... probably not the first time.

My cheeks heat at being caught, although thankfully from the other side of the classroom.

"Of course, I'm so sorry."

With a quick wiggle of the mouse, I bring the computer to life, quickly followed by the projector, and put up the first slide for her to talk through.

The second I'm done, my eyes drift to the window once more. But to my surprise, he's gone.

Relief floods me. I'm not sure I'd have coped with the next two hours if he insisted on standing there watching me like a grade-A stalker.

Feeling a little lighter, I twist around with the intention of refocusing on Melissa's lesson, but the second I catch sight of the doorway, my world tilts on its axis once more when I find Nico's imposing body filling the space.

"Ah, Mr. Cirillo, how lovely of you to grace us with your presence," Melissa quips, clearly unfazed by who Nico is.

I knew I liked her.

Ripping his eyes from mine, his entire expression softens when he looks at her.

"I'm sorry I'm late. Things have been a little..."

"I know," she assures him. "Come and take a seat. Did you manage to complete the revision tasks I emailed to you?"

I almost laugh out loud at that question, but somehow, I

manage to keep any reaction off my face. Or at least, I think I do. Nico's narrowed eyes when he turns them back on me once more makes me question myself.

But then, he shocks the shit out of me by saying, "Of course, Mrs. Hendrix. It's right here." And he pulls a whole stack of paperwork from his bag and slaps it down on the table.

Well then...

"Oh," Melissa squeaks, clearly as shocked as I am. "Well, that is fantastic. I'm glad you've been able to focus."

He grins at her. It's so fucking innocent—a look I never would have said he was capable of if I hadn't seen it with my own two eyes—that I have to question if I'm actually looking at the brutal, corrupt man I've come to know and hate.

Walking over, Melissa picks up the stack of paper ready to flick through, while everyone in the room waits for her to continue with her lesson.

"Miss Andrews, perhaps you could catch Nico up on what he's missed," she suggests, glancing over her shoulder at me.

Forcing a polite and professional smile onto my face, I rise from my seat and walk out from around the teacher's desk.

The second I emerge, Nico's eyes drop from holding mine in favour of the navy dress that hugs my curves. Not in the sexy kind of way that I'm sure he's used to from me, but in what I hope is a professional, I-own-this-teaching-elite-kids-shit, kind of way.

But I soon realise that I could be walking toward him wearing a fucking bin bag and it wouldn't matter. The way his eyes eat me up as if he's remembering every single second we've spent together without any clothes on, ensures my entire body is burning up with a mixture of hate, frustration and need by the time I get to his chosen desk at the back of the room.

"Miss Andrews," he drawls, leaning back in his chair and linking his fingers behind his head like the pretentious dickhead that he is.

My foot twitches with my need to kick his chair leg to send him flying toward the floor. I only just about manage to restrain myself. It's fucking hard, though.

My entire body trembles as I reach for the chair sitting unused at the desk beside him, and I pray to anyone who might be listening that he doesn't see it.

"Okay, so," I start after attempting to swallow down my unease.

The second mirth begins dancing in Nico's eyes, I know he isn't going to make this easy on me.

"Nice dress," he quips, cutting my explanation of what Melissa is going over. "Looks expensive."

My lips part but no words come out.

"Must have a nice sugar daddy who bought that for you. Or..." he quickly adds, "is it stolen?" My heart rate is so fucking fast I'm not sure how I don't pass out right here. The only reason I don't is because I know just how much he would love to know that I have such a visceral reaction to him.

"Screw you, Nico. We're not doing this now."

"Oh, so when do you propose we do? Lunchtime? I know a storage cupboard that's lockable from the inside that's perfect for—"

"Stop. Just stop," I beg.

His brow quirks but he doesn't say a thing for long, painful seconds. But when he does, predictably, it's enough to knock me on my arse—should I not be sitting, of course.

"Fucking love it when you beg for it, Siren."

My teeth grind, my fists curling on my lap as I continue to restrain myself from physically hurting him.

"Now, I came here to learn…" He sits forward, resting his corded forearms on the desk—because unlike what the uniform rules state, of course he's got his sleeves rolled to his elbows—and dips his head low, staring at me from beneath his lashes. "So tell me, Miss Andrews, when exactly did you steal my credit card?"

Tension crackles between us as I keep my mouth firmly shut on the subject.

A shadow falls over us, and I'm finally able to rip my eyes from his dark ones in favour of Melissa's most concerned ones.

Fuck.

"Is everything okay here?"

"Fantastic, Mrs. Hendrix," Nico says in a very uncharacteristically butter-wouldn't-melt voice. "Miss Andrews was doing a wonderful job of catching me up on everything I seem to have missed."

Melissa looks between the two of us suspiciously before she finally smiles.

"Okay, that's great. You're up to date to continue with today's task then?" she asks before giving me a look that says, *Shall we?* and nods toward the teacher's desk.

"You've got it, Mrs. H." He winks. Actually fucking winks at Melissa.

Something I really don't want to acknowledge stirs in my stomach. It doesn't matter that Melissa is old enough to be his mother, that one gesture affects me nonetheless.

"Thirty minutes to come up with an argument to the statement on the board," she repeats to the entire class while Nico's stare continues to burn into my back as I walk away from him.

"Was he rude to you?" she asks the second we're out of earshot.

"Uh…"

"Do you know who he is?" she asks, lowering her voice even more.

"I'm aware, yes."

Melissa sighs and my heart stops as I wait for what's about to come next. "Rhea told you, didn't she?"

I can't help but laugh at that assumption.

"No, actually she didn't. I know them through association. But it's nothing to worry about," I quickly add, praying it's true.

"Okay, good, because if that revision he just proudly handed to me is anything to go by, he's going to need all the help he can get to pass."

Shit.

"What can I do to help?" The words are out of my mouth before I even realise I'm saying them, and I kick myself immediately. Any other student in this school and I wouldn't question my intrinsic need to help them succeed. But Nico… The stunt he pulled this morning alone with that video should be enough for me to want to throw him to the wolves.

Melissa studies me for a beat, I assume trying to work out if I'm serious or not. It's at that point I really should tell her that I'm not. But then I glance over at Nico and find his attention not on me, but on the paper before him with a deep frown marring his brow. He's struggling. Really fucking struggling. I mean, it's hardly a surprise with what's happened recently, but there's no way I can just stand by and let it happen.

"His coursework is solid. He's capable of doing well, but his focus is elsewhere right now. I'm assuming if you know who he is then you're aware he lost his father only a few weeks ago?"

I nod but refrain from telling her just how painfully aware I am.

He just needs to find a way to push all of that aside so he can dig out everything he already knows. The knowledge is there. It's just... buried."

"What are you suggesting?"

"Let me check in with his tutor and compare both of your timetables, and I'm going to suggest he has a few extra sessions to help him solidify everything he already knows and give him the confidence boost he needs to do what he's really capable of."

"Y-you want me to do—"

"I thought that's what you meant when you asked what you could do to help?"

My head spins with the reality of what I've got myself into.

"Umm... y-yeah, I guess."

"I'm already mentoring a huge handful of year elevens and thirteens, but I'm sure I can fit him in if you—"

"No, no," I find myself arguing. "I've got this."

I look over once more, but he must sense my attention this time because his eyes lift from whatever he's managed to write and they lock with mine.

"Maybe you'll be able to get through to him. Hell knows most of the staff in this place have tried. He's a law unto himself. All the Cirillos are. They're hard work at times."

You're telling me.

"Not that we can really do anything about it. They basically pay our wages, after all."

14

———

NICO

Sitting in class with Brianna looking like a hot-as-fuck teacher that I'd like to... well... fuck was a whole new brand of torture I'd yet to experience. The only bit of satisfaction I got from the entire lesson was that she was entirely unsettled by having me there. Every few seconds her eyes would shoot to me, as if she was terrified that I might do something like publicly announce that I have very intimate knowledge about just how tight her cunt is, or how loud she screams my name when I make her come.

Having that little bit of knowledge locked away ensured the frustration that came with the work I was expected—and struggling—to do was that little more palatable.

"What the fuck, Nic?" Seb says loudly, slapping me around the back of the head before lowering himself beside me with his tray of lunch a second later.

"What?" I grunt, unaware that I've done anything recently to specifically piss him off.

"Didn't want to mention that your regular fuck buddy is

now wandering around school making all the virgin pricks come in their pants?"

The thought of anyone looking at her and imagining any of the things I do when my eyes find her sends a shot of jealousy through my veins that I have no right feeling.

She's not mine, and nor do I want her to be.

"What Brianna does has nothing to do with me," I spit.

"Oh shit. You didn't know either, did you?" he asks as Theo joins us.

"What doesn't Nico know? That jerking off in the common room isn't accepted?"

"Fuck you, man. It was one time."

Seb snorts a laugh. "Ah, good times, bro."

"She wasn't even that hot."

"I was having a dry spell and you motherfuckers were meant to be in class. Plus, it's not like you haven't got up to shit under this roof."

"Hell yeah, we have. There's one massive fucking differ-ence though," Seb argues.

"Go on," I prompt.

"We do it with our girls, not like creepy sex-starved losers."

"Is that why you wanted that footage from the lift? To jerk off over Miss Andrews in your free lessons?" Theo jokes.

"I bet she could teach you some lessons. Wait, what footage?" Seb asks the second he registers Theo's words.

"Nothing," I grunt, spearing a chip and stuffing it into my mouth.

"Oh yeah, because I'm totally going to let it slide with that shitty explanation," he quips, rolling his eyes.

"Nico chased Bri through the building on Friday night and assaulted her in the lift."

"I didn't fucking assault her. She was begging for it after sucking my cock in your bathroom," I point out happily.

"Motherfucker," Theo hisses under his breath.

"What? It could be worse. Seb fucked Stella on your sofa while you were busy with Em."

Theo's face turns tomato red as he stares daggers at Seb.

"You said you did it on the floor," he barks.

Seb lifts his finger to his mouth and bites down on it as he thinks, making himself look like a complete tosser, but it has the desired effect as steam practically starts billowing from Theo's ears.

"Floor. Sofa. Wall. Your bed... they all just blur into one, man." He shrugs and Theo launches himself across the table just as Alex appears and grabs him by the scruff of his neck.

"Down boy," he teases.

"You've fucked Stella in my fucking bed?" he shouts loud enough to gain the interest of the surrounding tables.

"Umm... like I said, they all just blur."

"I'm going to fucking kill you," Theo seethes. "Has anyone else fucked someone in my bed?" he asks, looking around at each of us.

"I haven't," Alex announces happily.

"Not getting laid is nothing to be proud of, man," Seb teases.

"Fuck you. I assure you, I'm not missing out on anything," Alex says cryptically.

"If you're going to try to tell us that Isla let you between her thighs on Friday night, then I gotta say, it's going to take a lot of convincing," Theo quips.

"I wasn't going to try to tell you anything. We don't all

need to fuck in front of each other to prove we're getting some, you know."

"Bro, jealousy isn't a good look on you," Seb laughs as Alex flips him off.

"So what the fuck is the deal with Brianna then?" Alex asks, unfortunately putting us right back on track.

"Nico's been jerking off in class to the security feed from the lift in our building of him fucking her," Seb helpfully informs Alex, right in time for the final member of our group to join us.

"You fucked her?" Toby baulks. "I thought..." I cut him a look. "Fine whatever," he mutters, backing down from immediately getting into it with me over Brianna. Again.

She's best friends with the love of his life. I get it. But shit. That doesn't mean he's her keeper.

"I didn't fuck her in the lift. Sadly, I don't have video footage of railing her all night in my bedroom though."

"Rookie mistake," Theo mutters. "You want me to hook you up with cameras?"

All eyes turn on him.

"You film you and Emmie going at it?" Alex asks, although I'm not sure if he's horrified or impressed.

"Yes, and no, you're not getting access, so don't even fucking ask."

Alex holds his hands up in surrender. "As if I would. She's not even my type."

"You're right. She's too good for you."

"Fuck you. So if you didn't screw her in the lift, can we see that?"

"Why did you even want it?" Seb asks, looking like a confused puppy as to why I might want a video that doesn't include me fucking her.

"Why not?" I shrug, playing it off as nothing as I pull my phone from my pocket.

Back in the day, we used to share all sorts of fucked-up shit that we'd recorded with girls. But since these saps all started falling in love and got protective and shit over their girls, it's becoming less and less.

I fucking miss it, shooting the shit with my boys when the five of us were all we had to worry about. Now we're expanding faster than I can cope with, and the boys who used to be my ride and dies are all finding others who are more important than us. It fucking sucks.

"Fucking hell, she doesn't look very into it," Theo points out when Brianna obviously doesn't kiss me back for a few minutes.

"She was trying to prove a point. She failed. See," I say when I finally grind against her and make her restraint snap.

"You look good together. Really good together," Seb points out.

"What are you trying to say?" I ask, ripping my eyes away from my screen and the way she claws at me as if she can't get close enough.

"That you could do a lot worse than Brianna."

"You mean, Miss Andrews."

"Yeah, about that... how exactly did she manage to score a placement here when Knight's Ridge never has student teachers?"

"Yeah, how indeed," I repeat, shoving my phone away and crossing my arms across my chest. "Wanna fill the boys in, Toby?"

"Jesus, you're acting like I let her move into your flat or something."

"At this point, I wouldn't put it past you."

"What? I just helped her out with a job. And a car."

"A car?" I bark, my eyes almost popping out at that confession.

"Yes, a fucking car. You know, if you spent less time worrying about the fastest way to get into her pussy, you might actually see that she needed a little help."

"That isn't what I'm thinking about."

"You're so full of shit," Theo mutters.

"Just stay the fuck away from her while she's here," Toby warns.

"What?" I ask innocently.

"I know you, Nico. I recognise that look in your eyes. If you fuck this up for her then I'll—"

"You'll what?" I ask, shoving what's left of my lunch back as I glare at my best friend.

"Just leave her the fuck alone."

"Yeah, we'll see."

Grabbing my shit, I dump it in the closest bin and take off across the restaurant.

"Who kicked your puppy?" Emmie asks when I nearly collide with her and Calli as I blow out of the vast room.

"Get out of my way," I bark, not in the mood to listen to their opinions on my life right now.

"Ooh, touchy. Anyone would think you haven't gotten laid recently," Emmie teases as I storm away from them.

"Nico," a softer, more concerned voice says before a small hand lands on my arm.

"I'm fine, Cal."

"Are you?" She rushes around me, blocking my exit from the building.

Her large blue eyes stare up into mine and a little bit of the frustration that was holding me captive is instantly released.

"Yeah, I am," I say a little softer and a hell of a lot more convincing. "I just need to go and get some air."

I give her a half-arsed smile before darting around her and heading out through the main doors to the building.

I come to a stop on a bench that just so happens to look directly into Mrs. Hendrix's office. When we were in year eight, it belonged to Miss Hancock, and we used to spend our lunchtimes out here perving on her like horny little arseholes.

I have no idea if Brianna's going to be in there with her, but it's the only guess I've got right now. If she's in the staff room, I've got no chance of spotting her. That place is nicely hidden away from us all with its private courtyard.

It only takes thirty seconds to discover that I'm in luck. Mrs. Hendrix is nowhere to be seen, but there is a certain blonde in a sinful navy dress sitting at her desk and staring down at something before her.

I watch her for the longest time while the world continues on around me. Voices and kids shouting and enjoying life hit my ears, but nothing registers. I'm too lost in her. That is, until a shadow falls over me and someone drops down at my side.

"Here," Theo says, passing a folded piece of paper over.

"What's this?"

"Open it and find out, maybe?" he suggests, his eyes focusing on the woman in the building beyond.

"This brings back memories," he teases as I open the paper.

"How'd you get this?" I ask, staring down at Brianna's timetable.

"You ask dumb questions, Nic."

"Why?" I ask.

"Because I thought you might want it. Just... don't do anything stupid with it."

"Me?" I ask lightly.

"Look, I know shit is hard right now. I know you're hurting and looking for ways to push that onto others. But not her, man."

"Jesus, you sound just like Toby."

"Yeah, because he's right. Bri has been there for him and Jodie, she's been here for you. Yes, this might be a little too close for comfort, but she really doesn't need you fucking this up for her."

"And what about what I need?"

"Do you even know what that is right now?"

I stare at his profile, wishing I could come up with an answer to that question.

What I need is for the pain and grief to subside for long enough that I can see straight. But that makes me sound like a fucking crazy person, so I just shut my trap and let my eyes wander to Brianna once more.

"How are you feeling about our exams?" Theo asks.

It's easy for him. He's been intelligent as shit since the day he was born. Toby too. I wasn't gifted with the ability to effortlessly succeed at everything.

Every decent grade I've ever got I've worked tirelessly for—something I fear I'm not going to be able to pull off in the coming weeks.

But Toby was right when he turned up the other day to study. Dad would be so disappointed in me if I fuck this up again.

I have to do it. No matter what it takes.

For him.

"Not great," I confess. Unease ripples through me at

being honest and vulnerable in front of the one person I never want to see it.

"I'm here, we all are, you know that, right? And if you ask her nicely," he says, nodding at Bri again, "then I'm pretty sure she will be, too."

"Thank you."

"Get these exams smashed, then we're going after the Italians."

"Can't we do that first?" It seems like the easier of the two challenges right now.

"That's down to Dad and Enzo. We need an opportunity, a solid one to take a swipe at them and try and unearth our snake, and until that comes, we're keeping our heads down. Just like they are. They have to know we have Daemon and Ant, but they haven't made a move."

"That makes me uneasy."

"You and me both, but what else can we do? We've got eyes and ears in their ranks. We have to trust it."

"You trust Ant and Enzo?" I ask.

As far as the meeting went yesterday, it seems that everyone is fully onboard with both of them wanting the same as us when it comes to Ricardo Mariano, but I can't help being concerned that we've already made enough mistakes when it comes to the Italians.

"I trust Calli and Daemon," he says strongly. "And Ant and Enzo seem to be on our side so far. We just need to keep a close eye on it all. We've got tracking on all Enzo's devices; we can literally see and hear his every move he makes. If he's playing us, we'll know instantly."

"I want to trust them. I want them to give us the in we need to overthrow that cunt."

"With or without them, Ricardo has a death wish for what he did to us. I fucking promise you that." His hand lands on my shoulder and he squeezes in support. "You need me, you know where I am, yeah?"

"Thanks, man. Appreciate it."

He's gone as quickly as he appeared, leaving me alone once more.

I stare down at my knees, wondering where all of this is going to end, and when I finally look up, I discover that my presence has been noticed, because Brianna is standing at the huge window of the office she's in, watching me.

I hate to think of what she's seen while I've been here with my shoulders slumped in defeat. But it's too fucking late to worry about it now. And she's seen worse.

Memories of the mess I was when she came to me the other night hit me like a truck, making my anger soar once more.

Pushing to my feet, I hold her eyes as the air crackles between us.

She wants me to do what the others are begging of me and allow her to do her time here in peace.

But all I want is for her to stop seeing so fucking deep. And her being here only gives her more access to all my failures. My weaknesses. My vulnerability. And I don't want her or any other person on this planet seeing them.

15

BIANNA

Despite spending my afternoon in a revision session with year eleven students, I've been unable to shake the prickling sensation that he's still watching me.

It's ridiculous, because I'm in a completely different building from where his last class of the day is. Yes, I may have printed myself a copy of his timetable so that I can keep tabs on him when Melissa excused herself from her office during lunch. Incidentally, it was collecting that from her printer that ensured I found him sitting out there like a fucking psycho, staring straight in at me.

Even now, as I pack up my stuff ready to head home for the day, a shudder runs down my spine.

Unable to stop myself, I glance over my shoulder, but both the doorway and the hallway beyond are deserted, all the students gone for the day.

After a few words with the teacher I was observing this afternoon, I throw my bag over my shoulder and make my way back to Melissa's office.

She's already told me that she's in a meeting this

evening, so I make the most of my peace and quiet and start work on lesson planning for next week.

I'm totally lost in what I'm doing by the time the door behind me opens a few hours later. I jump a fucking mile, my eyes shooting to the person marching inside, my initial thought that it's Nico coming to torment me over his 'stolen' credit card situation.

"Are you okay?" Melissa asks when I stare at her with wide eyes.

"Y-yeah. I just had my head in this and you scared me."

"Sorry." She winces. "What are you doing?"

"Planning this year seven project for your class. I have the first couple of lessons down, I think."

"Let's see." She walks over as I scroll up to the top of the document.

I watch her as she studies it, nodding at what she sees.

"It's good, Bri. I think the students will really love working on this."

Pride washes through me as she makes a couple of suggestions before asking me to email it all over once I have the set of eight lessons complete.

"You should head home. You must have something more exciting to do tonight," she says, tidying up her own things.

"Umm... sadly not. I've just got a uni assignment waiting for me."

"Ah, the life of a student," she laughs. "Feels like a lifetime ago for me now. I always said I'd go back and do my masters, but you know."

"Yeah, I think I might be done after this, to be honest."

"Just a few more weeks. And don't forget to send me your CV and cover letter so you're ready for any jobs you're interested in. They should start coming in thick and fast now."

"I will," I promise. My mentor at my last school helped me with it, but something tells me that Melissa will be able to tighten it up even more.

The thought of embarking on this as a real job, having classes that I'm responsible for without anyone looking over my shoulder every minute of the day is as terrifying as it is liberating. I'm also nervous as hell that I'm not going to be able to find a job at all and I'll have to resort to retail or restaurant work, after all.

"You've got this, Brianna. The perfect job will turn up. Promise."

"Thank you," I say before closing my laptop down and packing it away. "Have a good night, I'll see you in the morning."

"Have a good one." She waves me off and I slip out of her office and into the deadly silent building beyond.

The only thing to be heard as I walk toward the exit is the echo of my footsteps on the old flagstone floors. It's eerie and does little to help the unease that's had me on edge since finding Nico watching me earlier.

I once again look over my shoulder before I push through the doors, but there's no one there.

It's all in my head.

The walk to the car park is much the same as being inside the building. Almost all the cars are gone with just a handful of dedicated staff left. And I guess those who live on-site with the boarding students.

Pulling my phone from my pocket, I find three messages from Jodie and open them up.

Best bitch: How's it going?

Best bitch: No news is good news, right?

Best bitch: Toby said you had a class with
Nico. Was it okay? Did he survive it?

I can't help but laugh as my mind goes back to thoughts of kicking his chair out from under him earlier. Damn, it would have been priceless to watch his smug little expression falter as the world disappeared from beneath him.

But as I approach my new car, a pair of shoes enters my vision and any amusement I was feeling is swallowed up.

"What do you want?" I hiss, lowering my phone and finding his hard, angry eyes.

"What do I want?" he repeats like a dick.

"Yes, arsehole. What. Do. You. Want?"

A smirk curls at his lips. It's all I need to know that I really, really don't want him to tell me what he's thinking.

"Do you know what? I don't actually care. Just get the fuck off my car and let me leave."

"Your car?" he spits, refusing to shift his arse an inch.

"Whatever."

I continue moving forward, confident that I can round the bonnet that he's sitting on like he owns the fucking thing without getting within touching distance, my intention to drop into the driver seat and run him down if I have to just to get rid of him.

But, predictably, he's faster than me and his fingers wrap around my wrist before I manage to twist out of the way and I'm hauled over until I'm standing between his legs.

"You can't do this. Not here," I seethe, my eyes darting around for spectators.

"I can do what the fuck I like, Miss Andrews."

I try yanking my arm free of his hold, but it's pointless. He's got it in a vice grip.

I glare at him, silently pleading with him to let this go, but of course it gets me absolutely nowhere with this pig-headed, stubborn fuck.

"Don't you have better things to be doing than stalking me? You know, like revising? Don't forget, I've seen your work, your grades now. You're on the verge of failing, Mr. Cirillo."

It's not entirely true, after Melissa told me that his coursework was solid earlier; obviously, I went searching for it, and I've got to say, I was impressed. This fumbling buffoon can actually write a decent assignment.

But with revision like he so proudly handed in earlier, his upcoming exams are going to seriously let him down.

"Fuck you."

"Eloquent. That'll help. And here I was thinking that your argumentative skills were top notch."

His jaw tics in irritation as our eyes hold, neither of us willing to give into this little battle of wills we embarked on that very first night we hooked up.

I'd have thought us fucking like rabbits would have broken it, but apparently, it only gets worse each time we collide. Like we suddenly both have even more to prove to each other.

"I want my credit card back, Siren."

"Then you're going to have to let me fucking go, aren't you," I say sweetly.

It takes him a second or two, but he finally releases his hold on me, allowing me to reach into my bag and pull my purse out.

I dig out the card and hold it between us.

The second he reaches for it, I pull it back, like the child that I am.

"You might be many, many things, Brianna Andrews, but I never had you down as a thief."

"I'm not. Until I was handed this, the only thing I'd taken from you was pleasure and abuse," I state flatly. "And I only made use of this because you owe me."

His brows shoot up. "I owe you? Please explain."

"If you have to ask, then you're stupider than you look. Here," I say, thrusting his card at him. "Take your fucking credit card, your attitude, and your smug fucking face elsewhere. I'm fed up with being anywhere near you."

I take a step away but falter when his amused chuckle hits my ears.

"What?" I snap, unable to stop myself.

"Nothing, Miss Andrews. You run away like a good little teacher. But just remember..." he warns, his voice low and dangerous. "I'm not going to be very far away."

My breath catches at the unspoken threat in his words, but when I look back, he's already marching away from me.

"Fucking dickhead," I mutter under my breath before I pull my key out and lock myself safely in my car.

I close my eyes, blowing out a long, calming breath. But the knowledge that I have to come back here tomorrow and do it all over again never leaves me.

The second I closed my front door behind me, I flipped the deadlock for fear of him following me back and using his unending wealth of random skills to pick my lock and torment me some more. To be fair, he could still probably do it if he so wanted; there doesn't seem to be much that stands in his way. Entitled privileged prick.

I stripped out of my clothes, threw them in the general direction of my laundry basket, and put myself in the shower to hopefully wash the day away.

It did very little. When I got out, I was wrung just as tight as when I stepped in.

Memories of the day, of Nico's vicious stare, his silent promises, the evidence sitting on my phone that I've been doing things I shouldn't with a student all float around my head, refusing to release me from their clutches.

I drag on a pair of sweats and an oversized hoodie, twist my hair up into my heatless curler and make my way out to the kitchen with the intention of finding some carbs to lose myself in before I open my laptop and get to work, banishing all thoughts of Nico and his hot, arrogant arse from my head as if he doesn't exist.

With my phone on aeroplane mode, my laptop on one knee and a bowl of noodles on the other, and one of my favourite playlists filling my flat, it doesn't take long to fully immerse myself in my final uni assignment. That is, until my buzzer rings out through the flat.

"Fuck," I bark when my still-half-full bowl wobbles off my knee, spilling noodles over my cream sofa.

I do the best I can to pick it up as my buzzer continues to ring.

"All-fucking-right," I shout, assuming it's just Jodie and that she's freaking out because she can't get through on my phone.

It's better to assume it's her than the other option.

"Yeah," I say frustratedly when I finally make it over to the pad on the wall and jam my finger against the button.

"Hey, baby," a deep, familiar voice purrs down the line. "Miss me?"

Tipping my head back, I close my eyes and curse this fucking day. Why is it not over yet and still throwing shit my way?

"Hey, Brad," I say through gritted teeth.

Brad isn't a bad person. Actually, he's a pretty fucking decent one. One that I shouldn't have caved to when he wanted a repeat of the first night we hooked up. But he made it so easy. He isn't like the other fuck boys. Something that should have set alarm bells off when he found me online after our first night. But he was nice, treated me well, made me come hard. He's just... well, boring. He doesn't set my world alight. Not in the way that—

Nope. Do not go there, Brianna.

His cock is fucking magical though so... yeah. I've not put all that much effort into getting rid of him because he does come with some serious stress-relieving benefits.

"Are you going to let me in, baby? I've missed you."

"I'm not really dressed for guests," I confess. "I'm studying."

"You know I don't care about that. I can help," he offers like the nice guy that he is.

Leaning forward, I rest my forehead against the wall and reluctantly press the button that will allow him entry to the building.

"Good girl," he says softly, but unlike when those two words came from someone else's lips, my body doesn't react in the slightest.

Pulling up my big girl knickers, I unlock my front door and crack it open so he can let himself in before I head back to the sofa in an attempt to clean up the mess I made properly.

I hear him before I see him. The door closes and his footsteps make their way across the flat to where I'm washing up.

"Noodles for dinner, really, Brianna?" he chastises when he spots the packet on the counter.

He steps up behind me, his hands on my hips, and his lips land on my neck, sending a shiver right through me, but it's not the kind of shiver he thinks it is.

"You need to look after yourself, baby. You deserve better than a fifty-pence packet of noodles."

"Eighty-pence," I correct. "I've got a lot of work to do and I didn't have time to—"

"It's a good job I'm back then, isn't it?"

He twists me around so I have no choice but to face him.

He really is incredibly handsome. Especially when he's dressed in his sharp suit like he is right now. But still, those flutters and that 'I must have you now' reaction I'm so addicted to just aren't there.

He really is just a friend with benefits. Even the term 'lover' seems a little far-fetched.

Unfortunately, though, I fear that he's got images in his head of me in a white dress, a house with a picket fence and little Brads running around.

I have never once misled him or allowed him to think that there could be anything more than a few hookups between us. But he's like a dog with a fucking bone. He seems to think he can 'change' me or some bullshit. That I'll fall so hard for him I'll forget everything else in my life and suddenly become a good little housewife. Un-fucking-likely.

I told him from... well, day two, I guess. That we were not exclusive, that I didn't want a relationship, that while he might be a repeat, he wasn't to think for even a second that he was my only one.

He agreed quickly, I assumed because the sex was pretty insane, but as time has gone on I'm realising that it's more than just sex. For him at least.

But, at this point, I'm figuring that that's on him, not me. I've laid down my intentions for my future and his place in it time and time again. What else can I do?

"You look stressed, baby," he says, his eyes tracking every inch of my face.

"Yeah, well, life is like that," I say, twisting out of his grasp before he does something stupid like try and kiss me.

"Let me take you for dinner," he offers.

"Seriously?" I ask, looking down at myself.

"Yes. Go put something sexy on and I'll take you out."

"I can't," I say, gesturing to my laptop and the books littering my coffee table.

"I can order ahead. You need a break and it'll help clear your head. Then you can come back and continue."

My stomach growls, mourning the loss of the noodles.

I should say no, send him on his way and order a pizza. Not that I can afford to. My rent is due in a few days, and it's already touch and go as to whether I'm going to have enough. I do still have *his* credit card stored in my app though... I could order myself a feast at his expense.

"Fine. But we're going Italian because I want carbs. Call that place you took me to that's only a few streets over and place an order." I rattle off what I want as I rush through into my bedroom.

"That's better," he says with what should be a knee-weakening smile when I return in a pair of skinny jeans, a fitted jumper that shows off a little cleavage, light make-up, and my freshly curled hair. "Damn, I missed you," he says, rushing toward me and slamming his lips down on mine before I have a chance to react.

Thankfully—and probably for fear of wearing my lipstick—it's only a chaste kiss, but it's enough to make me feel all kinds of icky after the past few days with Nico.

It's never bothered me before. But something has changed since I acquired my place at Knight's Ridge and I find that I'm now questioning everything. And as much as I might like men—okay, more specifically, their dicks—I'm almost at the point where I'm going to swear off all of them in favour of my vibrating friends for a while. They deliver nearly as much pleasure and a hell of a lot less drama. And that's exactly what I need right now.

Proving me right, the second he pulls back, he wipes the back of his hand across his mouth, inspecting for stray make-up.

Nico would never do that, a little voice says in my head. He'd wear it like a badge of honour.

Cursing myself for letting my head drift back to him once more, I let Brad take my hand and lead me out of my flat.

The second we're out and I've locked up, he throws his arm around my shoulders and starts telling me about the work trip he's just been on. I immediately zone out.

At least I'm going to get decent carbs out of this. It's just a shame that I'm going to refuse any sex-ercise to burn it off after.

16

———

NICO

"What the fuck?" I breathe when I push through my front door and the floral scent of cleaning products hits my nose a beat before freshly baked— "Jocelyn?"

I kick my shoes off and dump my bag beside them as I walk deeper into my flat.

And just as I suspected, standing in the middle of my kitchen, wearing her standard uniform and apron that Mum always insisted on, is the woman who's almost single-handedly kept me somewhat sane over the past few years. She can't really take the credit for being the one to bring Calli and me up. We had nannies and many, many housekeepers before her. But there was something special about Jocelyn that we both saw on her very first day.

She smiles softly at me as I continue to cut through the room toward her.

"I hope you don't mind. Calli said you could do with a little help and—"

I cut her words off with a hug that I'm not entirely sure she's expecting.

A nervous laugh falls from her as I hold her small frame tightly.

"You should have called me," she chastises. "You know that I'd have been here in a heartbeat."

"Thank you," I whisper before finally releasing her.

"This place was a dump," she says, pinning me with a disapproving look. "Although it hasn't seemed to put the girls off, has it?"

I can't help but laugh at the thought of her finding Brianna's knickers twisted up in my bedsheets where I left them.

"Just one girl," I confess. "And she's... different."

I regret the words the second they fall from my lips, because her expression softens and hope seems to enter her eyes.

"Oh no," I say. "Do not start getting any of those ideas. She's not *that* different."

An annoyed humph falls from her lips.

"So what have you cooked? It smells amazing," I say in the hope of distracting her from thoughts of me settling down.

Calli has started giving her hope.

There's a steak and ale pie in the oven—well, there are three, actually—but I promised Calli, Daemon, and Anthony them."

"Ant?"

"Sweet boy," she muses. "Needs all the support he can get right now."

My lips part to say something, but I soon find I don't have any words.

"There's also a fresh batch of cookies in that tin, and a salted caramel cheesecake in your fridge."

"Shit, I missed you, J."

"There are some of the green junky drinks you like so much to counteract all the sugar."

"You're the best, J. When you're ready to leave Mum behind, just say the word," I tease.

"Funny, Calli said the same thing."

"That's because you're the best thing left in that house now, J. She can rot in hell for all we care."

"Nico," she sighs. "She's not that bad. She's hurting too." But even as she says the words, I can see the hesitation in Jocelyn's eyes to defend our selfish cunt of a mother.

"Is she, though? I always thought she loved him. But now I'm not so sure."

I slide onto one of my bar stools as Jocelyn pushes a can of Coke toward me.

"Love comes in many, many forms, Nico. It's hard to understand people's relationships from the outside. They were together almost all their adult lives. That kind of relationship doesn't last without love, respect, and mutual understanding and goals."

"I guess."

"It worked for him, whatever it was."

"But it's like she hasn't even realised that he's gone."

"Maybe she hasn't," Jocelyn offers softly. "Death, grief. It affects everyone differently. There's every chance she's living in denial to put off having to deal with it all."

"If that's the case, she needs a good psychiatrist."

"She has one," Jocelyn says, but from the gasp that follows, I'm not sure she was meant to tell me.

"Oh?"

"She's been seeing someone weekly for quite a while. It's not public knowledge."

"Right." More lies and secrets. Just what we all

need. "Well, I hope he isn't very expensive, because I'm not sure he's doing much good."

Jocelyn just smiles at me, refusing to offer up any more information.

"Is there anything else you need me to do before I go and deliver these pies?" she asks, grabbing an oven glove and pulling it open.

"I think you've already done more than enough."

She places three golden, bubbling pies on the counter and my stomach growls.

"There are vegetables in the fridge, you just need to boil them. You can handle that, right?"

"I can," I assure her.

Those might be the first homemade pies my oven has ever seen, but contrary to popular belief, I can actually use it.

"Okay, so call me if you need anything. But seeing as you've locked your usual cleaner out, and that devilish boy of your sister has granted me access to your inner sanctum, I'll pop back in a few days to ensure things are clean and tidy. Just... remember our old deal. I don't touch rooms with drugs or johnnys."

"You got it, J. No johnnys." I wink at her and she groans.

"N-no, no. That's not what—"

"It's cool, J. There will be no baby Cirillos heading our way anytime soon."

"Uh... good. That's good. Enjoy the rest of your night. Be good," she warns before heading off with her two steaming hot pies balanced expertly in her hands.

Our class is in silence when a quiet, hesitant knock comes.

Every single head in the room looks up from the dull-as-shit exam questions we're working on and not a second later, a tiny year seven pokes his head into the room.

I want to say that he looks on the verge of shitting his pants at being forced to step into a sixth form classroom, but I'm pretty sure he already has.

"Hello, can I help you, young man?" Mr. Wilson says softly, which still makes the kid trip over his own feet as he moves into the room.

The guy sitting beside me snorts a laugh, which sends an inferno racing through me.

Shoving my chair back an inch, I steal his attention and his eyes find my deadly ones.

No words are spoken between us. They don't need to be. He can read the threat that's written all over my face clear as day.

He swallows nervously before returning his attention back to the exam paper in front of him instead of the little boy trembling in front of Mr. Wilson.

The boy doesn't say anything, he just nervously holds out the note in his hand.

Mr. Wilson looks up and immediately finds me watching.

He nods his head in my direction and my stomach twists as I realise that whatever is on that note is for me.

The boy turns to me. I thought he looked terrified before, but the look of pure fear on his face now is actually unnerving.

Clearly, he knows who I am. To be fair, there aren't

many walking around these halls who don't. But I'm in class; what does he really think I'm going to do?

He walks over, albeit reluctantly. I also want to call Mr. Wilson out on the fact he sent this poor kid over here when he could have taken the note and given it to me myself, but I keep my mouth shut, wanting to see how this is going to play out.

The guy beside me, Jamie Carmichael, shifts in his seat again as amusement covers his features.

My fists curl beneath the desk, my need to pound them into his face almost too much to deny.

"Hey," I say to the boy when he gets close. "Is that for me?"

He nods, thrusting the note at me.

"What's your name, kid?"

"B-B-Benjamin R-Reynolds."

I take the note from his trembling hand. "Thank you," I say genuinely. "Hold your head high, Benjamin Reynolds. You have nothing to be scared of."

A scoff comes from Jamie, only this time, he's joined by a couple of his dickhead friends. They have to know it's a dumb-arse move in front of me, but apparently mocking this terrified kid is worth the pain that will inevitably come.

"Th-thank you, sir."

This time, someone full-on barks a laugh at him.

When I cut a look to my right, the laughter quickly dies.

"Have a good day." I smile at him as he takes a step back. He glances at the dick beside me before looking back at Mr. Wilson and then practically running from the room.

"Pussy," Jamie coughs as the door swings closed behind the kid.

"You got a death wish, Carmichael?" I breathe, my voice low and deadly.

He sucks in a sharp breath but doesn't reply as Mr. Wilson barks at us to continue with our work.

I watch him as he follows orders like a good little puppy, ensuring he's completely on edge and regretting his life decisions before I open the note that's still in my hand.

Nico Cirillo
Meeting in the sixth form library at the beginning of fourth period for an English lit revision session.
Mrs. Hendrix.

"Brilliant," I hiss, earning myself a warning from Mr. Wilson.

Glancing at the clock behind his head, I find that we've only got ten minutes left. This was meant to be my last lesson of the day. I told myself before I even arrived this morning that I was going to leave and revise at home. Try and do the right thing where Brianna is concerned and stay out of her way. It seems fate has other issues. Plus, I've now got some games to play with Jamie. And I guess watching him cry for being a prick to that kid is worth sitting through a revision session for.

I don't do any more of my exam paper. I'm too lost in thoughts of the girl who shouldn't be anywhere near my head. But it seems she's managed to worm her way in despite my attempts to keep her out.

It's all Toby's fault. If he never went on that revenge mission, then I never would have met her.

Then Toby never would have got vengeance on the cunt who claimed to be his father and find the love of his life.

Ugh, why does he need to be so worthy of all the happiness Jodie brings him? It makes it really fucking hard to hate him.

"I want these exam papers completed in exam conditions and handed in tomorrow. No excuses, no textbooks and no Google. It will not help you in the long run," Mr. Wilson warns as everyone begins noticing the time and starts to fidget in their need to escape.

The bell rings out as I'm stuffing the paper into my bag and before everyone else, I stand from my chair and make for the door. But I don't walk through it straight away. Instead, I pause and look back. My eyes collide with Jamie's, the promise of unbelievable pain for tormenting that kid earlier crackling between us.

With that silent warning delivered, I take off, heading toward the toilets to take a piss before I go in search of Mrs. Hendrix in the library.

17

BRIANNA

"Do you have the resources you need?" Melissa asks as I gather up everything she's given me. "Yes." No.

There is nothing in the world that would help me be any kind of prepared for what's about to happen.

My heart is in my throat, blood is racing past my ears, and my hands are trembling.

I haven't even left her office yet.

"If you can nail this, then you'll be able to handle any student here at Knight's Ridge."

Nail...

If I can nail this student. Pretty sure our heads are in entirely different places right now.

"I've got it under control," I lie, hiking my bag up over my shoulder and scooping up the books and papers Mrs. Hendrix printed out for me.

"I have every confidence in you. And I'm sure it'll be much more entertaining than the meeting I have."

Entertaining would be one word for it.

"There will be biscuits, right?" I ask, having learned

over the past few days that the teachers at Knight's Ridge don't do anything without being fuelled by sweet treats.

"Oh, you can guarantee it. Good luck," she calls as we walk out of her office and head in opposite directions, her toward the main building where all the senior management offices are, and me toward the sixth form building.

My head spins as I make my way over.

But it's nothing compared to when I walk through the huge double doors to the sixth form library.

I've been inside the one in the main building that the rest of the school uses. That was... mind-blowing. Much like everything in this place, it was massive, over-the-top, and ostentatious. But while this one might be smaller, it's still as impressive. The second I step inside, the scent of books hits me, instantly settling something inside me.

Despite appearances and what I know everyone thinks of me, deep down, I'm just a bookworm trying to find her place in the world.

When I was a kid, life was... well, I try not to think about it. My mum, Jodie's aunt, was young, too fucking young when she had me. I've since learned that she point-blank refused to do what her parents deemed to be the right thing, something I can understand. But in doing so, she caused a massive rift between her and my grandparents. They were traditional and idealists. Both Joanne and my mum were meant to be perfect ladies, save themselves for marriage and then just lie back and think of England while bringing up a handful of brats and keeping the house clean.

Joanne had already fucked them over by falling in love with a mafia soldier—a fact I'm not sure they were aware of at the time, but Jonas was a bad boy through and through, from what I've heard. And while she was defying the rules and shattering the expectations put on her, my mum, her little sister, got pregnant with me. At fourteen.

From what Joanne has told me, she hid it for a long time. But obviously, she—or I—was a ticking time bomb and eventually, her swollen belly was unignorable, and my grandparents flipped their lids, insisting I was put up for adoption and handed over to loving parents the moment I was born.

Needless to say, that didn't happen. My mum ran and ended up in a home for young vulnerable mums. I don't remember most of it, but we moved around different homes and assisted living places for years. Mum was a mess, an addict, desperate to find a connection to someone, and in doing so, I was mostly left to my own devices.

We had no money, no food, no heating or even electricity in some of the places we were forced to call home. But no matter where we went, there was always a library. Sometimes it took a little finding, or I was forced to use the rubbish ones at the schools I was enrolled in, but they were always there to offer me an escape. Books were the one reliable thing in my life. I could always count on them to help me forget how cold I was, how hungry I was, and to provide me with images of another life. I didn't even care what the story was. As long as it was a distraction from my life, I was in.

Mum didn't get it. She used to tell me that I lived with my head in the clouds in a fantasy land that wouldn't help me in the real world. I often wanted to ask her how she thought the things she did helped her in life, but I was never brave enough. Or maybe it was that I never really wanted to hear the truth. That I wasn't enough for her.

All those years before, she'd been so adamant that she wanted to keep me, yet she did nothing for me. It didn't make any sense. If she cared so much, then you'd think she'd want me warm, fed, safe. But that wasn't my reality.

When I found her in the middle of a seizure in our damp and fousty living room after school, it was probably the best thing that ever happened to me.

By the end of the day, I'd found a family, people who cared, a sister in Jodie, and Mum finally got the support she needed. But still, the books remained. When things got too much, and they did often, I fell back into my old routine, pulled a blanket over myself and grabbed any book I could find and jumped in with two feet.

I smile at the librarian as I pass, my eyes scanning the tables of sixth form students. I recognise a couple from the English lit lesson, but none of them pay me any attention.

As instructed, I walk to the back of the vest space where I find doors that lead to private study rooms.

My stomach knots. Being anywhere private with Nico is a bad, bad idea. But I could hardly stand in front of Melissa and demand we have our study session in the middle of the busiest place on campus because I don't trust myself around him, despite the number of times I've tried to convince myself to forget about every second we've spent together, every touch, every cry, plea, and moan of his name.

Goddamn it, Brianna.

Pushing the door handle down, I slip inside the room.

The second the door clicks closed behind me, I struggle to suck in the air I need.

He's not even here yet and I'm already freaking the hell out.

The bell rang as I was walking here, and my heart beats out of rhythm as I lay out everything we need, anxiously waiting for that door to open.

Melissa booked this room for him so I have no doubt

that he'll be directed down here the second he turns up—should he turn up, that is.

There's every chance that he'll have taken one look at the request, screwed it up and tossed it in the bin.

Or would he have suspected that I might be behind that note?

If he does, I have every confidence that he'll show his face, probably just late to ensure I'm already pissed off before he graces me with his presence.

Nine minutes and forty-three seconds.

That's how long I sit there questioning my terrible, terrible decisions when it comes to Nico Cirillo before the door handle twists and my heart jumps into my throat at the same time my stomach sinks to my knees.

The second he steps into the small room, I swear he sucks all the air out of it.

Just like yesterday, he's shed his blazer and stands before me in just his fitted white shirt with his sleeves rolled up his strong arms and his tie loose around his collar. His shirt is tucked into a pair of slim-fit trousers which are tight enough to tease me with what I know is hiding beneath, and I don't just mean his solid thighs.

"Well well well, what do we have here? Mrs. Hendrix sent the lackey, huh?" He prowls closer, his tempting scent filling my nose and making the butterflies that are already going crazy in my stomach begin to riot.

"Mrs. Hendrix had nothing to do with this," I confess.

"Oh," he says, one side of his mouth kicking up in a smirk. "So you needed an excuse to get me alone? Missing me, Miss Andrews?"

I watch his every step as he moves closer, but eventually he closes in behind me, proving that I made a stupid mistake in choosing this seat.

"N-no, I—" My gasp of shock rips through the air when his large, burning-hot hands land on my shoulders and I'm wrenched backward.

The front two chair legs leave the floor, my knees skimming the edge of the table as I have little choice but to surrender to his mercy.

Swallowing down my unease, I look up.

My breath catches once again when I find his dark, angry eyes boring down into mine.

"Admit it, Miss Andrews. It's been three days and you're desperate for my cock, aren't you?"

"Nico." I want it to come out like a warning, but even I can admit that it misses the mark by a mile.

He chuckles, hearing it exactly like I do, and my cheeks heat.

"Do you think Mrs. Hendrix has any idea what a filthy little whore you are, Siren?"

"Nico, stop," I beg, my breathing increasing as my frustration levels soar.

He pauses, his eyes searching mine before they drop to my lips.

His tongue sneaks out, swiping over his full bottom lip before they drop lower.

My nipples pebble behind the confines of my bra and satin shirt, and I just pray the fabric is enough to hide my visceral reaction to him.

"I really hope you haven't been leaning over any students' desks today, Miss Andrews."

My body burns up as he stares down my cleavage.

"But then again, I can't imagine a better inspiration to do some work than getting a go on your tits." I breathe a sigh of relief when one of his hands leaves me, but it's short-lived because I quickly discover where it's heading.

He flicks my top button like a pro, exposing my silver bra.

"It really doesn't come as a surprise to me that you'd be willing to let all the boys lust over your body."

"I'm not— That's not—"

"Try arguing with me when you don't look like a shameless slut who's desperate to get on her knees for a student."

"You should be so lucky," I breathe. "I'm not going anywhere near your shrivelled dick ever again."

He chuckles, fucking chuckles, before thankfully righting my chair. It wobbles before it settles, and by the time my head stops spinning, he's sitting opposite me with his forearms on the table, looking at me as if he's impatient to start.

"You're assuming I'd want you anywhere near me, Siren."

My brow quirks, a comeback about him already being hard and aching for me on the tip of my tongue, but the librarian walks past the small window behind his head and I'm reminded of where I am and what I'm doing.

"Right, well. I marked those revision questions you handed in yesterday. They're not good, Nico. The smug arrogance you handed them in with was certainly not warranted.

"We're going to start by going through your answers and comparing them with what would be expected to hit both A and B grades."

He rests back, placing his hands behind his head, and studies me.

"Go ahead, Miss Andrews." His gaze drops to my chest and I'm reminded of the fact that I'm showing off my bra. "I'm fully focused and ready to blow your mind."

I lift my trembling hands and, much to his amusement, fumble to do my shirt back up.

Arsehole.

By some miracle, he actually lets me do my job. Although I'm not entirely sure if that's because he actually cares and wants to improve his answers, or if he's just humouring me, waiting for an opening to bait me some more, or to do something that's going to pull the rug from beneath my chair like he did with that fucking video yesterday.

Each tick of the clock rocks through me with every second that passes.

I study Nico as he writes an answer to one of the questions I've given him.

I should look elsewhere, do some work of my own, but I can't. I'm enthralled by this enigma of a man.

We've never spent time like this. Time where we're either not at each other's throats or so consumed by each other that the rest of the world fails to exist.

Whenever we've hung out, there has been alcohol and debauchery. Not him allowing me to see this vulnerable, less-than-perfect side to him.

My heart races as I continue to stare at the top of his head, wondering how things might have been between us if we met at a different time, if the situations surrounding us were different.

It's pointless, all of it, but it floats around in my head anyway.

Until something brushes up the back of my calf.

My breath catches, but for some fucked-up reason, I don't move.

I also don't breathe as I wait to see what he's going to do next.

"Keep staring at me like that, Siren, and I'll start to think you have other intentions for this private room." His foot keeps moving higher, and I quickly discover that he's slipped his shoe off when he gets to the inside of my knee.

"Nico," I warn.

"Here," he says, spinning his paper around and sliding it to me. He sits back in his chair with a smirk playing on his lips and crosses his arms over his chest.

His foot stops, allowing me to read what he's written.

My eyes dart between his answer and his smug, over-confident face.

"This is good. Really good," I confess. "It's—" Realisation hits me and a laugh tumbles from my lips.

"You smug fucking bastard."

My fingers curl around the edge of the chair ready to push back, but his foot finally moves and I'm rendered useless as he slides it under my skirt and right between my thighs.

"I have no idea what you're talking about, Miss Andrews." He says innocently as his foot gets higher.

I should stop him. I need to stop him. I—

The sound of his phone cuts through the air like a knife.

"Would you look at that," he taunts. "Saved by the bell."

Without moving his foot, he reaches for his phone, glances at the screen and then puts it to his ear.

"Yes. Yes. Yep. Coming right now."

His eyes burn into mine as he talks to whomever is on the other end. When he lowers it once more, he looks away and I finally manage to find some inner strength and shove my chair back, ensuring his foot falls from me as I stand and move farther away.

He chuckles as he gathers up his things.

"Anyone would think you can't be trusted in a room with a student, Miss Andrews. Letting me touch you like that. How inappropriate," he taunts.

"Just go," I hiss, desperately trying not to show how much I'm freaking out right now.

Anyone could have walked into this room just then and saw what he was doing, the look on my face as he did it.

Get a fucking grip, Brianna.

"Go? But we haven't arranged our next session."

"You don't need it. That answer you just gave me was perfect."

That sadistic smirk returns.

"Oh but I'm not sure my classwork with Mrs. Hendrix will look that way. I think I definitely need some more one-on-one time with the teacher who helps me understand it in a way no one else ever has before."

A low growl rumbles deep in my throat.

"What? Are you going to refuse to help me, Miss Andrews? That wouldn't look good on your CV or upcoming job applications, would it?"

"Fuck you, Nico. I won't bow down to your threats."

"I really suggest you reconsider. Because I never, ever dish out empty ones."

He prowls around the table, throwing his bag over his shoulder as he goes, closing the space between us and making the air crackle.

I back away, but there's only so far I can retreat before my back collides with the wall.

"You need to stop."

His smirk turns into a sneer as he stares down at me.

"I don't need to do anything, Miss Andrews. I rule this school and everyone in it. And now, you're right here in the middle of my kingdom. Don't be thinking you hold any power here. You don't. I have it all. And if you want to walk out at the end of the year with the chance of a teaching career in your grasp, then you need to do as I say."

"What did I ever do to you, Nico? Why do you hate me so much?"

"Who said I needed a reason? Maybe I just like this look in your eyes right now."

Lifting his hand, he trails a fingertip down my cheek before ghosting it over my bottom lip.

"Maybe I just like having you at my mercy."

"Sadist."

"Oh, Siren. I thought you already knew. I'm so much worse than that."

18

—————

NICO

"The fuck?" Theo barks the second I rip his passenger door open and drop into the seat. "I called you like ten fucking minutes ago, saying it was urgent."

"All right, keep your fucking knickers on. I'm here now, aren't I?"

He glances over at me, the promise of pain oozing from his eyes.

Gunning the engine, we fly out of the car park and quickly speed away from Knight's Ridge and toward the centre of town.

"What the fuck was so important that you made me wait?" he barks after long, painful seconds of seething in silence.

A smirk pulls up at my lips.

"I had a revision session."

"What the fuck were you in the middle of studying? Lylah's cunt? I swear to fuck, Nic. The boss won't take that as a good enough excuse."

"Yeah, he wasn't overly thrilled the last time we turned up with our dicks still wet," I deadpan.

"Seriously?" he hisses.

"You need to lighten up. Emmie not putting out or something?"

I'm baiting him, and he knows it. But he's also too highly fucking strung to let it go.

I get it. Of course I fucking get it.

If we've been summoned by Damien, then the chances are he has news on the Italians. And I'm fucking desperate to hear exactly what we're going to do to bring Ricardo motherfucking Mariano to his knees. Preferably in front of me while I press the barrel of my gun to his temple.

No. Shooting him would be too easy. I want him to go through everything Daemon did and worse.

I might even be a good friend and let Daemon start him off. I'll fucking end him, though.

"Fuck you, my girl is fucking perfect. Although it seems that Lylah must have upped her game if she's left you feeling this chipper."

"I wasn't fucking that whore."

"So, who were you studying? Because we both know it wasn't book pages you were spreading."

"It was, actually. English lit, if you want specifics."

"Engli— You motherfucker," he hisses, putting two and two together and almost coming out with the right answer. "I thought you were going to let her do her job."

"I was," I say innocently. "And then I got this note about a revision session, and who should I find waiting for me in one of the private rooms of the library?"

"I'm assuming not Mrs. Hendrix," he mutters under his breath. "You need to stop, Nico. Brianna is a decent person and if you fuck this up for her then—"

"Since when has what I do with one of my fuck buddies been any of your business?"

"Because Brianna isn't just a fuck buddy, is she?" He glances over at me and I fucking hate the look in his eye.

"Isn't she?" I ask innocently. "As far as I see it, she's a good fuck that I have zero intention of settling down with. Although, I don't like her all that much, so buddy might be pushing it."

"You're so full of fucking shit, Nic," he says, pulling off the main road and disappearing into The Empire's underground car park.

"So this is serious business then if it's just the two of us?" I ask, looking at the guys' empty allocated spaces.

"Maybe he's officially making me his underboss," Theo taunts.

I keep my mouth shut until I step out of the car and he attempts to go ahead of me to the lift on the other side of the vast space.

"Ow, you motherfucker," he barks when I punch him in the arm.

"There's only one man for that job, and you know it."

"Do I? As far as I can see, the dickhead who thinks he deserves it is too busy playing games with a woman he refuses to admit he wants."

"I don't fucking want her. I don't want any woman."

"And you think that's going to fly?" he asks as the doors close and he flips open the secret panel above the standard buttons to take us to the very top of the building.

"What the fuck is that meant to mean?"

"The boss is going to want to see that you're committed to something before he even considers you for the position you secretly want."

He's right. I've never once declared my wish to take over

Dad's position since we lost him. There's a part of me that doesn't want to admit it out loud because it's just another thing that will make the whole situation more real. But I do want it. Of course I do. I'd be fucking honoured to step into my Dad's shoes and stand beside Damien, running this Family.

But I'm also not fucking stupid. I'm nineteen, soon to be twenty if we're looking on the positive side of things. And I can be somewhat of a liability, I can admit that. And I guess that my behaviour, my inability to cope with losing Dad over the past few weeks, hasn't exactly shown my loyalty and dedication to the Family.

But I've never considered the possibility that he'd want to see more from me than just being a good soldier. Surely, he doesn't give a shit if I'm in a serious relationship?

"Stop yanking my chain. He won't give a fuck."

"Won't he?" Theo taunts. "Might be time for you to find yourself a nice little Greek girl to warm your bed at night."

"Like your sister? Ow," I bark when he retaliates with a solid punch to my shoulder.

"That's your fucking cousin you're talking about. And she's fourteen, bro."

"You do remember what we were doing at fourteen, right?" I say, quirking a brow.

"Rhea's not like that," he argues.

"Mate," I say, clapping him on the shoulder, "take it from a guy who's just discovered his little sister is getting railed by the devil. She *is* like that. And the sooner you come to terms with that, the easier it will be."

"Rhea's a good girl," he continues to argue.

"Bro, are we even talking about the same person? She's walking around looking like she's raided your girl's wardrobe these days. There's no way she's not—"

"Shut the fuck up," he growls darkly, making me chuckle.

Thankfully, the lift dings and the doors open, cutting off our conversation.

Delusional idiot seriously needs to take a closer look at his sister, though.

"Afternoon, lads," Jason, Seb's oldest sister's husband says when he glances over his shoulder and spots us approaching.

"You had a promotion, Gabris?" I ask, not used to finding him up here in the inner circle.

He swallows nervously before confessing, "The boss made a few adjustments after..."

"Right," I mutter quietly, not needing him to say any more.

Dad wasn't our only loss that night. And seeing as I've buried my head in the sand ever since and refused to rejoin the real world, I have no idea what's been happening around here.

My first taste of work was the other night when I sat down with everyone in Theo's flat.

Regret twists my insides. I should have been present and useful in this fight the Italians have started, not hiding like a pussy in my flat, unable to focus on anything but the pain.

"Come on, the boss is waiting for you," Stefanos says up ahead, marching toward Damien's office door and opening it for us.

But unlike I was expecting, he doesn't leave us to it. Instead, he slips inside where we find Damien, Charon, and Galen.

My breath catches, a massive fucking lump climbing up my throat as both Stefanos and Galen move to stand behind

Damien. The exact spot that my father used to fill as Damien's underboss.

My stomach turns over, and for more seconds than necessary, I'm convinced that I'm going to throw up on Damien's ugly-as-fuck carpet.

"It's okay, man," Theo says, sensing my distress.

His hand lands on my back in support and he gently pushes me toward the two chairs that are waiting for us.

"Boss, Galen, Stefanos, Charon," Theo greets politely while I continue to hold it together.

"Take a seat."

"What's going on?" I ask, ripping my eyes from the two men over the boss's shoulders and trying to focus on the reason they called us here.

"The Italians have taken the right side of Walker Street."

"What?" Theo booms, his grip on the arms of the chair turning his knuckles white.

"It's okay. We knew it was coming." We all knew it was coming. It was what Enzo told us about Saturday night. But no one said a fucking thing about just letting the Italians' plans play out.

"Yeah, but you didn't need to let it happen," Theo snaps, echoing my thoughts.

"And what would you have proposed we do instead, Son?"

"He's right," I say, agreeing with Damien. "If we stepped in at this point, they'd know we have someone in their inner circle. This is the smartest thing to do."

"I get that, I do, but fuck. That means they have Marco's."

"And they're going to be disappointed when they get

down to the basement, because Marco shut up shop on his little side business a few weeks ago."

"And that won't ring alarm bells?" Theo asks suspiciously.

"They've been trying to take that bit of our territory since Ricardo got into power. It's only sensible of us to move that part of our business elsewhere. Should have done it before now," Damien explains.

"So what now?" Theo asks. "We sit back and watch them take our businesses one by one?"

"For now, we continue what we're already doing. I don't want to make the first move. I want to intercept theirs."

"And what if they don't make one?"

"They will," he says confidently. "They're trying to drag us into it. But we're not going to bite. But at some point, they're going to want to really hit us for Daemon and Anthony."

"Should we be moving out?" I ask, thinking of my sister and the other girls living in our building. There's no fucking way I'm putting any of them at risk. They've all already been through too much.

"No. We've already started to drip intel through the family of their location, and it's nowhere near your building."

"And what if they suspect we're lying?" I ask, not liking this at all.

"Have you told anyone about where they are?"

"No, of course not. But there are plenty of us who know. And not just soldiers. Isla, Carolina, Jocelyn, Gianna." Theo glances over at me as I name-drop Daemon and Alex's mum. Yeah, okay, she's unlikely to do anything to risk her sons. "Brianna," I reluctantly add. Theo's brow lifts knowingly.

"Well, then I suggest you do whatever you need to ensure their lips stay firmly shut. Although, all the former have been a part of this Family for years and are trusted. There is only one name in that list which could be a liability, don't you think, Nico?"

"Brianna wouldn't do anything to put us at risk," Theo says.

"How much do you know about her? Have you done a thorough background check?"

"Of course I have," Theo scoffs, making my brows hit my hairline.

"Oh? And why have I not seen this information?"

"Because you were too busy dipping your dick in her to think rationally," Theo deadpans.

"And I assume you're also going to tell me that you had Emmie checked out before—"

"Yes. I knew all her secrets long before I got tangled up with her." Theo shoots his father a glare. Although he's happy that Emmie belongs to him, I'm not sure he'll ever get over the fact he never actually got to make the choice himself.

I've never seen Theo as a romantic, but something tells me that he might just be deep down, and the fact he's had his moment to drop to his knee and ask Emmie to be his properly taken away from him doesn't sit right.

"Right, well, I'm going to need to see all of that."

He rolls his eyes at me and turns back to his father.

"Are you going to tell us any of the real details of Daemon and Ant's supposed location?"

"It's inconsequential right now. What I need from you all is your full focus on your future. We have everything under control here."

"And what does that future look like, Dad?" Theo asks.

He's doing it for my benefit mostly, although I know he's curious about how he fits in the Family's reshuffle now Dad is gone.

"I'm still mulling things over. But for now, both Galen and Stefanos will be picking up your father's duties, Nico. But please, don't think for a second they're replacing him. It would be impossible to even try.

"Focus on your exams. Take the time you need to move past everything that's happened," he says, staring me dead in the eyes. "And then we'll talk seriously about what comes next."

My lips part to dig deeper, to understand where his head is at. But I know better than to question him, especially when he's all business like he is now.

"You got it."

"And do what you need to do with Brianna to ensure our secrets are locked up tight. Having her at Knight's Ridge sure helps, but there are plenty of ways for her to sell us out for the right price."

"She needs security," Theo says, referencing the fact that the rest of the girls have details appointed to them, although not to their knowledge. Something I'm sure Theo and Seb are going to pay for with pain when Emmie and Stella find out.

But as amusing as that's going to be, I can't help but agree with Damien's decision. The girls are our weakness and Ricardo is no fool. If he wants to get to us, he knows exactly where to hit next, and we'll be damned if he's going to get a chance to lay even a finger on them.

My chest aches at the thought of someone going after Brianna, but I can't deny that the risk is real. Not only has she been openly fucking me, but she's a direct line to Jodie and Toby.

"I'll speak to our team, see who they've got to watch her."

My teeth grind with my need to demand that I'll do it. But even I know that I don't have the time for that right now. And the thought of someone following her around, watching her every move sends some weird, violent reaction shooting through me that I don't want to even attempt to identify.

"If that's all?" Theo asks, apparently more than ready to get the hell out of here.

"That is all. Call us if you hear or see anything. And focus, yeah? Imperial is waiting," he says, staring at his son with something akin to pride shining in his eyes. "And I know your father would want to see a solid set of results to your name in a few months' time," he adds, turning to me.

"You got it, Boss," I say, pushing to stand as Theo does the same before we walk away and head straight for the lift.

19

———

BRIANNA

"He's in a right state," the year twelve closest to me says instead of completing the task Mrs. Hendrix has set her. I should probably chastise them for gossiping, but I can't help but lean forward a little and listen.

The tension in sixth form was noticeable from the moment Melissa and I stepped inside before this lesson. But it wasn't unexpected. There was gossip flying around Melissa's year ten tutor group, and it didn't take much guessing to figure out who they were talking about.

There are only five boys who rule this school and lay down the law to anyone who doesn't fall into line.

"They jumped him on the basketball court apparently," she continues.

"Does anyone know why yet?"

"Nope."

"It must have been bad though."

"Probably tried hitting on one of their girls. Jamie has never been the smartest tool in the box."

"Girls," Melissa snaps, noticing their lack of progress.

Not wanting to be caught eavesdropping, I force my attention back to the computer screen.

"What has Mr. Middleton done about it?" the girl whispers.

"What do you think?"

"Fuck, I wish I had even half their power."

"Right, time is up, year twelve. Let's go through those answers."

I don't move for the rest of the lesson in the hope of overhearing something else, but sadly Melissa monopolises all their attention.

By the time she lets them all go for lunch, I'm no further forward and desperate to find out the truth.

Jodie was useless when I messaged her at break, so clearly, Toby wasn't in on whatever happened after school last night.

"My meeting has been cancelled this afternoon, so if you want me to do that study session, I can."

Thoughts of how Nico left our previous session makes it seriously tempting to push the job off on Melissa, but something tells me that Nico won't have any of that. Plus, I'm too desperate to know what they've been getting up to to not show my face. It's probably another really, really bad idea when it comes to Nico Cirillo, but I figure, what's one more to add to the already very long list of fuck-ups?

"No, it's okay. I'd like to continue with what we did yesterday. If that's okay?"

"Of course, I'll never say no to an extra free lesson to play catch up. You should drop a couple of your observation lessons this week, though, so you don't fall behind with your planning."

"I've got everything under control," I promise her before we tidy up and head out to get some lunch.

Unlike my previous placements or the many, many schools I've been to over the years, the food here is edible. And even better than that, it's free. Perfect for my current situation.

I can fill up here and then not have to worry about what to feed myself at night, assuming Brad doesn't show up to take me out for something fancy.

Just like I told myself I would, I sent him away Monday night with nothing more than a thank you kiss at the main door to my building.

He wasn't happy about it, and when he finally walked away he looked like I'd just kicked his puppy.

I understood why. Whenever he's been away on business in the past, I've always been more than happy to see him when he's returned. Now it's different. Although, I'm struggling to understand why.

With a stomach full of today's incredible cottage pie, fresh greens and more cake and fruit than I could eat in a week, I make my way back toward the sixth form block.

Unlike when we walked out before lunch, students are loitering around, ready to move toward their final class of the day.

Everyone I pass is talking about the same thing.

The boy who's walking around after having his face rearranged by... well... I'm yet to find out by who exactly, but I have my suspicions.

There's a 'closed to students' sign on the door, but I think nothing of it as I push inside and find the entire library deserted.

Unease ripples down my spine, but I figure the librarian is just having a well-deserved lunch break and I make my way toward the back of the space, breathing in the scent of books.

A sign for the young adult section reminds me of what I said to Rhea last week when she showed me around this place and a little excitement stirs in my belly.

Instead of lingering with the books, I rush to the room that's once again booked for Nico's session, and the second my arse hits the chair, I pull my notebook and phone from my bag.

I've got a couple of notifications from Calli, but I push those aside in favour of writing this list.

Opening my Goodreads app, I scroll through my bookshelves until I find the one I want.

"Yes," I hiss as I write 'Books Rhea Must Read' at the top of a blank page.

I've got a list of at least ten books, most of them series that I think she'll love based on our conversation the other day, by the time the door clicks open and the air around me changes.

"You're late," I snap without looking up.

Honestly, I have no idea what time it is. The second I started thinking about books, the minutes just slipped away, just like when I'm reading.

"What's that?" he asks, walking over and staring down at my list.

"None of your business," I snap, slamming my notebook closed. But I'm not quick enough with my phone and he snatches that up and starts scrolling.

"I guess it should come as no surprise that a filthy whore like you should love nothing more than reading porn."

"It's not porn," I argue, reaching out to snatch my phone from him. "It's romance, with some red-hot smut thrown in for shits and giggles."

"So... porn?"

"Because all that shit you watch to make yourself feel

less lonely at night has any kind of romance in it?" He opens his mouth to argue, but I'm quicker. "A plumber turning up to service a girl's pipes does not count as romance. Nor does Daddy's friend who appears to have a sympathetic ear and shoulder to cry on."

"Oh?" he asks, reading through something. "So this review that I assume you've written is the opposite of that, is it? *I'd happily call him Daddy and let him spank my arse raw.*"

"That is one part of it. Not the entire thing," I hiss, finally able to snatch my phone back before he reads any more.

"Think I might need to check out some of these books. Might learn a few things."

I pause with my phone half in my bag at the words, *You don't need any more skills*, right on the tip of my tongue. Thankfully, I manage to swallow them down. The less sex talk we have in here, the better.

"Feel free to read all you like. It's good for the soul."

"The soul, riiight. So did you want to tell me why you're writing a list of 'romance' books for my teenage cousin?"

"I'm recommending her a few things in the hope of sparking her love of reading."

"By corrupting her?"

"You have met Rhea, right? I'm not sure anything I'm going to suggest will teach her new skills."

"She's fourteen."

"And at what age did you lose your virginity, Nico?"

His lips open and close like a goldfish as he tries and fails to come up with a suitable lie.

"Sixteen, obviously."

"Obviously." I roll my eyes hard. "Me too. Shall we?" I

ask, kicking my handbag under the desk before reaching for my tote that has the folder we need.

My gasp of shock rips through the space as Nico's hand smacks against my arse.

"Nico," I shriek, standing bolt upright. "What the fuck are you—"

Mirth dances in his eyes as he slips around the other side of the table and drops into the chair.

"Just testing your theory about getting spanked raw. You just creamed your knickers, didn't you?"

"No," I state confidently. Although I can't deny that I'm feeling a little hot down there after that move.

"You're a terrible liar, Miss Andrews. But I'll let that slide for now. So what have you got for me today?"

I lower myself to the seat opposite him and quickly discover that his eyes aren't focused on my face, but my tits.

"Nico," I hiss.

"Just wondering if it's the silver one again, or black, maybe. Red? It's sheer, isn't it? So sheer that I'll be able to see your hard nipples right through the fabric."

"Are you done?" I snap.

"Maybe, maybe not." With that, he moves, resting his elbows on the table, leaning closer and forcing his already tempting scent deeper into my senses.

My eyes drop from his amused ones to his hands, which are now resting on the tabletop.

"So the rumours are true then?" I ask, taking in his busted knuckles. There might have been some lingering damage there yesterday, but it wasn't that bad.

"There are rumours? Care to share, Miss Andrews?" His eyes glitter with amusement and his lips twitch into a smirk.

"You're such a—"

"Careful, Miss Andrews. You wouldn't be about to verbally abuse a student, would you?"

"What the hell is wrong with you today?"

"Me?" he asks innocently. "Nothing. I'm cushty."

"Right, so did you want to tell me why you beat the shit out of Jamie Carmichael on the basketball courts last night?"

"My, my, you really have been paying attention to the gossip mill, huh?"

"Hard not to when it's literally the only thing everyone is talking about."

"Well, I don't know what to say, Miss Andrews. I spent last night at Mickey's beating the shit out of Theo, fucking pussy." Moving his hands, he makes a show of his busted knuckles by running his thumb across his bottom lip, incidentally managing to remind me of just how soft that part of his body is.

All the muscles south of my waist clench.

"You really expect me to believe that?"

"Sure. Why not?" He shrugs nonchalantly.

"You're lying."

"So... prove it."

"You're an arsehole, Nico." If my insult affects him in any way, then he doesn't show it.

"Why should I tell you anything, Miss Andrews? I have no reason to trust you. In the past few days, you've stolen my credit card, you've lied to me about working here, and despite knowing that you were about to be my teacher, you let me fuck you. Do I need to go on, Miss Andrews?"

"Will you stop calling me that?" I hiss, hating the mocking way my name rolls from his tongue.

"Why? It's your name. Or would you prefer filthy little whore, or dirty lying slut?"

I shoot up out of my chair, my palms slamming down on the tabletop as red-hot anger surges through me.

"Fuck you, Nico. Do you want my help or not?"

He stands, although his movements are much slower and more composed than mine.

His eyes hold mine, and I hate that he can see right beneath my defences. There aren't many people I've met in my life, but damn it, he's one of them.

"You won't leave."

"Won't I?" I challenge. "I don't need to be here right now. Mrs. Hendrix offered to take you off my hands so—"

"Yet, here you are. You couldn't bear for me to spend an hour with her instead of you, could you?"

"You're talking shit. I just want you to do well."

"Bullshit. You hate me, remember? Only useful for a good fuck. So why do you care?"

"Because I do. You're Toby's friend. You deserve to succeed."

"That's nice of you," he taunts. "But I think after yesterday, we both know that you don't really need to be here."

"Mrs. Hendrix—"

"Bull. Shit." In a moment of weakness, his eyes drop from mine in favour of my lips and somehow, I realise we're both closer than we were a few minutes ago. There's barely half a foot between us despite the table that's stopping us from colliding. Then, he startles me by demanding, "Sit back down, Siren." His deep, raspy voice hits me exactly where he intends.

Unable but to do as I'm told, and aware that putting my arse on the chair will help with the space we so desperately need, I follow orders.

"Good girl."

Goddamn this prick.

His eyes crinkle with amusement.

"Now, I really do want to learn some things in here this afternoon, and I think we need to start with you trying to convince me that I can trust you. Because right now, the evidence isn't stacked in your favour."

"How about the fact I know more secrets than you're probably aware of and yet they have never once left my lips," I seethe, thinking of all the things I've been party to with regards to their 'business' since things between Jodie and Toby became serious.

"Ah, now we're talking," he says, suddenly looking much more interested in what I have to say.

"Who the hell would I tell, Nico? I don't exactly have a massive circle."

"There's the question. As far as I'm aware, you've got a whole harem of fuck buddies. Obviously, they all pale in comparison to me, but we can't all be gifted like I am."

"Arrogant much?" I mutter.

"Tell me I'm wrong. I dare you."

"Brad's better," I say happily, aware that I've already taunted Nico with Brad's skills before. He doesn't need to know that the guy literally bores me to tears and that the only good thing he can do with his mouth is eat me with it.

"About Brad..."

"I haven't told him fuck all, if that's what you're insinuating. Your business is just that. Your fucking business. I couldn't give a shit about the little gangster games you run around playing. My focus is here, on teaching, on my career, on the kids' lives I can hopefully have an impact on and make better in some way."

"But do you want that bad enough not to sell us out?"

"Where the fuck is this even coming from, Nico? You haven't given a shit about me knowing stuff before."

"Times are different now."

"Oooh," I say, realisation dawning on me. "You think I'm going to go running to the first corrupt Italian I can find and spill all your dirty secrets? Jesus, if I was going to tell them that I know where their missing soldier is, I'd have done it long before now, don't you think?"

"Depends on what they might offer you in return."

"Wow," I say, an unamused laugh bubbling up my throat. "You really don't trust me, do you?"

"I don't even know you, Brianna Andrews."

"Go on then. Ask me. Anything you want to know."

20

NICO

I stare at her for a beat, thrown by her openness.

I guess if I had bothered to dig beyond the surface and the pleasure Brianna offered me in the past, then I might already know some of the stuff that Theo showed me last night.

I should have known that he'd have pulled everything he could find about this woman the second both she and Jodie entered our lives. But I was probably too pussy blind to even consider it.

"Tell me about your mum," I demand, my voice hard and cold.

As I walked away from Damien last night, the thought of her being the leak dripped through my veins like poison to the point, I almost bailed on our session at Mickey's and marched over to her flat to have it out with her. But I didn't want to do it there, in her home where she's comfortable, I wanted to do it here. Where she's out of her comfort zone, surrounded by people she struggles to relate to and is trying to impress.

The insane outfit she's wearing today—bought by me,

obviously—is just another reminder of how different life here is compared to her usual one. I just never realised quite how big that divide was. Until last night.

And I'm not sure if reading the truth helped settle my unease or just make it worse.

"M-my mum?" she stutters.

"Sure, why not. If I want to know if you're as trustworthy as you make out, where better to start than the very beginning?"

"Uh..." She hesitates. I kind of understand why now I know the truth. It's not a great story to tell. "My mum was... well, she was a kid herself when she had me. She rebelled against all the rules and expectations placed on her and she ran to stop my grandparents from forcing her to put me up for adoption."

Reading that little fact on paper was hard enough, but hearing it from her own lips? Ouch. Not that I'm going to allow her to see that reaction.

"So where did you live?"

"To start with, we lived in various sheltered accommodation that was designed for teenage mums. Obviously, I don't remember any of those. But as I got older, we continued to move around, mostly in council flats."

"Your mum, she sorted herself out?" I ask innocently, making Brianna bark a laugh.

"My mum was a dreamer. She knew exactly what kind of life she wanted, but unfortunately, she had no clue how to get it. So she ended up with every kind of scumbag in the country as long as he made the right promises. She tried to find her answers at the bottom of a bottle or an empty baggie of whatever she could get her hands on.

"Pretty sure she never actually worked a day in her life,

unless you count lying back and spreading her legs for kicks."

"She was a prostitute?" I ask, having not seen that in her background check. Although, I can't say I'm surprised. That's not usually the kind of job anyone puts on their tax return.

Brianna laughs again. "No. She was just a whore. She didn't have the patience to go out touting for work or finding clients. She just made use of anyone who happened to stumble into her path."

"So what happened? How'd you end up here?" The one thing I do know from listening to her, Jodie and Toby talking is that Brianna spent many years living with Jodie and her mum. And that little fact was only confirmed when I ran my eyes down the list of schools she's attended. At about thirteen, everything seemed to settle down. She stopped moving about and only attended one school right through to her A Levels. It didn't take much research to discover it was the same one that Jodie went to.

Brianna slumps back in her chair and folds her arm over her chest, making her cleavage fucking mouth-watering and giving me a real hard time focusing on her eyes.

"She finally took it too far and overdosed," she says, her voice void of any emotion. "I found her, called an ambulance, and I was finally taken away."

"By Jodie's mum?" I ask, getting a little too sucked in by this story.

Her eyes flash with surprise. "Yeah, Auntie Jo didn't bat an eyelid about taking me in. She'd have done it before, if she knew where we were."

"And your mum?" I ask.

"She survived. But that's about all I know. She discharged herself from the hospital before she should have and just... disappeared. Haven't seen or heard anything from her since."

"And Joanne just took you on as if you were her own?"

"Yes. Why does any of this matter exactly?"

I pause, mulling that question over in my head.

"It all just paints an interesting picture."

"Interesting, really? I just thought it was fucking depressing. I have nothing, Nico. No parents, just an aunt who thankfully will do anything for me. I have nothing to my name. Everything I own I've worked for myself."

"Apart from what you stole from me," I deadpan.

She leaps up out of her chair in a rush. "Do you want it back?" she asks, her hands lifting from her sides. "Is that what this is about? You want to rub my past in my face, prove to me that I'm not good enough for the likes of you and the elite students of this school?"

"Wha—"

"You can have it," she snaps angrily. "All of it. Have it all fucking back, because it means nothing. Nothing," she hisses as she reaches behind her to pull the zip of her dress down.

The top half immediately falls away from her body, revealing what I was desperate to know not so long ago. Her white lace bra does show me her rosy pink nipples beneath.

"Brianna," I start, but my words are quickly cut off when she shimmies her dress over her hips, letting it pool around her waist and leaving her standing in just her lingerie and heels.

"NO, Nico. You wanted to prove a point. Well, consider it proved." She bundles up her dress and throws it at me. "I know I am not worthy of all of this. I know I'm just a council estate kid who grew up freezing cold and starving hungry. I can't possibly understand the lives of you and all the other students in a place like this, just like I don't expect you to be able to understand me either.

"All I want to do is make a difference. I want to help kids who have been born into something, or who are living through something that makes them miserable. And quite frankly, it doesn't matter how much money the parents have. Kids still suffer. Lives are still ruined."

She surges forward as if she's actually about to flee this small, enclosed room in just her underwear.

"I don't fucking think so, Siren," I growl, reaching for her as she tries to dart around me to the door.

I wrap my arm around her waist and drag her into my body.

"What are you doing?" she gasps, staring up at me with her big blue eyes.

"Not letting you walk out there in your fucking underwear is what I'm fucking doing. No one gets to see this but me."

All her breath leaves her lungs in a rush before she reaches up and slams her lips on mine.

I'm rendered useless for a second, not expecting her to throw caution to the wind and do something quite so risky. But as ever with Brianna, my self-restraint doesn't last long and I soon find my hands slipping to her arse and dragging her even tighter to me as my tongue plunges past her lips.

Her taste explodes in my mouth, taunting me with all the things I want but point blank refuse to acknowledge or accept.

Instead, I focus on what happens when we collide like this.

Her grunt of surprise fills my mouth as I slam her back against the wall, sweeping her feet from the floor. I wrap her legs around my waist and she gasps as she discovers just how hard I am for her.

"Been five days," I groan into her kiss. "Fucking dying."

"You've been counting?" she breathes, disbelief flooding her raspy voice.

"Addicted to your tight cunt, Siren."

Leaving her suspended against the wall by my hips, I reach up, tuck my fingers under the straps of her bra and tug them down.

The cups give way, allowing her breasts to spill out.

"Look at you," I murmur, staring down at the flushed skin of her chest and the tight buds of her nipples. "Such a seductive little whore."

"Nico," she moans, arching her back, offering herself up to me and grinding against my length, forcing me to grit my teeth.

"You fucking love it, don't you?" I groan. "Anyone could walk in here right now and discover the truth about who Miss Andrews really is."

"Oh God," she moans as reality hits her and she starts shoving at my shoulders. "Nico, stop. We can't—"

"We can. And we will."

"Nico," she cries.

"What's wrong, Siren? You can't tell me that you haven't been craving my cock. I know you have. I can feel your cunt burning through my trousers. You're fucking desperate for it."

"N-not here."

"Oh yes. Right fucking here."

She squeals as I peel her from the wall in favour of the table. Holding her with one arm, I sweep her folder and the work she was going to give me to do from it and let it fall to the floor with a thud.

"Nico."

"Fucking love it when you scream my name, Siren."

Lowering her to the cool wood, I immediately dip my head, sucking one of her nipples into my mouth, once again making her arch for me.

I lap at her, teasing her hard peak with my teeth as my hand cups the other one, pinching her and making her moan and mewl for me.

My cock aches against the confines of my trousers, desperate to be set free and sink inside her tight heat.

He's never been in a pussy as spectacular as Brianna's before, and the fussy fucker doesn't seem to be all that interested in a mediocre replacement.

"Oh God, please," she begs, making me even harder, if that's at all possible.

"Never fucked anyone in the library before," I confess.

"Oh shit. We can't— NICO," she screams, entirely too loudly given where we are when I drag her knickers aside and plunge two fingers into her burning heat.

"It's almost like you want to get caught, you filthy whore."

"N-no. P-please," she begs almost incoherently, fidgeting on the table as if she's going to attempt to roll off it.

"I don't think so."

The rip of her lace knickers is loud enough to fill the space around us as the flimsy fabric falls away from her body.

"Oh my God, you did jus—"

Balling her underwear up in my hand, I stuff it into her mouth mid-sentence to shut her the fuck up.

"Oh Siren. I'm pretty sure the only time you've looked better is when you're bouncing on my cock."

She moans around her knickers as I curl my fingers inside her, hitting that spot that makes her really scream. And fuck if I don't want that sound echoing off the walls around us like I need my next breath.

But even I'm not that fucking stupid. I might be confident that we're not going to be discovered, but there is always a risk.

One that Brianna is apparently brave enough to ignore.

Well, I guess I am just that good.

With that little ego boost making my chest puff out, I finger-fuck her like a man on a mission, causing her to moan and cry out the best she can.

"That's it, Siren. You're gonna come so hard for me in here, aren't you?" I encourage.

Her back arches, her hips rolling in her need for more to push her that final step into her freefall.

"Fuck, you're running all over my fingers."

She screams out as I focus on her G-spot, my thumb circling her clit as I lean forward once more and suck on her nipple.

"Come for me, Siren," I growl against the softness of her breast.

Her cunt tightens down on my fingers as her cries get louder before she falls.

"Fuck me," I grunt as she squirts all over my hand, her juices dripping to the tabletop beneath her.

"You're a filthy whore, Siren. Just think, the next students to work in here will be doing so exactly where you've just come and covered the table."

She groans at my dirty words.

"I bet they'll still be able to smell you. They can't have you though. This cunt is mine."

I drop to my knees and drag my fingers from inside her.

She moans at the loss, but I ignore her demands as I press my hands against her inner thighs and spread them wide.

The sight of my bite mark still lingering makes me feel like a fucking king, but I'm not thrilled about the fact it's starting to heel.

Before I've even thought about my next move, my teeth are sinking into her skin once again, the taste of copper filling my mouth as I rebrand her in the same spot.

Mine. All fucking mine.

Brad and his magic dick can fuck right off if he thinks he has any kind of ownership of my siren.

And the sooner he finds this and discovers the truth, the better.

She thrashes against my bite, but all she really achieves is tempting me with her glistening cunt that's right in my eyeline.

"Fuck, I need to taste you," I confess as I release her thigh and dive for her pussy, cleaning her up and savouring her taste.

She screams, or at least she would if her mouth wasn't stuffed with her own underwear. It doesn't escape my attention that her arms are free at her sides and she could have pulled the lace free by now. But my siren is nothing if not a good girl when I'm lavishing attention on her sinful body.

She continues moaning as I lick up the length of her heated flesh before focusing on her clit, my need to feel her coming for me bordering on an obsession.

"Come for me, Siren. Show me how much you love me eating you. Show me how much you like being a naughty, naughty girl."

Her fingers thread into my hair, twisting as she drags me closer in her need for more.

Pushing two fingers back inside her, I find her G-spot as I up my pressure on her clit.

She chants something as she gets closer to shattering for me. I like to think it's my name, but it's impossible to make out with her gag in place.

"Such a good girl, Siren."

At my praise and with the vibrations of my deep voice flowing through her, she finally falls, her muffled screams filling the room.

"Fuck yes. Now you're going to take my cock like a good girl, Miss Andrews," I growl as I push to my feet and rip my fly open, fisting my aching cock and sweeping up the precum leaking from the tip with my thumb.

Brianna's eyes flare with fear, but I don't let it stop me and I push my thumb into her mouth with her underwear, giving her little choice but to taste me.

"I know you're desperate for a taste too, Siren."

She shamelessly licks at my skin, or at least, the most she can in her predicament.

Pulling my hand free, I grab her hips, dragging her so her feet hit the floor and flip her over.

My palm collides with her arse, a bright red handprint appearing on her pale skin.

"Is that how you like it? You want Daddy to spank you raw like that?"

She screams like a whore when I do it again, and again.

My cock bobs against her cunt, her juices running over it as she gushes with every spank of her arse.

Her moans get more and more desperate, and eventually, I can't take it anymore and I sink inside her with one quick thrust of my hips.

A low growl rumbles in the back of my throat as her heat surrounds me and her muscles try to drag me deeper.

"So. Fucking. Good, Siren. FUCK."

With one hand clamped around her hip, I twist the other in her curls and drag her head from the desk, giving her little choice but to look at the window before her.

A violent shudder rips through her, her fear about what —who—is on the other side of that thin wall palpable. It feeds something inside me that it really shouldn't.

Fisting her hair harder, I drag her from the tabletop.

"Imagine if someone were to look through that window, Siren," I growl in her ear. "What do you think would happen if they did?"

She shudders again and lifts her hand as if she's finally going to free her knickers.

"Uh-uh, I don't think so," I chastise, catching it before she manages to get to her mouth. "All of this, everything you've worked for would be for nothing, wouldn't it? Ruined because you couldn't control your need to be my dirty whore. Unable to resist the lure of my cock and the pleasure it gives you."

She screams, her body vibrating with its fierceness.

"And then what? You'd be left with nothing. You'd go back to that point in your life when you literally had nothing or no one who cared about you. Your reputation would be in the gutter. The only student teacher Knight's Ridge let in, and you fucked it up on your first week by coming on to a pupil. Corrupting one of their most presti-gious students."

She screams again, thrashing and fighting against me, but I'm stronger than her and she stands no chance of getting away from me.

"You're sure putting a hell of a lot of trust in me right now, Siren." I tell her, letting my lips brush against the smooth skin beneath her ear. This time, her reaction is less angry and more desperate as she shivers in my hold, her skin erupting in goosebumps. "This could be our little secret. Or... I could tell everyone who would listen how I fucked you in the library. That sure would make the gossip about whoever taught Jamie fucking Carmichael a lesson go away fast, huh?"

She screams something that sounds suspiciously like, 'you're a fucking cunt', but it's nowhere near enough to stop me.

Releasing her wrist, I slide my hand down her stomach to find her clit.

Her pussy immediately clamps down around me, making my teeth grind with my need to hold off. I have every intention of her coming all over my cock before I allow myself to fill her up.

"Come for me, Siren. You've ignored the rules, the law, this far. Might as well go the whole hog."

I pinch her clit and slam into her one more time and she finally falls, screaming as her release crests.

"Fuck. Such a fucking good girl, Siren," I grit out before my balls draw up and my cock jerks deep inside her, filling her with my cum and ensuring she won't be able to forget about this little tryst for a good few hours.

A feral roar rips from my lips and I shove her forward, pressing her against the table once more.

"You know, you're not all that much better than your whore of a mother really, are you, Siren? One hint of some mindless pleasure and you open your legs and forget about the world around you.

"You make out that you're all noble and want to do all this good in the world. But deep down, you're not that different from any of us. Your weapons might not be knives and guns, but what you hide between your legs is just as dangerous, and not just to those you let touch it."

Finally, she reaches up and pulls her knickers free.

"I fucking hate you, Nico," she spits. "Get the fuck off me."

She kicks and thrashes, and for a few moments, I hold still, but eventually, I take pity on her and finally step away, tucking myself back into my trousers and smoothing down my shirt and tie as if nothing happened.

She spins around and glares at me, but it has little impact. All I see is my seductive siren in her natural state. Freshly fucked and desperate for round two.

Well, this time she's going to be disappointed.

"Enjoy the rest of your day, Miss Andrews. And just remember, trust is a very fickle thing."

With that warning hanging in the air, I drag the door open and march away from her.

21

BRIANNA

The second the door slams closed behind him, I stumble back, colliding with the wall. My legs give out despite my desperation to keep it together and before I know what's happening, I'm on my arse with my arms wrapped around my legs and silent tears streaming down my cheeks.

It is not my finest hour.

What the hell was I thinking, allowing him to touch me? Allowing him to taunt me, to shame me, to degrade me like he just did.

And all because he suddenly doesn't think he can trust me. Where the fuck does he even get off?

I have done nothing since the moment we met to make him think I'm untrustworthy. I've been party to more than a few of their more-than-illegal secrets, and I've never muttered a word of them to anyone. Hell, there are ones that haven't even passed my lips within their inner circle.

I have no idea how long I sit there having a pity party for one that is full of regrets and my never-ending list of mistakes, but eventually, a bang from the other side of the door has me jumping to my feet.

I wipe my cheeks with the back of my hands before I set about covering myself up.

The second I swipe my knickers from the floor, I remember that it's pointless even trying to put them back on. They're ruined.

I stuff them into my handbag before pulling my bra up and then my dress on.

Anger surges through me as I shove my arms through the holes and zip it up.

This is the reason all that fucking happened. At least, it's easier to blame the item of clothing than it is to dig deeper into what I just allowed to take place.

After finger-brushing my hair and attempting to fix my make-up, I throw my bags over my shoulder, hold my head high and drag the door open.

The silence beyond the small room that holds a whole heap of my sordid secrets doesn't register to begin with, but the second I emerge from the back row of books, I find row after row of empty tables and chairs. And I soon discover that the librarian station is as deserted as when I walked in here.

A weird foreboding sensation washes over me as I walk toward the exit, the lining of my dress tickling against the bare skin of my arse like it wasn't before.

Fucking prick.

As if fucking me in one of my favourite places in the world wasn't enough, he's now forcing me to walk around a school with my cunt on show for anyone who might care to attempt to look up my skirt, and his cum running down my thighs.

I suck in a deep breath when I reach for the door handle.

The final lesson of the day might still be in action, but that doesn't mean the hallways are going to be as deserted as the library.

Thoughts of Nico having something to do with our solitude float around my head, but I refuse to give him the credit. Nothing about what just happened says that my career, my future, registered in his plans to fuck me like a brute in that back room. Organising clearing out the entire place for an hour seems like way too much effort for him to prove his entirely futile point.

I'm still shaking my head at that insane thought when I finally get brave and step out of my safe haven.

Thankfully, there's no one to be seen as I make my way down the hallway, but that doesn't mean that the sixth formers are far away, I can hear them all talking inside the common room.

With my eyes locked on the double doors that will take me away from this building and everything that's happened in the last forty-five minutes, I focus on getting the hell away from him.

Should he still even be here.

I'm about two metres from freedom when a shiver of awareness races down my spine.

I don't need to turn around to know that he's there.

Was he waiting for me?

Did he really think I needed the knife driven any deeper into my chest?

"That's it, Miss Andrews," he drawls, making my heart jump into my throat. "Run away like a naughty little girl who's been caught with her fingers in the biscuit tin."

My teeth grind as anger surges through me at his audacity. Shaming me in private is one thing, but in public? In the middle of the fucking sixth form?

No. Just fucking no.

Spinning around, I search the hallway before me.

But there's nothing.

Not until his amused chuckle fills my ears.

Dragging my eyes up, my fists curl at my sides as I find him leaning against the railing of the first floor with a smug-as-fuck grin on his face.

Without thinking, I spit the only thing I can think of at him that will hurt.

"You don't think you can trust me? How about you go and speak to your sister about how good I am at keeping secrets."

His expression falters, and I hate that a surge of victory races through me. He's still trying to process my words when I spin on my heels and run from the building. Guilt slams into me, and my heart races as I realise what I've just done.

I'm a flustered, sweaty mess by the time I crash through into Melissa's office where the rest of my stuff is.

"Brianna, what's wrong?" She gasps in shock, her eyes as wide as saucers as she stares at me.

"I-I'm sick."

"You should go home. You look…" She hesitates, too polite to tell me that I look like a piece of chewed-up dog shit.

"Y-yeah, is it okay if I do?"

"Of course. Go."

"Thank you," I mutter as I dive for my things and stuff them all into my bag haphazardly.

In only minutes, I'm racing toward my car, ready to put this nightmare behind me.

But before I can put it into reverse and speed away, a fresh wave of guilt rips through me and I pull my phone from my bag.

Opening my conversation with Calli, I ignore what she's sent me and type out a message of my own.

> Brianna: I'm so sorry. I might have dropped you in it with Nico. He's probably heading your way right now.

With a trembling hand, I drop my phone into the cupholder and finally make my escape from Knight's Ridge.

T he second I dumped my bags beside my front door, I stripped out of my dress once more en route to the bathroom.

I turned the shower on as hot as it would go and stepped under the spray in the hope that it would wash all my regrets and bad decisions down with it.

It didn't.

And two hours later I'm sitting on my sofa, staring at reruns of *Friends* on the TV but not really seeing any of it as I run the events of the afternoon through my head.

My stomach is one big messy knot of anxiety, and every time my phone buzzes with an incoming message or call, it sinks even deeper that it might be Mr. Middleton telling me that he no longer wants my presence in his school, my uni tutor telling me that I've been kicked off my course only weeks before the end.

Or worse, the police.

I retch at that thought alone, bile burning up the back of my throat.

A knock at my front door startles me to the point I actually let out a little shriek of fright.

"Bri, it's me. Open up," the concerned voice of my best friend calls. "I've got a key and you know I'll use it."

"Fuck," I hiss.

It's not that I don't want to see her. I do. More than anything. But it's going to mean reliving it all out loud, and I'm not sure I have the strength to confess all my sordid sins.

"Brianna Andrews," Jodie warns darkly as if I could ever be scared of her. "If you've got the deadlock on, you know I'll just get the guys here to break it down."

The mention of them is enough to get me moving.

And after releasing the deadlocks she accused me of hiding behind, I pull the door open and find myself instantly in the supportive embrace of my best friend.

"What did he do?" she breathes in my ear as her hug tightens.

"You don't want to know," I confess.

"I do, or I wouldn't be here. I brought your favourite," she says, releasing me and holding up a bag full of pink prosecco and chocolate.

"Well, I guess you'd better come in then," I mutter, stepping aside and then instantly relocking the door.

"Expecting to be burgled or something?" she quips, watching my every move.

"Or something." Right now, having a stranger rummaging around my worthless things seems a hell of a lot better than having to face Nico again.

Leaving her to it in my kitchen, I curl back up on my sofa, pulling the blanket around me as if it's armour.

"Here you go," Jodie says, handing over a full glass of bubbles.

Despite having an empty stomach, all that food from lunch well worked off thanks to my afternoon exercise, I down the entire glass before Jodie's arse has even got close to the cushion.

"I'll get the bottle, shall I?" she teases before walking back to the kitchen and refilling my glass.

The bubbles pop and fizz down my throat before settling in my stomach. The promise of the haze they can deliver means I make almost as quick work of the second glass.

"Jesus, Bri," Jodie breathes, her eyes locked on my face, concern darkening them.

"When you hear what's happened, you'll understand."

"I'm ready. Hit me with it."

By the time there's another pounding on my front door hours later, I'm drunk.

And not just a little bit.

"Make him go away," I whine.

"You don't even know it's him."

"Of course it's him. Why wouldn't he want to come back and drive that knife a little bit deeper in my chest? Maybe twist it for good measure."

"It's not him, Bri. He's been warned to stay the fuck away."

"Oh yeah? And you think he listens to anyone?"

"I do."

Placing her glass on the coffee table, she crosses the room, twists open my deadlock and pulls the door open.

"No, Jodie. No," I cry, leaning forward in an attempt to stop her and rolling straight off the sofa with an audible thud. "Ow," I complain.

Deep, rumbling laughter hits my ears, and anger blooms.

I scramble to my feet, ready to go toe to toe with Nico if necessary. Any fear of facing him after what happened earlier has been drowned by prosecco.

"NO," I bellow. "You do not get to turn up here and—" My argument comes up short when my eyes land on Toby and Alex, who are staring at me as if I'm some unknown creature. "Oh."

"Having a good night, Bri?" Toby asks with a smirk.

"No. No, I am fucking not. And do you know why?" I slur, poking him in the chest. "Because your best friend is a fucking cunt. How do you put up with him? How? You don't even get the added benefit of orgasms. Why bother keeping him around?"

A snort of amusement fills the room before I turn to his buddy.

"Oh, you think that's funny, do you?" I glare pure hate at Alex, but honestly, it's hard to keep it. He's too bloody cute for his own good when he's fighting laughter.

Letting my eyes drop down his body that's wrapped in a navy polo shirt and a dark pair of jeans, I take a step closer.

"You know," I drawl, "I think I might have settled for the wrong boy."

He tenses as my hands land on his chest and slide up until my arms are looped around his next.

"Oh yeah?" he asks, his smirk getting wider.

"Shame I don't know anything about your skills. I'm not sure you could handle me, cutie."

"Cutie?" he asks, his eyes wide as Toby and Jodie laugh.

"Yeah. You're not as bad boy as the others. There's something softer about you."

"Well, I can assure you, there is actually nothing soft about me," he quips.

"Alex," Toby warns, but even that dark edge to his voice isn't enough to stop me.

"Well, let's see about that shall we?"

Pulling my arm back, I let my hand trail down his body.

Excitement licks at my insides as I descend, but it all comes to a grinding halt as my fingers touch his waistband.

"I like it attached to my body, Brianna. And Nico would fucking kill me if you found out mine was bigger than his," Alex teases, his fingers wrapped around my wrist in a vice grip.

"Pussy," I taunt. "When was the last time you got laid so good you couldn't remember your own name?"

His eyes darken.

"Recently enough that I'm not about to take you up on the offer."

"Oh?" Toby asks, clearly in the dark about what his friend has been up to recently.

"You know, I don't need to give you a play-by-play of every person I hook up with."

"I know. But when? You've been with us or at school."

"Seriously?" Alex hisses.

"Well, are you going to make my day better or not?" I ask, hopefully.

"Not. Sorry, Bri."

Taking both my wrists in his hands, he pushes me back.

"Ready to go home, Demon?" Toby asks Jodie as I stand there, suddenly feeling like I don't belong despite the fact we're in my flat.

"Uh..." Jodie looks back at me with her brows pulled in concern.

"It's fine. You go and get your brains fucked out by your sexy man. I'll be okay with Viv the Vibe."

Alex snorts again. "Viv? You call your vibrator Viv?"

"Why not? What do you call yours?" I ask, glaring at him with my hands on my hips as if he's actually going to answer that question.

"I don't need vibrating plastic shit to get myself off," he scoffs.

"Lucky boy," I mutter. "Well, don't say I didn't offer."

"Jesus, we should go before she jumps me."

"What? Don't you think you can handle me, big boy?"

"Tobes?" he says, looking to his friend for help.

"I can stay if you want," Jodie offers, ripping through the tension in the room.

"No, I'm good. I'm just going to finish this bottle off," I say, swiping the half-full bottle that's left over and tipping it to my lips.

"Maybe you should call it a day and go to bed."

"Or maybe I should go out dancing. Find someone who isn't too scared to fuck me." I shoot Alex a look.

"I'm not scared of you."

"Sure you're not."

"Go to bed, Brianna. Or I'm not leaving."

"Such a fucking spoilsport," I mutter. "Fine." I huff, clutching my bottle and stumbling in the direction of my bedroom.

"I'll lock the door," Jodie calls.

I mumble a reply that isn't even fathomable to my own ears as I crash into my bed.

Voices filter around for a few seconds before my front door slams and the lock engages.

With a pained groan, I flip over, successfully tipping a generous amount of prosecco over myself.

I right the bottle and lift my head from the bed. My oversized hoodie is around my hips, exposing my bare legs and—

"Holy fuck," I gasp, my eyes locked on the angry bite mark on my thigh.

He really fucking bit me.

It hurt when I was in the shower, but I was so blinded by rage and my mistakes that I didn't pay it any attention. But fuck.

Needing more alcohol to deal with this shitshow, I tip the bottle to my lips again, forgetting that I'm practically lying down and sloshing it all over my face. But it's not enough of a mess to make me move, and the second I get my lips around the bottle, I chug it down like it's water.

22

NICO

"Where the fuck is Calli?" I bark when I race into the common room and find Theo, Toby, and Alex sitting around chatting like everything is fucking rosy.

"She went home about twenty minutes ago," Theo says calmly, the complete opposite of how I'm feeling.

Spinning on my heel, I march back out the way I came in only seconds ago.

The only thing spinning around my head is what Brianna could be keeping secret for Calli. What could she possibly be hiding from all of us that she let Brianna in on and no one else?

"Nic, wait," Theo calls, the heavy footsteps behind me telling me that he's following.

His fingers grip onto my upper arm as he attempts to stop me.

"What the fuck is going on?" he barks.

"I don't know. That's what I'm about to find out," I spit cryptically, refusing to stop and talk to him.

"Is she okay?"

"Fuck knows."

"I'm coming with you."

Before I get a chance to argue with him, he's ripped open my passenger door the second I unlock my car and he's dropping his arse into the seat.

He doesn't say another word as the engine comes to life and I floor it out of the parking space.

"So do I need to ask why your hair is a mess, your lips are swollen and your uniform is all fucked up?" Theo asks with a teasing lilt to his voice.

I glance over, shooting his question down with a single look as I focus on my sister.

"Okay then. I'll let my imagination run wild, but I'm assuming it has something to do with why the library was suddenly out of action this afternoon. Didn't you have a revision session booked in there with—"

"Shut up. Just shut the fuck up."

"It went well then, I assume. On your way to full marks, huh?"

My teeth grind at his teasing and my grip on the wheel turns painful.

"I certainly passed some kind of test, that's for sure. Not sure about my teacher," I mutter under my breath.

"You're playing with fire, man," Theo warns.

"Isn't that how we usually roll?"

"We might run Knight's Ridge, but I'm not sure even that will get Brianna out of the shit you're trying to get her into."

"I'm just trying to do what the boss suggested," I counter.

"You're not still seriously questioning her loyalty?"

"We've been screwed over by too many people we trust recently not to suspect her. Plus, with her background, I—"

"You're not actually suggesting that just because she had a shitty childhood, she would be willing to sell us out for a pretty penny?"

"I dunno, man. People have done it for less."

I glance over to see Theo's lips part as if he's going to argue, but he soon realises that he doesn't have a leg to stand on.

"So what happened in the library that's led you to Calli like a barely restrained bull?" he asks, changing the subject.

"Just something Brianna said."

"Care to enlighten me?"

"Not really no," I say as I spin the car into our building's car park and then drive down the ramp toward our underground parking.

"Fine. Be like that," he mutters.

"Oh because you're always so fucking forthcoming with your shit," I bark.

"All right, no need to be a dick about it."

"You're a cunt," I hiss as we make our way to the lift.

"Fuck you, knobhead. Calli might be your sister, but she's my cousin, and if you're about to go in there shouting and screaming then—"

"Daemon will probably shoot me. I don't need you as extra protection."

"So you're accepting their relationship now then?"

"Do I have a choice? They're fucking living together."

Without bothering to knock, I press my hand to the biometric scanner that will grant us entry to their flat, and the second the little light turns green, I shove the door open and storm inside.

And it's then I realise my fucking mistake.

Daemon is fucking my sister, my little fucking sister, over his dining table.

And both of them are so fucking into it, they haven't even noticed they've got visitors.

"Fuck, Nikolas," Calli moans.

Shock surges through me, but I'm not sure if it's because of what I'm witnessing or the fact she just called him by his real name and he didn't freak the fuck out.

No.

It's definitely what I'm seeing.

A throat clearing beside me drags me back to reality and I turn around right at Calli realises that she's got an audience.

"Oh my God, what the fuck are you doing?" she screeches, although I don't miss the raspiness to her voice that I'm not sure I've ever heard before.

Daemon has ruined my sister.

Movement beside me lets me know that Theo has also turned their back on them.

"Haven't you ever heard of knocking, prick?"

"Ignore them, Angel," Daemon growls. "Let's go finish up in the bedroom. Something tells me they won't follow."

A deep, violent growl rumbles in the back of my throat before Daemon laughs.

"You fucking—"

"Whoa," Theo says, reaching to grab my arm before I throttle the motherfucker who just had his hands all over my sister. "Calm the fuck down."

"Imagine if it were Rhea," I spit.

"Rhea is fourteen. Any motherfucker doing that to her would already be dead. Calli is an adult."

Shock renders me useless. He's always been on my side

when it came to protecting Calli, but it seems things have changed.

Is it her age, or the way Daemon stares at her like she's literally the best thing in existence?

Maybe a bit of both.

My heart pounds, blood rushing behind my ears in my attempt to drown out the noises we just walked into.

"Go and get cleaned up. We need to talk," I seethe.

"Give us ten," Daemon says, making Theo scoff.

"You have two, or I'll come and drag her out. And if I snap your cock off in the process, all the better."

Daemon's deep laughter rumbles through his home as their footsteps retreat, but it does little for the fury that's racing through my veins.

"I swear if he takes her in there and tries finishing—"

"It's what you would do," Theo points out helpfully.

I spin toward him, a deadly expression on my face that would scare any other motherfucker. But not my cousin, or any of the guys—and some of the girls—who live under this roof.

Sometimes I fucking hate how well they know me. Although, in this case, Theo might be wrong. He doesn't think I'll hurt him for suggesting my sister is getting fucked six ways from Sunday right now down the hall. But I fucking will.

"Why should Calli be any different?"

"Because she's my little sister," I force out through gritted teeth.

"Who's in love with Daemon. She's moved in with him, Nico. What did you think they were doing in here, playing fucking Scrabble and reading each other bedtime stories?"

"I prefer not to think about it," I confess.

"I get it, I do." The second that final words leaves his

lips, a loud female scream fills the flat and he winces, probably wondering if he's going to be the one on the wrong end of my anger.

"I appreciate the sentiment, but you can't. Until you walk in on Rhea with some cunt balls deep inside her, you can't get it."

Without another word, I stalk through the living room in favour of the kitchen and rip the fridge open in the hope of finding some alcohol.

"What the fuck is this?" I ask, my eyes scanning the rows of bottled water, caffeine-free Coke and a bigger array of fruit juices than you'll find in most supermarkets.

"Try this cupboard," Theo offers, hinting at the fact he's spent more time here recently than I have. "Oh," he breathes when he finds that empty. "Must be on some kind of detox."

"Brilliant. Just what I fucking need. Go get me something," I demand. "Alex will have enough vodka next door to wake the dead."

"Fuck you, I'm not your little bitch."

"Well, I'm not leaving. I need to speak to Calli."

"You know, there is such a thing as a phone."

"There's also knocking," a deep voice rumbles. "But he seems to be pretty shit at that too."

When we look up, we find Daemon sauntering toward us with a shit-eating grin on his face, now fully dressed in his signature colour.

"You do not need to look so fucking smug," I grunt.

"I think you're wrong," he says, an unusual smile pulling at his lips, and damn if the sight of it doesn't soften something inside me. Something really, really fucking small.

He marches past me, shoulder checking me as he goes and mimics my gesture of pulling the fridge open. Only, he's not disappointed by the contents and pulls out an orange juice and cracks the top open, chugging it down in one.

"Where the fuck is your alcohol?"

"Gone. Calli is focusing on her exams and eating and drinking better will help her focus."

"And her sex drive," Theo mutters behind me, earning himself a fist to the gut.

"Yeah, can't say we've ever really had an issue with that, to be honest."

"You motherfu—"

"What do you want, big brother?" a soft voice rings through the air. "If you just wanted to show your face and prove what a massive fucking hypocrite you are, then it's really unnecessary and you can leave as fast as you entered."

My teeth grind at her words. She's thrown similar ones at me for years, and I've never been able to deny that they're true.

Everything I've always told her not to do, I've always been doing.

But she's my little sister. I never wanted her to be a part of the dangerous life, having to possibly put her safety on the line when she could make a nice, less risky future for herself.

But maybe she has been right all along. She was born into it as much as I was. It's her right to be a part of it.

I just hate that that cute little blonde girl who used to run around with a teddy stuffed under one arm and a doll under the other has to face our reality.

All three of them stand there glaring at me, waiting to

hear what was so fucking important that I had to barge in on them mid-fuck.

A violent shudder rips down my spine as I remember that scene only minutes ago.

Ugh.

"You're lying to me," I spit, making everyone's eyes widen.

"I'm sorry?" Calli asks at the same time Daemon steps forward, ready to protect her.

"You're hiding something."

Calli doesn't so much as flinch as she walks around her bodyguard and stares up into my eyes.

"So what if I am, Nico? That's my prerogative. It's hardly like you've been honest with me all your life."

"I've never lied to you."

A look of pure disbelief covers her features.

"Sure, you keep telling yourself that if it helps you sleep at night."

"What... that's... I've protected you," I argue. "It's different."

"Is it? Is keeping me in the dark about any part of our lives, what's happening around me protecting me? Really? I was clueless, Nico. Utterly vulnerable without even so much as the basic knowledge to even try to protect myself.

"I'm a part of this as much as you all are, but the only ones who seem to see that are Daemon, Stella and Emmie.

"You guys need to fight, I want to be right there with you. Helping you in any way I can."

A deep, angry growl comes from Daemon behind but, but she doesn't stop to address it.

"I'm allowed secrets, Nico. Contrary to what you seem to believe, you are not my keeper. I am eighteen. I can make my own choices and live my life the way I see fit. The only person who has any right to an opinion seems to have checked out, so feel free to do the fucking same."

She stares at me with determined and defiant eyes that I'm not used to seeing while her hands rest on her hips, more than ready to continue sparring with me.

"You'd think that orgasm would have chilled her out, huh?" Theo quips, making me want to spin around and plant my fist in his face.

"So what's it going to be, Bro?" she hisses.

"What secret is Brianna keeping for you?"

Her expression falters, some kind of emotion flashing through her eyes, but she locks it down as quickly as it appears. It seems she might just have what it takes for this life if she's going to be able to remain almost emotionless while facing off against me.

"What's that got to do with you?"

My lips part to respond, but she doesn't let me get a word in.

"If she wanted to spill my secrets, she'd have already told you."

My eyes narrow when hers flash with amusement.

"You know, if you treated her better, she might not feel the need to be on my side."

"Who the fuck said anything about sides?" I bark.

"You drew the line between us when you decided I wasn't good enough to live the same life as you. There have been sides ever since."

"That's bullshit, Calli."

"Is it?"

Silence falls around us as the tension becomes unbearable.

Her eyes flick over my shoulder and a lightness enters them as I assume she looks at Daemon.

There's a part of me that wants to hate him for giving Calli this strength. But there's a bigger part of me that's so fucking proud to watch her stand up for what she wants that I find it hard to hold onto the anger I first felt when I discovered their relationship.

"I-I just—"

"She knew about us before anyone else did," Calli blurts, finally cracking. "I spent the weekend you raided the Italian compound here with Daemon. Things got... things were intense back then, and I might have drugged him and ran away."

"WHAT?" I roar, ripping my eyes from my sister and instead focusing on the motherfucker behind me. "What the fuck did you do to her for her to drug you?"

"Nico," Calli soothes as her small hand lands on my upper arm, forcing me to look back at her. "It's old news now and doesn't matter.

"The point I'm trying to make is that when I ran from the building, Brianna was there. She looked after me, took me home, and promised that she'd keep my secret for as long as she needed me to.

"She's loyal, Nico. So fucking loyal. She never breathed a word to anyone so—"

"FUCK," I bark. "Fuck. Fuck. Fuck."

"Maybe you should go grovel, man. Preferably on your knees. From what I've heard, Bri likes that," Theo teases, with what I can only assume is a shit-eating grin on his face. Fucking prick.

"Fuck you," I hiss before spinning on my heels and marching out of what is now my sister's flat without landing a punch on either motherfucker who's watching me with amused eyes.

The door crashes back against the wall as I throw it

open and storm through the building with thoughts of what happened today spinning around my head.

The second I'm in my flat, I drag my freezer open and pull out the bottle of vodka chilling in there and twist the top.

"Fuck you for doing this to me, Brianna Andrews."

23

BRIANNA

Ripping my eyes open yesterday morning and forcing myself to look at the brightness of the phone screen so I could call in sick to both school and uni was almost more than I could handle.

The second I'd hit send on the email to my tutor, I dropped my phone into the sheets and immediately passed back out again.

I've had some hellish hangovers in the past, but this one was right up there.

The only saving grace was that Melissa saw the state of me the day before and would never question how legitimate my actual sickness is.

When I woke sometime during the afternoon feeling a little better, guilt for bailing on my job not even a week in because I couldn't handle my own reality and reached for the bottle—just like my mother did—had me rushing to the bathroom faster than I thought possible before I emptied the contents of my stomach into the toilet.

I sat there on my cold bathroom floor, my skin slick with sweat and my veins filled with regrets, for the longest time that I somehow fell back to sleep. And by the time I woke again, I was shivering, curled up on the floor with drool running from my mouth.

If I needed any more evidence about how shit my life is right now, then there it was.

When I eventually discovered my phone buried in the sheets, I found a whole heap of notifications, mostly from Jodie and Calli. I sent them both a message to let them know I was alive, and after stuffing my face with an entire bag of cheesy Doritos, I fell back into bed covered in an orange dusting, hoping that when I woke again everything would be okay.

With everyone believing I've got a stomach bug and unable to attend school again for forty-eight hours, I turn my alarm off when it goes off the next morning and flip onto my back.

Staring up at the ceiling, I appreciate that for the first time in a while, it doesn't spin before me.

Hangovers are not fucking fun in your twenties.

I remember being seventeen and going on weekend binges and being okay for school on a Monday morning as if nothing had happened.

If my recovery is this bad now, I can only imagine what it'll be like when I hit my thirties. It doesn't even bear thinking about and is nearly enough to put me off drinking.

I almost allow myself to believe that's possible. That is until his face flickers through my mind and I realise that while he's in my life and firmly on his quest to ruin everything I've been working toward, or whatever it is he's doing, then it's not going to happen.

"You know, you're not all that much better than your whore of a mother really, are you, Siren?"

Bile burns up the back of my throat as his deep, raspy voice fills my ears.

I've spent years trying to ensure I don't turn into the mess my mother used to be. I barely remember how hard my early life was now, but the memories that do haunt me are enough.

I'm not like her. Not entirely, anyway.

I have qualifications, a future. Hopes, dreams, and desires that don't revolve around getting wasted and high at every opportunity.

Rolling out of bed, I drag my fluffy onesie from under my bed, grab some clean underwear and pad out through my living room, turning the coffee machine on as I pass the kitchen in favour of the bathroom.

I feel a hell of a lot better once I've cleaned my teeth, and after stripping off, I throw myself into a red-hot shower to hopefully burn the scent of the past forty-eight hours from my skin.

I spend time exfoliating, shaving, anything to try and make myself feel better, and by the time I get out, I smell like fresh mangos. It's just a shame my stomach is still knotted up. Although, I think most of that is probably hunger at this point. Those Doritos didn't really do it for me last night.

Wrapping my hair in curlers, I apply my moisturiser, pull my less-than-sexy onesie on and head out to the scent of rich coffee brewing.

The need for some fresh pastries burn through me as I go in hunt of my phone once more. The temptation to open up my UberEats app and make use of Nico's card is seriously high.

The second he gets a notification of it being used though, it's going to bring him straight to my door.

Is that a bad thing or...

I slam that thought down as my vagina attempts to take over my thought process.

Yes. Yes, it is a very, very bad idea.

But those pastries from the bakery a few streets over are so freaking good...

Before I know it, my thumb is flying over the screen and I'm ordering more buttery delights than one person should ever eat in a day, but fuck it. He owes me, and if he wants to turn up and try to punish me for it, then he can have it out with me through my locked front door.

With a weird kind of success—not that making him pay for my breakfast in any way makes up for the bullshit he's pulled—I grab my coffee and curl up on my sofa to wait for my goodies to arrive.

I work my way through my notifications, shocked by the state of the messages I sent to both Jodie and Calli yesterday. They're barely intelligible, and I can't help but wonder why they didn't turn up here demanding to check on my mental state.

Maybe they did, a little voice says in my head. Jodie has a key, and something tells me that I'd have slept through a tsunami with the amount of prosecco that was in my system.

I send them both new messages that make a little more sense before opening up another conversation. One I'm not so excited about.

> Brad: I miss you, baby. Let me take you out tonight.

My heart sinks as I look at the time of his message and realise he sent it this morning and I haven't slept through his invite.

> Brad: You there, pretty girl?

> Brad: Is dinner not a good enough offer? How about I promise to eat you after until every one of your neighbours knows my name?

"Pretty sure they already do, but whatever," I mutter to myself before my eyes drop to his next message.

> Brad: Is something wrong, baby? Did I do something wrong?

"Jesus, get a clue."

I'm about to reply when my buzzer goes off and my heart jumps into my throat.

Would that have been enough time for Nico to get from Knight's Ridge to my building? Or is it just my breakfast?

Questioning my impulsive decision to use his credit card again, I make my way over to the small screen by the door which will allow me to find out the answer.

I breathe a sigh of relief when I just find a man standing there with my order.

Hitting the button to allow him entry, I unlock my door, finding the deadlocks haven't been engaged and making me question whether Jodie did make an appearance yesterday or not.

Footsteps sound on the stairs as I step out, ready to intercept the delivery guy on his way to my flat.

"Carl," I say with a smile when he gets closer. "Long time no see."

"Hey, Bri. Looking good. It's been a while since your name popped up on my screen." His eyes glitter with wicked intent before they drop down to take in my less-than-desirable outfit.

"Been trying to be good, you know how it is," I tease, unable to rein in the flirting.

Carl and I have hooked up once. He used to deliver to me almost weekly, and after a few heavy flirting sessions, he finally returned after his shift one night and rocked my world. Well, he thinks he did. I can be a good actress when I want to be. But needless to say, there hasn't been a repeat of that night despite his best attempts to lure me back in.

"Well, it's working. You're smoking." His eyes take another leisurely trip around my body, but despite his best efforts, there are zero tingles or flutters in my nether regions. My vag remembers his flappy tongue and lost fingers all too well.

"Thanks," I say with a friendly smile.

"So, who's the lucky man who was allowed to stay for breakfast?" he asks, hanging the large box from Betties over.

"Umm... they're actually all for me."

His brows lift in shock.

"I've just been ill and—"

"Ah, I see. Well, if you want to give me his name, I'm more than happy to go and deliver a painful goodbye message."

"W-what?" I ask in confusion.

"You've had a breakup, right? Eating your feelings? I've got sisters, I get it."

"No, you really, really don't. I don't do mornings after, remember? I certainly don't do boyfriends or breakups."

"R-right. Shit, I—" Thankfully, his phone beeps, giving him the perfect excuse to hightail it out of my building and away from the massive hole he's digging himself.

"Have a good day, Carl," I call as he practically runs down the stairs.

I'm still shaking my head as I make my way back into

my flat, kick the door closed behind me and sink down onto the sofa with my box of goodies.

With a morning chat show playing quietly on the TV, I lose myself in comfort food and attempt to eat my feelings.

I have no idea how I manage it after sleeping for almost twenty-four hours, but when my buzzer rings out around my flat, I'm startled awake.

"Shit," I hiss, pushing the notes from my lap where they must have fallen as I untangle myself from the pillows I've twisted myself up in and stumble toward the door.

I have my finger on the button to speak to whoever it is before I remember why it could be a really bad idea.

Quickly glancing over my shoulder, I find that it's gone six o'clock. School is long over. There's every chance he's been biding his time, hoping to build the suspense and—

"Bri, baby, are you there?"

All the air rushes out of my lungs as I lean forward, pressing my brow to the cool wall.

"Yeah, I'm here. What's up?"

"Well, I was hoping to be let in," Brad says lightly. "I've managed to get us a table at Twenty-Five."

"How the hell did you manage that?" I blurt, successfully being pulled in by him name-dropping a bistro that's taking reservations months in advance.

"I have my ways, baby. Now, are you going to let me up? I might have another little surprise for you too."

Shit.

"Yeah, sure." Regretfully, I press my finger against the button and grit my teeth when the buzzer sounds out.

His footsteps bound up the stairs like a puppy who's excited to see its owner after a day away.

I should be excited too, but right now, I feel nothing.

"Oh." My lips form an O when he emerges dressed in his standard sharp suit and clutching a dress bag with another expensive card slung over his shoulder.

"Surprise," he says, a wide smile splitting across his face.

"Brad, you really didn't need to—"

"I know. But I saw it and all I could think about was how hot it would look on you, and I couldn't resist."

"I hate you spending money on me like I'm some cheap—"

"Don't you dare," he warns, backing me toward my flat with what I think he believes is a dangerous glare. But honestly, it's nothing compared to the one Nico can turn on when he's truly pissed off.

Thoughts of him cut through me like a knife.

I really thought he'd have shown his face at some point today.

There's no way he's satisfied with the threat he made me on Wednesday afternoon in the library. That's not Nico's style.

Unless he's waiting until I return on Monday...

Dread slowly drips through my veins.

"Go and put this on, let your hair down," he says, his eyes jumping to my curlers and reminding me that they're there, "and then we're hitting the town."

"Brad, I'm still not feeling—"

"You told me earlier you were feeling better," he argues.

He's not lying. I did tell him that when I finally replied

to his messages, but I didn't say it expecting him to turn up and pull this stunt.

"It's Friday night, Brianna. Don't you want to go and enjoy the beginning of the weekend?"

My lips part, my refusal right on the tip of my tongue. But with the way he studies me, I know that he'll question me if I say no.

I never say no.

I'm always up for a good time. Or at least I was until Nico turned the tables on me and started making me question everything I do that doesn't involve him. If he is part of the decision making my brain apparently fires differently.

"O-of course I do," I stutter like an idiot. "It's just been a tough few days."

"Even more reason to dress up and feel better about yourself."

Hanging the dress bag over my bedroom door, he pulls the zip down and reveals the contents.

Inside is the slickest, most stunning little black dress I think I've ever seen.

It is so my style, but it probably cost more than a month's rent.

And it was selected by Brad. That little fact takes away some of its charm.

"It's stunning," I say, my eyes eating up the soft looking fabric.

"It's nothing on the hanger. On your curves though..." He fists his mouth as his gaze drops down my onesie-clad body as if I'm already wearing it.

His green eyes darken as he tugs his full bottom lip into his mouth.

But just like Carl earlier, I get no reaction.

That's never been an issue with Brad before. He's hot.

Really fucking hot. Even more so if he keeps his mouth shut, especially when talking about his dull fucking job.

There's only one answer for all of it.

Nico has fucking broken me.

He and his perfectly sculpted cock that hits every single spot just so…

"I like where your mind just went, baby. And we will certainly get to it later. It's been too long since I fell asleep with your taste coating my tongue."

He takes a step closer, his large hand cupping my cheek, but as his thumb brushes across my bottom lip, it's not him I'm imagining being close to me but a guy I should never allow anywhere near me after what he did to me Wednesday. But while my head might be fully on board with that plan, it seems my pussy is on an entirely different page.

"Go get dolled up," he says, taking a step back from me. "I'm pretty sure that dress will be too tight for underwear too." He winks at me and something sinks inside me.

I should refuse his offer, send him on his way and maybe call for another takeaway in the hope of luring Nico from his hiding place. At least, that's what my pussy wants to do. My head… she knows that taking up Brad on his offer is the most sensible choice if I don't want to spend a Friday night alone in my flat. Especially when I'm feeling better and have had more sleep than I usually get in a week.

"I think you might be right," I purr, forcing as much lust into my voice as possible.

Maybe I just need to play the game. Get him between my thighs and let his talented tongue distract me and remind me that he's the safest choice here.

A smile that should probably melt my underwear graces Brad's face as he backs out of my doorway and heads toward the kitchen with the other bag still over his shoulder.

"What else did you bring?"

"Champagne, obviously," he says, barely containing his eye-roll at my apparently stupid question as he lifts the bottle from the bag. "And accessories to finish your look."

"Brad, you—"

"Enough, Brianna. You deserve it. And if it makes you feel better, you can sell it all after I've fucked you in it."

A frown crinkles my brow. "That does not make me feel better. It makes me sound like an upmarket whore."

"Which is about as far from the truth as possible, so get those stupid thoughts out of your head."

My chin drops to argue, but he cuts me with a look and I swallow my words.

Unhooking the dress from the bag, I fold it over my arm and make my way across my flat to the bathroom. But I don't get that far, because Brad pauses his search for my champagne glasses, wraps his fingers around my wrist and tugs me into his body.

"You'll crease the dress," I argue in a futile attempt to stop the inevitable.

"It'll be worth it," he mutters before his lips land on mine.

He's insistent as his hand skims down my side, grabbing my arse and pressing us closer so I have no choice but to feel what my presence does to him, but I refuse to deepen the kiss, much to his irritation.

"What time is the meal booked for?" I ask, trying to extract myself from his hold.

"Seven-thirty."

"I'd better get a move on then." This time when I twist away from him, he lets me go without argument. He has plenty of experience of how long it can take me to get ready when I have a reason to waste time.

I have to hand it to him, he might be dull as dog shit, but Brad knows how to pick a good dress.

Standing in front of the full-length mirror in my bathroom, I twist this way and that, admiring the designer dress he selected for me.

He'd already taken the tag off, so I have no idea how much it cost him. But as the saying goes, if you have to look then you can't afford it. And I know that's the case here.

His suggestion of selling it after this night is done floats around my head, but I can't help feeling seriously weird about it.

I like sex, and I like trying it out with as many different guys as I can. I always have. But that does not mean I'm willing to be a whore for any man.

Even a man as wealthy as Brad.

I might be riding the edge of bankruptcy right now with my rent due and still too long until my next bursary payment, but I still refuse to sell myself. Things aren't that fucking desperate. Not yet, anyway.

Aware that my time is coming to an end, I smooth my hands over my hips, feeling more than aware of my missing underwear.

Brad was right, the dress is too fitted to be wearing anything underneath. Something I have no doubt he's going to try to take advantage of. It's just a shame that I'm not on the same page.

If this were a few months ago, I'd be buzzing with excitement for what a night with him might hold. He knows how to show a girl a good time with exclusive reservations and drinks in the best bars before a night in a flashy hotel somewhere or other.

But now, I think I'd rather stay hiding in my flat.

Okay, so maybe not. But I don't really want to be spending the night out with Brad.

"You must be nearly done in there, surely?" Brad shouts, proving my previous thought right about how long I've been locked away in here.

Sucking in a deep breath, I check my make-up once more in the mirror and pull the door open.

A low whistle comes from him when he gets his first look at me. His pupils dilate as he runs his gaze over my curves appreciatively.

"I knew that would look knockout on you, baby."

My cheeks heat under his scrutiny.

"You need shoes."

"Brad," I sigh, but I don't bother saying any more as he rushes toward the kitchen counter where he abandoned the bag. The second he pulls out a shoe box, I panic. "You just put new shoes on the counter," I screech, racing forward and snatching the box from him, despite it being too late.

"Uh..."

He looks between me and the box I'm now hugging.

"It's bad luck," I state, horrified by his actions.

"Umm... isn't it a table?"

"What?" I snap.

"Putting shoes on a table is bad luck. Not a kitchen counter."

"Semantics. I've had enough bad luck recently, I don't need you adding any more."

His brows lift in surprise. "What don't I know, baby?" he says, the teasing lilt to his tone vanishing as he steps closer.

"N-nothing. It's nothing. Just uni shit," I confess, not

willing to dive into the whole Knight's Ridge-slash-Nico issue with him.

He wouldn't understand. Hell, I'm not sure I even understand.

"It's almost over," he says encouragingly. "You need to tell me about your new school."

I just about manage to swallow the groan that wants to rip up my throat at the prospect of having to spend any part of my night talking about Knight's Ridge, but I know I'm on borrowed time. I managed to put it off the night he took me to the Italian restaurant, but something tells me that he might actually want details about my life tonight.

"Sure," I say, finally lowering the shoe box in my hands to the sofa. "Oh wow," I breathe, taking in the black strappy sandals. They would look right at home wrapped around a pole in Hades.

"Sexy, right? Put them on," he encourages.

Unable to deny the lure of the gorgeous shoes, I undo the clasp as I sit down.

They fit perfectly, and Brad annoys me that much more because of it.

Why does he have to be so perfect on paper? He should be my perfect man.

Intelligent, successful, good in bed. Back in the day, we had killer chemistry, although that has mostly withered and died now. Or at least it has for me.

But there's something missing. There always has been, and it's only becoming more and more obvious when we spend time together these days.

"Can't wait to see them over my shoulders later," Brad mutters absentmindedly as if he's fully invested in his fantasy. I'm concentrating on doing up the fiddly straps, but the second I look up, I find myself at eye level with his tented trousers.

"We really should be leaving," I say, getting to my feet before he decides that he'd rather stay here and let me suck his cock instead.

The thought alone makes my stomach turn over.

"Y-yeah," he mutters, rubbing his jaw.

Making my way toward the door, I grab my clutch and stuff my purse and phone inside, and when I look back over my shoulder, Brad is busy adjusting himself.

"Do you need a few minutes?" I ask with my fingers wrapped around the door handle to make a point.

"No. I'm hoping you'll fix my issue later. It's all my own fault for buying you that sinful dress, baby."

His eyes drop down my body once more, but I quickly turn my back on him and step out of my flat.

It's safer being out in public when he's looking at me like he's about two minutes from devouring me.

Brad might be kinky in the bedroom, but public displays aren't really his thing. Thank fuck.

24

NICO

The second I discovered Damien had put a security detail on Brianna to ensure her safety, I demanded that Theo hack into the system and tell me which motherfucker it was.

Relief flooded me when I heard the name of one of our older guys who has years of experience popped up. He's also, hopefully, not going to be someone Brianna looks twice at. That thought made the relief vanish quicker than it arrived, instantly turning to anger.

I shouldn't care if she finds the security tailing her hot. I shouldn't give a fuck if she wants to screw him six ways from Sunday...

But you do.

Anyway, I want to say that it's his fault that I'm sitting outside her apartment like a grade-A stalker on Friday evening when I could be literally anywhere fucking else enjoying life. But it's not. He might have called me to tell me she'd invited a guy inside, but I've been sitting here much, much longer than that.

Since about ten minutes after she ordered those fucking pastries, to be precise.

I watched the delivery guy go inside, stay for longer than necessary, and then shamelessly rearrange his junk the second he emerged once more.

If I didn't have the notification sitting on my phone to tell me that I had paid for that little treat, then I might wonder if she paid in another form.

If she did, he really fucking needed that. Because while he might have been gone for longer than the delivery would have taken. It wasn't that fucking long.

Brianna has skills, but surely no man in his right mind would allow it to be over that fast.

But then, more hours later than I'm willing to admit to, Brad the bellend parked his rich-boy Porsche in front of her building and sauntered in like he owned the fucking place.

The second I saw him, my fingers curled around the wheel, my grip turning painful and my knuckles white. My heart rate increased and the heavy weight of my gun sitting in my waistband became almost impossible to ignore.

It wasn't the first time I'd seen him. Seen them.

Only minutes after she taunted me with this Brad and his magical cock, I went on a hunt through her socials to find him. It wasn't hard to locate the sleaze, and when I did, I had Theo run a check on him.

I was hopeful we were going to find something I'd be able to ruin him with. But his profile was boring as fuck. No criminal records or even warnings, no evidence of any wrongdoings. Just a solid sleazeball who had regular access to the pussy I was quickly becoming addicted to.

Everything he does, every move he fucking makes only goes to prove everything Brianna has said about him. And I fucking hate him for it.

I hate him with a passion I don't usually feel. It's reserved for special motherfuckers like Ricardo Mariano, not Brad the fucking bellend who thinks he owns my girl.

Yeah, we'll fucking see about that.

It's almost two hours later when there's finally movement at the front door.

Thoughts of them up there rolling around in Brianna's bed had my stomach twisted up in knots, jealousy surging through my veins, slowly poisoning me from the inside out. But even still, I never moved a muscle.

I couldn't.

But the second they both emerge from the building, I lean forward, my eyes eating up Brianna's body.

"Fuck me, Siren."

The black fitted dress is so tight, it shows off every one of her mouth-watering curves. But that's nothing compared to the fuck-me shoes on her feet.

"Shit," I hiss, shifting around in my seat and tugging at my jeans to give the big guy a little space to breathe.

With his hand resting on her lower back, Brad guides her toward his pretentious Porsche. My teeth grind, my eyes locked on that one innocent bit of contact he has with her. The desire to hack that limb off with a blunt saw washes through me until I realise that I sound about as deranged as Daemon and I lock it down.

I don't need any reminders of what a twisted motherfucker my sister is currently in bed with. I just need to focus on the fact he'd protect her until his dying day. And seeing as he seems to have as many lives as a cat, we should be good for a while.

Brianna disappears inside the prick's car before he closes her door and stalks around the front to the driver's side with a smug-as-fuck grin on his face.

He can't have any idea he's in the middle of a battle here, so he has no reason to believe he's winning anything other than her company for the night, but he seems to be celebrating nonetheless.

Yeah, let's see how long that lasts.

I don't see Brianna's security detail anywhere, but that doesn't mean he's not here.

We pay the best for a reason. There's every chance that when all of this is over, she won't even know someone was following her around. Well, aside from me, obviously.

The second his car comes to life, so does mine, and I take off, following him at a distance.

If I get too close then I'll ruin my chances of a surprise because one look at my Mustang Shelby GT500 and she'll know exactly who is on her tail.

He cuts through the busy Friday night traffic with ease as the image of his hand resting on the bare skin of Brianna's thigh exposed by the high split in her dress keeps my blood simmering at dangerous levels.

I'm hardly surprised when he pulls up into an awaiting space outside Twenty-Five.

He's really going all out tonight.

Thoughts of how Brianna might repay him for spoiling her so thoroughly flicker through my mind as I'm forced to park a little too far down the street. By the time I climb out of my car, they're being greeted by the maître d'.

Glancing down at my jeans and polo shirt, I take off in the opposite direction.

Twenty-Five might be a Cirillo business, but I'm not sure even I will be allowed inside without adhering to the dress code, it's that exclusive a place.

In only twenty minutes, I'm marching back down the

street decked out in a black Armani shirt and a pair of Dolce and Gabbana dress trousers.

Smoothing the fabric over my stomach, I hold my head high and saunter toward the maître d' with a dangerous smirk playing on my lips.

"Mr. Cirillo," he greets, which shocks me.

I can't have been inside this restaurant more than a handful of times. But it's nice to know that my reputation precedes me.

"What can we do for you this evening, sir?"

"The couple that just came in. Woman in the black dr—"

"Bradley Whitlock?" he interrupts bravely.

"That's the one," I agree. "I want to see them, but—"

"I've got you covered, Mr. Cirillo," he says confidently before looking down at the tablet in his hands and tapping away for a few seconds. "Please follow me. A glass of our best whisky is already on its way to your table."

My only response is to nod, not that he sees it, as I follow him inside, my eyes scanning the restaurant. With all the dividers and thoughtfully placed plants to allow guests privacy as they enjoy their insanely priced meals, it's hard to see much, but as Raoul leads me to a secluded table, another appears before me through a tall, spiky potted designer plant.

"How is this for you, sir?" he asks politely as another member of staff lowers a crystal glass to the table filled with a generous measure of the whisky I was promised.

"Couldn't be better, Raoul," I state, keeping my expression neutral as I pass him a fifty for his trouble.

I know an ally when I see one, and I fully intend on keeping as many as I can.

"Will you be eating with us tonight, sir?" He offers me

the menu, and after a couple of awkward seconds while I study Brianna through the plant, he finally places it on the table.

"The steak tonight is especially exquisite, sir."

"I'll have that then, please," I say, still refusing to avert my eyes.

"Fantastic. Rare?"

"You've got it."

He melts away from my table, leaving me to slouch low in my seat, slide my glass from the table and take a sip.

An appreciative moan rumbles in my throat as nostalgia of better times slams into me like a truck.

This whisky was Dad's favourite.

Pain slices through me, threatening to rip my heart out from inside my chest right here, and it's only made worse when Brad the bellend reaches out and tucks a lock of Brianna's hair behind her ear as she sips on a glass of champagne.

It hurts to suck in a breath as she smiles back at him, her eyes soft and full of want.

My jaw tics with irritation and I throw back the whisky, fighting the grief and darkness that threatens to consume me from the taste alone.

Their starters come and go while I'm lost, just staring at her like a fucking creep. But eventually, Brad excuses himself from their table and leaves her alone.

The second he's gone, Brianna reaches for her handbag and pulls her phone out.

And I do exactly the same, more than ready to start messing with her.

After selecting a small snapshot I had pulled from the CCTV in the library, I upload it to our chat and hit send before I lower my phone to the table to watch her reaction.

I know the second the notification pops up on her screen, because her eyes widen and her jaw pops with frustration.

I can't help but smirk, watching as my name alone affects her.

You're so fucked, Siren. Probably more than I am, because I'm the one in control here.

The second she opens the message and finds the video, her chin drops in shock and she lowers her phone beneath the table. Filthy little whore that she is though, she doesn't close it. Instead, she watches as I lick and suck her nipples and thrust my fingers into her tight pussy while she writhes around on the table in our little private room.

Her hand lifts and she bites down on her finger as she continues watching.

I. Am. Hard. As. Fuck.

Movement in my periphery makes me rips my eyes from my siren, and a smirk covers my face as her dickhead date returns to his seat. She startles, and I'm pretty sure an actual shriek passes her lips when he lays a hand on her shoulder.

The second reality hits her, she stuffs her phone under the table so the bellend can't see it, and after dropping a kiss to her cheek that makes me want to rip his lips clean from his face, he lowers his arse back to his chair.

Not two seconds later, their mains arrive, quickly followed by mine.

I wasn't hungry when I ordered it, my stomach too knotted up watching that motherfucker touch what's mine to think about food, but as the scent of the steak and fancy chips hits my nose, my mouth waters and my stomach growls.

With them distracted by their own food, I pick up my cutlery and dive in.

"Fuck," I groan when the steak practically melts in my mouth. The only thing that could possibly make this better would be if she were sitting opposite me in that sinful dress.

"How is everything, Mr. Cirillo?" Raoul asks, seemingly making it his sole job tonight to ensure I'm happy.

I get it. Having me here could be make or break for him.

"Fantastic, just as promised. Listen, Raoul, I need a favour."

"Anything, sir," he agrees happily before listening intently to my plan.

It doesn't escape my attention that Brianna nurses the same glass of champagne throughout the whole meal. And while I might like the fact that she's not getting wasted and is instead keeping her wits about her, her lack of visits to the bathroom is seriously hindering my plan.

Needing something to sate my twisted desire for her, I find the next part of the video and hit send.

Her bag is resting on her thighs, and the second the message is delivered, her spine straightens.

It's all I need to feed that beast inside me.

The bellend is busy talking, probably about his boring little life. He's so lost in his bullshit story that he hasn't noticed that Brianna isn't paying attention, and he also doesn't notice when she pulls her phone out and focuses on that instead.

She sucks in a sharp breath as she watches me rail her

from behind. She had no idea, but she was staring almost right at the camera with my fingers fisting her hair.

My cock jerks as she continues watching, and I can't help myself but to up the ante.

Nico: You're getting wet watching us together, aren't you, Siren?

25

—————

BRIANNA

My heart pounds so hard I can feel it in my toes as I stare down at his words.

He's not fucking wrong, though.

Those videos. They were... Hot. Wrong. Forbidden.

Did I mention hot?

Us together might be all kinds of disastrous, but there is no denying that we look fucking good. If his mafia life weren't to work out and I lose my job over all this bullshit, we could definitely get into porn.

My hands tremble with my need to reply.

His messages are the single most exciting thing that has happened since I opened that shoe box back in my flat.

Obviously, the food has been incredible. Beyond incredible. It should be really, considering the astronomical prices.

Thank fuck Brad earns an eyewatering amount of money or I'd have a serious issue allowing him to treat me to something like this.

I'm mostly a simple girl, and I'm more than happy with

a date that consists of a movie and Pizza Hut as long as what comes after is mind-blowing.

I glance up, finding him still talking about something to do with... something.

Honestly, I've barely listened to a word he's said tonight —not that he's noticed, or cares.

He makes no secret of the fact he doesn't really have any friends outside of work colleagues, so I think he's just glad to have someone to unload on.

Lucky me.

Since the moment we walked out of my building together, I've been on edge.

It's because of my stupid decision this morning to order those pastries. I'm still expecting Nico to pop up from behind one of these insane plants and pull the rug from beneath me.

But there's been no sign of him. Not that I've really gone out of my way to search. I've been too scared to find out what might happen if he does show his face and introduce himself to my 'date'.

A shiver of dread races down my spine as Brad continues to drone on.

Needing some excitement, I find my thumbs flying over my screen.

> Brianna: No. I'm wondering what I was thinking, allowing you to touch me.

I have every intention of stuffing my phone back into my bag and placing it on the table so I have no idea if it goes off again, but his reply comes too quickly.

> Nico: See... I was wondering the same thing about the prick who's been touching you all night...

This time, my gasp is loud enough that it actually distracts Brad from his tireless chatter and he looks over with concern etched onto his features.

"Are you okay, baby?"

"Y-yes, sorry. Ignore me."

His eyes narrow as he continues to study me.

"Could I get another drink?" I ask, reaching for my glass and swallowing the generous amount of champagne that's still in there.

I might have been holding off, with the lingering memory of my recent hangover from hell ever present in my mind, but after reading that message, aware that he's seen us, is potentially watching us, I need it. Hell, I might need the bottle.

"Of course."

I cringe hard when Brad lifts his hand and clicks for the server like a pretentious prick who thinks the world owes him something.

And while he's distracted playing the big man, another message comes through.

> Nico: That dress though. *drooling emoji* I hope your date is aware that he isn't the one who's going to be peeling it from your body tonight...

> Brianna: I don't know where you are, but you need to leave. Who I spend time with, or what I do, has nothing to do with you. You told me what you think of me quite clearly the other day. Go and find someone else to torment.

Feeling satisfied with my achievement, I successfully shove my phone into my bag and place it on the table as my fresh glass appears before me.

Without wasting a second, I reach for it, allowing the mass of bubbles to explode on my tongue.

"Better?" Brad asks softly.

"Yes, thank you."

Delusional idiot doesn't even know what the issue was but is clearly happy it was fixed with a glass of Cristal.

"Are you ready to order your desserts?" the server asks.

Quickly grabbing the menu, I scan it while Brad rattles off his order as if he'd planned it before we even arrived. To be fair, he probably did. Spontaneous is not his thing.

"Could I get the torte?" I ask, mentioning the first thing I recognise. The menu is well beyond what I'm used to.

"Of course, and would you like a dessert wine with that? I can recommend—"

"No, I'm fine thank you," I say, quickly cutting him off.

As he walks away, I try to scan my surroundings discreetly, but I can barely see any of the other diners, let alone anyone I recognise. And there's a reason—this place has clearly been designed with diners' privacy in mind.

On any other day, I might appreciate that. But while I'm trying to find the man who's watching me, taunting me, I have a very different opinion.

"I can't wait to get out of here," Brad drawls, his eyes dropping to my chest.

My lips part to say something, but I quickly find that I have no response to that. Well, no response that he wants to hear, anyway.

"Excuse me," I say, needing to get away from his heated stare. "I need to visit the ladies'."

Grabbing my bag, I push my chair back and walk away without so much as looking back at him.

As I put some distance between us, the more aware I become that I'm being watched. My skin prickles with what feels like a million pinpricks as I move toward the bathroom sign at the back of the restaurant. But no matter how much I look around, I don't find him.

He's here though. I know he is.

My eyes land on a woman sitting alone at the bar in a sequin-covered silver dress and a pair of red-soled shoes. Her hair is immaculately styled, and despite being unable to see her face, I just know she's perfect.

I may have put plenty of effort into my appearance tonight, mostly to waste time, but I can't help feeling like I don't fit in.

I might be wrapped in a designer dress like the rest of the patrons, but this isn't me.

Tiny portions of fancy—albeit incredible—food really isn't me.

Noticing my attention, the woman glances over her shoulder, but her eyes never actually find me. Instead, they find the man I've left behind.

Fine by me.

The thought of escaping out of the back door of this place and leaving them to it flickers through my mind as I continue forward, and I can't deny that I'm more excited about the prospect of running away right now than I was coming here in the first place.

With my sight set on the ladies', I push thoughts of everyone else around me aside and focus on just a few minutes of alone time so I can try to figure out my next move.

Brad wants more from me tonight, he's made that more than obvious. But I really, really don't want to invite him back to my flat or let him lead me into a fancy hotel room to act out whatever fantasies are floating around his head right now.

Pushing into the ladies', I find it gloriously empty. It's huge and totally over the top with deep purple flocked wallpaper and smaller versions of the plants that fill the main restaurant. There's even a fucking chaise longue. Who the hell wants to hang out in the toilets longer than necessary, even if said toilets are this fancy?

A woman content on hiding from her date…

My phone buzzes once more on the small shelf behind the toilet as I go about my business. The sound makes my heart jump into my throat.

It's him. I know it's him.

He'll have seen me walk in here…

Maybe this was a bad idea.

I finish up with trembling hands, thoughts of everything that happened between us Wednesday in that library as clear in my mind as if they happened only hours ago.

Much to my relief, the main area is still empty when I emerge and walk toward the sinks. I wash and dry my hands before reluctantly pulling my phone out, but I don't get a chance to see who it is because movement in the mirror before me forces my head up, and when my eyes focus, I find a dark, angry pair staring back at me as he emerges from the other stall I hadn't even realised was occupied.

He moves silently, like a ghost in the night, closing the

space between us and making my heart rate spike to the point I wonder if I'm about to pass out.

"W-what are you doing?" I breathe when he's almost in touching distance.

"I could ask you the same question, Siren." His deep voice hits a place deep inside me that Brad has come nowhere near touching tonight with his dreary stories. My lower stomach clenches in desire, reminding me of everything I felt while watching those videos.

Placing my phone on the side, my fingers curl around the marble counter before me, my nails bending under the force of my grip. But while I'm locked in his heated stare, there's nothing more I can do.

I can't move. I can't think. Well, not with any other part of my body than my slutty pussy.

"You shouldn't be here."

"And you shouldn't be here with another man," he throws back instantly.

My chest heaves as I watch him stalk closer. My skin prickles, my blood beginning to boil as if I'm standing here before him naked, ready for him to take me.

You should be angry. You should be lashing out, a little voice says inside my head. But all I can focus on is him. What he can offer. And what he's allowing me to escape from.

I don't want to go back out there. I don't want to go anywhere else with Brad.

But I also shouldn't want anything to do with this twisted fuck, either.

I really never have been all that good a judge of right and wrong.

"It's just Brad," I argue as if it's going to make this any better.

"I don't give a fuck if it's Jesus. He's spent all night eye-fucking you in this dress, planning what he's going to do once he gets you out of it, and touching you."

His voice is deep and gravelly as if he's barely restraining himself. It should probably terrify me, but that's not the reaction I have as a rush of excitement heads straight between my thighs.

"Careful, Nico. You sound awfully jealous."

A loud growl rips from his throat and he suddenly surges forward.

He's on me barely before I've registered that he's moved. His giant hand wraps around my throat, hauling me back into his strong, muscular body as his other hand clamps down on my hip, ensuring I'm not going anywhere.

His chest heaves against my back as his increased breaths tickle over my neck, ensuring every inch of my skin is covered in goosebumps.

"No one else is allowed to touch my toys, Brianna," he says dangerously.

"Fuck you, Nico. I don't belong to you. I never have, and I never will. I'm nothing but a cheap whor—"

All the air rushes from my lungs as my back collides with the wall beside me.

His hand finds its home around my throat once more before he makes the most of my parted lips by slamming his own against them.

I claw at his shoulders, shove at his chest—anything to push him away, because my head tells me that is what I should be doing.

But nothing deters him, and his tongue continues to lick deep into my mouth, his grip on my hip biting as he begins to cut off my air supply with the hand around my throat.

I've been known to dabble in a little breath play in the

past, but no one has ever been brave enough to take it as far as Nico. It's fucking mind-blowing.

"Stop fighting, Brianna," he warns into his kiss.

"Fuck you," I hiss.

"Yeah, Siren. That's the fucking idea."

His fingers tighten, making lights flash behind my eyes. But it has the desired effect, because combining that with hitching my leg up around his waist so I can feel his arousal and I'm fucking gone.

I fling myself right over the edge into crazy town without even bothering to kick my shoes off.

I stop fighting and give in to the kiss, matching his desperation with every stroke of my tongue.

His hand slides up my thigh, his fingers disappearing beneath the fabric and finding my arse.

"Siren," he growls into our kiss as he finds the bare, soaked flesh between my thighs. "You've been sitting out there with him like this." Anger laces his voice, and it sends a violent shiver of need through me.

"He told me not to wear any," I taunt, throwing fuel on his already out-of-control fire.

"And you listen to everything that motherfucker says, huh? Maybe we should get him in here, let him see what a filthy little whore my siren really is."

Panic slams into me.

I've already been gone longer than normal. If he were to come and find me—

"What's wrong? Worried about what he'll think about the real you? The corrupt teacher who gets off on fucking her student?"

"I don't give a fuck what he thinks of me."

"Can you afford to lose him, though?" he taunts. "Or is

this one of the ones I bought?" he asks, glancing down at my dress.

I'm unaware that I react to his taunts in any way, but when his eyes flash with something I'm too scared to try and acknowledge, I know he's read the answer to his question in mine.

"So what is it you do here... let him buy you designer clothes and dress you up as his little doll before you lie back and open your legs to pay him back?"

Crack.

I don't even realise I've hit him until the pain blooms on my palm, heat from the slap rushing up my arm.

He stares at me, his jaw working overtime and his eyes two black inky pools as dread settles in my stomach.

But that's all smashed a second later when he jerks forward, stealing my lips once more.

"Fucking whore," he groans into our kiss. But I'm too far gone. He's cast his spell and I've fallen like the fucking fool I am.

Pushing my thigh up and fully opening me up for him, he plunges two thick fingers inside me.

I cry into his mouth as he curls them perfectly, hitting that spot almost without trying.

"Nico."

"So fucking wet for me, Siren. Have you been sitting out there dripping for me?"

"Yes," I cry, entirely too honest as he finger-fucks me to oblivion while keeping his tight grip on my throat.

"I know you were. I was watching you. I saw every reaction you had to those videos."

"Oh God," I whimper as I think about the one of him fucking me from behind. "More. Nico. I need more."

"Beg like a good little whore and you might just get it, Siren."

He pulls back a little, watching me close in on my orgasm with hooded, desperate eyes.

"Fuck me, Nico. I need your cock."

"Need or want?"

"Both, whatever. I just—"

His fingers tighten on my throat, finally cutting off my breathing as he fucks me harder.

I fall almost instantly into one of the most intense releases I've ever experienced.

Pleasure sweeps through my body, my back arches, and I throw my head back, screaming out his name as lights flash behind my eyes.

I swear he murmurs, "So fucking beautiful," but I'm too blissed out to recognise anything but the mind-numbing pleasure he's providing me with.

This. This is why I love sex so much.

Nothing else in the world exists right now, and since so much of my life has been full of nothing but bullshit, I crave it. I'm fucking addicted to the high. And no one delivers it quite like Nico Cirillo.

I'm pretty sure I actually black out at some point, because when the world comes back to me, my dress is around my waist and the thickness of Nico's hard cock is pressing against my entrance, teasing me with the promise of more.

"Good," he states when he finds me looking back at him. "I didn't want you to miss this."

Then he slams into me with one powerful thrust, making me lose all sense of everything once more.

He doesn't pause to give me a chance to adjust to his width. Instead, he just pulls out and slams back inside me, making my foot leave the floor, sending me sliding up the wall.

"Fuck, you never look better than when you're impaled on my dick, Siren."

His fingers flex around my throat, although his grip is nowhere as tight as before. And I can't help feeling that it's more of a hold of ownership than anything else.

That thought does weird things to my insides that only bring my second release closer to the surface.

"Yes, yes," I agree because quite honestly, I never feel better than when I'm bouncing on his dick either.

It's dangerous. Too fucking dangerous, which is how I ended up starring in my own high school porn movie.

Fucking hell.

"Nico, w-we can't—" I start, attempting to do the right thing.

Anyone could walk in here right now. Brad could walk in.

"Trust me, Siren. I'm not sharing you with anyone tonight."

"Trust you?" I scream as he thrusts into me again. "You have to be fucking—"

His grip on my throat tightens, cutting off my words.

"It wasn't a question, Siren. It was a demand," he growls in my face before smashing his lips to mine and fucking me deeper.

His fingers dig into my arse as he holds me exactly where he wants me, and I lose myself in the mixture of pain and pleasure that saturates my body until I'm exploding around him.

"Fuck," he barks. "Fuck. FUCK." And then his cock is jerking inside me, filling me with his seed, marking his territory like a wild fucking animal.

Dropping his head to the crook of my neck, he sinks his teeth into the same patch of skin his thumb was just pressing into. The possessive move sends aftershocks shooting around my body.

"Did you want to piss over me too, really drive your point home?" I hiss as the high of what we've just done begins to seep from me.

A deep chuckle spills from his lips as he pulls back and sadly removes himself from my body.

"I don't think that's really necessary. We both know the truth."

"Oh yeah?" I ask as I tug my dress down to cover up my nakedness as the evidence of him being inside me begins to slip down my thighs. "And what's that?"

"You belong to me."

An unamused laugh bubbles up my throat.

"Yeah, sure. You keep telling yourself. You can let yourself out," I say, looking over his shoulder at the exit. "You sure found your way in here okay. My date is probably wondering where I am."

I move toward one of the cubicles, ready to clean myself up, but I pause when he speaks again.

"Don't worry, I arranged for him to have some of his own entertainment while you were otherwise engaged. You saw that woman at the bar, right?"

I swallow thickly.

"Seems like our Brad is going to be spending his night with two whores, only, the one out there takes straight-up cash."

Anger burns through me and an argument about me not being Brad's whore teeters on the tip of my tongue, but I fight it back.

It's not worth it.

He's not worth it.

"Goodbye, Nico."

I swing the door closed behind me and flip the lock—not that I really think it'll keep him out if he wants to get to me.

Hiking my dress up once more, I lower my arse to the toilet and pull a whole heap of loo roll from the dispenser. My frustration with the man who's caused this mess burns through me, and it only gets worse when I don't hear him fucking leave.

I clean up and I'm about to flush when the buzz of my phone cuts through the silence, reminding me of what I was doing before I was rudely interrupted.

Finishing up, I unlock the door once more and step out.

As I predicted, Nico is still here, only now, he's standing with my phone in his hand, his face tight with barely restrained anger.

"Why are you still here?" I ask, ignoring the fact that I'm pretty sure steam is literally about to billow from his ears.

My voice seems to bring him back to himself and he rips his eyes from my phone and glares at me. Although, I'm not even sure he's really seeing me, but instead looking right through me.

Stuffing my phone into his pocket, he reaches for my bag and then my wrist.

"Let's go," he barks, his grip on my arm instantly painful.

"Nico, what the fuck?" I shriek, having little choice but to be dragged along behind him as he marches from the bathroom. "Slow down," I beg, barely able to keep upright with the height of my heels and his speed.

"Shut the fuck up," he growls as the level of danger that emanates from him makes even me a little wary.

I've yet to be physically scared of this brutal soldier. But I have it on good authority that he's capable of things that would horrify me.

As much as his aura might turn me on, I'm not sure I want to witness him in action. I think I like the idea, the fantasy, of it more.

He blows through a fire exit at the back of the building and we immediately get pelted with rain.

It might be almost summer, but the cool, stormy air makes my exposed skin prick with goosebumps and sends a shiver skating down my spine.

Nico drags me through the dark back alley and I stumble and trip over the uneven ground, but he never lets up or attempts to help me.

"Nico, please," I beg when my shoe gets stuck in a crack in the concrete and I almost face-plant in a puddle.

"Keep moving," he demands, his low voice barely audible over the pounding rain.

Eventually, we spill out of the alley a little way down from the entrance to Twenty-Five and right in front of Nico's Mustang.

"You followed us here, didn't you?"

"Get in," he demands, gripping the back of my neck and practically shoving me inside.

My soaked hair sticks to my face and neck, and rivulets of water run down my cleavage.

I glance up just in time to see him swing the door closed, and I can't help but notice that while I'm here looking like a drowned rat, he looks as hot as ever.

Prick.

"ARGH," I scream as he jogs around the bonnet in the hope of expelling some of this pent-up anger that always seems to explode within me whenever Nico is close.

He doesn't say anything as he drops into the driver's seat and brings the engine to life.

A squeal rips from my lips as he spins the wheel and floors it out of the space in front of oncoming cars in both directions.

"Are you fucking insane?" I scream, my heart in my throat as I reach for my seat belt and rush to put it on.

Unsurprisingly, he ignores me as he white-knuckles the wheel and drives through the city like a fucking maniac.

"Put your fucking seat belt on," I hiss when he shows no sign of calming down as we get closer toward his side of the city.

"Where are we going?"

"You don't need to worry about me, Siren. You, however, are about to discover hell."

He glances over at me and my stomach lurches as he takes his eyes off the road.

"NICO."

One look at his speedo tells me that he's going way too fast even if he was paying attention.

I've never been a nervous passenger, but this is testing my fucking limits.

He looks back at the road at the last minute and takes a corner so quickly, I get thrown into the door. Pain explodes in my shoulder and down my arm.

"Will you calm the fuck down?" I scream as he does a seriously dodgy overtake, barely missing the oncoming car.

Rain lashes against the windscreen. The wipers are unable to keep up and our vision is getting worse and worse.

"Nico, please. You're going to kill us."

"Then maybe it's time to start confessing all your sins, Siren," he taunts.

His face is still pulled tight with anger, a vein in his temple looking dangerously close to popping, and his chest heaves as he throws us back into the main stream of traffic before we collide with a bus.

"I don't know what you're talking about," I shriek. "If I did, I would tell you to stop this insanity."

A dark and dangerous chuckle rips from his lips.

"I know, Siren. I know what you're hiding."

His words blur into one as the lights we were slowing for turn green and he floors the accelerator once more, taking off before all the other cars.

Thankfully, the traffic thins out as we close in on their building, and I just start to relax when I spot a guy up ahead swaying about on the pavement.

"Nico, that guy," I scream, watching as he stumbles out onto the road.

"Fuck. FUCK," Nico bellows, yanking the wheel to the right to avoid him.

One second, he has everything under control and I breathe a sigh of relief that we're not about to kill the guy, but then we hit a puddle and we aquaplane across the road.

Nico frantically turns the wheel to try to get control back as his foot presses the brake as hard as he can.

But it's no good. It's over, and I send up a silent prayer that whatever happens next isn't going to be too painful.

Suddenly, one of the wheels finds some traction and the car begins spinning out of control as my screams fill the space. Not that I hear them—blood is rushing past my ears too fast to register anything but the sheer terror of what's about to happen.

The moment we collide with something, a building I guess, the sound of crumpling metal turns my blood to ice.

My entire body is slammed to the side, crushed against the door, as the space around me seems to close in.

My head collides with the window, and I have to fight to stay conscious as the darkness creeps in.

"Nico," I cry, desperately trying to look to my right, but my body won't comply with my head. "Nico, please. Tell me you're okay?"

Nothing.

Pure unfiltered fear seeps through me.

"Nico?" I sob, finally finding the strength to look over. I fucking wish I hadn't, though, because he's slumped forward over the wheel with blood dripping from somewhere. "NICO," I scream, "NICO, WAKE UP," I demand, focusing on his back, desperate to see some movement to tell me that he's—

My stomach turns over and bile rushes up my throat.

"No, no. Please, Nico."

My eyes drop as my adrenaline begins to slip, allowing the pain to descend as they lock on the corner of my phone sticking out of his pocket.

I need to get it. But he's so far away, and as every second passes, the pain throughout my body is increasing to the point it's becoming unbearable.

I have no idea what I've hurt, if I'm bleeding or anything. All I know is that I need to get that phone. I need to call someone.

Summoning some strength from deep down, I manage to lift my arm from my lap and reach over.

My fingers just brush the glass of my screen, but I can't quite reach it.

"Fuck. Nico, come on. Be useful for once in your fucking life," I beg as I throw my weight to my right, pain screaming from my back and up my neck, but that isn't anything compared to the pounding in my skull. That is like nothing I've ever experienced before. Black spots swim in my vision, but I can't let them win. I can't. Not until I have that phone.

Finally, I manage to grasp it and wiggle it free from Nico's pocket.

Bringing it in front of me, the brightness of the screen makes me wince and I find two messages staring back up at me.

> Calli: Had another scan. Everything is perfect with little blob.

And then there's a photo of the ultrasound.

Right there. On. My. Lock. Screen.

Images from the past twenty minutes flicker through my head like a movie.

"I know, Siren. I know what you're hiding."

The darkness comes faster as reality hits me.

Maybe he was trying to kill me.

My thumb hits my screen, in my head, I'm ringing Calli to warn her, but in reality, I have no idea what I'm really achieving as I sink into the darkness where pain and panic don't exist.

"Calli," I cry. "He knows. Nico knows. And it's all my fault."

And then, everything finally turns black.

**Nico and Brianna's story continues in
Corrupt Princess**

ABOUT THE AUTHOR

Tracy Lorraine is a *USA Today* and *Wall Street Journal* bestselling new adult and contemporary romance author. Tracy has recently turned thirty and lives in a cute Cotswold village in England with her husband, baby girl and lovable but slightly crazy dog. Having always been a bookaholic with her head stuck in her Kindle, Tracy decided to try her hand at a story idea she dreamt up and hasn't looked back since.

Be the first to find out about new releases and offers. Sign up to my newsletter here.

If you want to know what I'm up to and see teasers and snippets of what I'm working on, then you need to be in my Facebook group. Join Tracy's Angels here.

Keep up to date with Tracy's books at
www.tracylorraine.com

Trick You #2

Defy You #3

Play You #4

Inked (A Rebel Ink/Driven Crossover)

Rosewood High Series

Thorn #1

Paine #2

Savage #3

Fierce #4

Hunter #5

Faze (#6 Prequel)

Fury #6

Legend #7

Maddison Kings University Series

TMYM: Prequel

TRYS #1

TDYW #2

TBYS #3

TVYC #4

TDYD #5

TDYR #6

TRYD #7

Knight's Ridge Empire Series

Wicked Summer Knight: Prequel (Stella & Seb)

Wicked Knight #1 (Stella & Seb)

Wicked Princess #2 (Stella & Seb)

Wicked Empire #3 (Stella & Seb)

Deviant Knight #4 (Emmie & Theo)

Deviant Princess #5 (Emmie & Theo

Deviant Reign #6 (Emmie & Theo)

One Reckless Knight (Jodie & Toby)

Reckless Knight #7 (Jodie & Toby)

Reckless Princess #8 (Jodie & Toby)

Reckless Dynasty #9 (Jodie & Toby)

Dark Halloween Knight (Calli & Batman)

Dark Knight #10 (Calli & Batman)

Dark Princess #11 (Calli & Batman)

Dark Legacy #12 (Calli & Batman)

Corrupt Valentine Knight (Nico & Siren)

Ruined Series

Ruined Plans #1

Ruined by Lies #2

Ruined Promises #3

Never Forget Series

Never Forget Him #1

Never Forget Us #2

Chapter One

Letty

I sit on my bed, staring down at the fabric in my hands.

This wasn't how it was supposed to happen.

This wasn't part of my plan.

I let out a sigh, squeezing my eyes tight, willing the tears away.

I've cried enough. I thought I'd have run out by now.

A commotion on the other side of the door has me looking up in a panic, but just like yesterday, no one comes knocking.

I think I proved that I don't want to hang with my new roommates the first time someone knocked and asked if I wanted to go for breakfast with them.

I don't.

I don't even want to be here.

I just want to hide.

And that thought makes it all a million times worse.

I'm not a hider. I'm a fighter. I'm a fucking Hunter.

But this is what I've been reduced to.

This pathetic, weak mess.

And all because of *him*.

He shouldn't have this power over me. But even now, he does.

The dorm falls silent once again, and I pray that they've all headed off for their first class of the semester so I can slip out unnoticed.

I know it's ridiculous. I know I should just go out there with my head held high and dig up the confidence I know I do possess.

But I can't.

I figure that I'll just get through today—my first day—and everything will be alright.

I can somewhat pick up where I left off, almost as if the last eighteen months never happened.

Wishful thinking.

I glance down at the hoodie in my hands once more.

Mom bought them for Zayn, my younger brother, and me.

The navy fabric is soft between my fingers, but the text staring back at me doesn't feel right.

Maddison Kings University.

A knot twists my stomach and I swear my whole body sags with my new reality.

I was at my dream school. I beat the odds and I got into Columbia. And everything was good. No, everything was fucking fantastic.

Until it wasn't.

Now here I am. Sitting in a dorm at what was always my backup plan school having to start over.

Throwing the hoodie onto my bed, I angrily push to my feet.

I'm fed up with myself.

I should be better than this, stronger than this.

But I'm just... I'm broken.

And as much as I want to see the positives in this situation. I'm struggling.

Shoving my feet into my Vans, I swing my purse over my shoulder and scoop up the couple of books on my desk for the two classes I have today.

My heart drops when I step out into the communal kitchen and find a slim blonde-haired girl hunched over a mug and a textbook.

The scent of coffee fills my nose and my mouth waters.

My shoes squeak against the floor and she immediately looks up.

"Sorry, I didn't mean to disrupt you."

"Are you kidding?" she says excitedly, her southern accent making a smile twitch at my lips.

Her smile lights up her pretty face and for some reason, something settles inside me.

I knew hiding was wrong. It's just been my coping method for... quite a while.

"We wondered when our new roommate was going to show her face. The guys have been having bets on you being an alien or something."

A laugh falls from my lips. "No, no alien. Just..." I sigh, not really knowing what to say.

"You transferred in, right? From Columbia?"

"Ugh... yeah. How'd you know—"

"Girl, I know everything." She winks at me, but it

doesn't make me feel any better. "West and Brax are on the team, they spent the summer with your brother."

A rush of air passes my lips in relief. Although I'm not overly thrilled that my brother has been gossiping about me.

"So, what classes do you have today?" she asks when I stand there gaping at her.

"Umm... American lit and psychology."

"I've got psych later too. Professor Collins?"

"Uh..." I drag my schedule from my purse and stare down at it. "Y-yes."

"Awesome. We can sit together."

"S-sure," I stutter, sounding unsure, but the smile I give her is totally genuine. "I'm Letty, by the way." Although I'm pretty sure she already knows that.

"Ella."

"Okay, I'll... uh... see you later."

"Sure. Have a great morning."

She smiles at me and I wonder why I was so scared to come out and meet my new roommates.

I'd wanted Mom to organize an apartment for me so that I could be alone, but—probably wisely—she refused. She knew that I'd use it to hide in and the point of me restarting college is to try to put everything behind me and start fresh.

After swiping an apple from the bowl in the middle of the table, I hug my books tighter to my chest and head out, ready to embark on my new life.

The morning sun burns my eyes and the scent of freshly cut grass fills my nose as I step out of our building. The summer heat hits my skin, and it makes everything feel that little bit better.

So what if I'm starting over. I managed to transfer the

credits I earned from Columbia, and MKU is a good school. I'll still get a good degree and be able to make something of my life.

Things could be worse.

It could be this time last year...

I shake the thought from my head and force my feet to keep moving.

I pass students meeting up with their friends for the start of the new semester as they excitedly tell them all about their summers and the incredible things they did, or they compare schedules.

My lungs grow tight as I drag in the air I need. I think of the friends I left behind in Columbia. We didn't have all that much time together, but we'd bonded before my life imploded on me.

Glancing around, I find myself searching for familiar faces. I know there are plenty of people here who know me. A couple of my closest friends came here after high school.

Mom tried to convince me to reach out over the summer, but my anxiety kept me from doing so. I don't want anyone to look at me like I'm a failure. That I got into one of the best schools in the country, fucked it up and ended up crawling back to Rosewood. I'm not sure what's worse, them assuming I couldn't cope or the truth.

Focusing on where I'm going, I put my head down and ignore the excited chatter around me as I head for the coffee shop, desperately in need of my daily fix before I even consider walking into a lecture.

I find the Westerfield Building where my first class of the day is and thank the girl who holds the heavy door open for me before following her toward the elevator.

"Holy fucking shit," a voice booms as I turn the corner, following the signs to the room on my schedule.

Before I know what's happening, my coffee is falling from my hand and my feet are leaving the floor.

"What the—" The second I get a look at the guy standing behind the one who has me in his arms, I know exactly who I've just walked into.

Forgetting about the coffee that's now a puddle on the floor, I release my books and wrap my arms around my old friend.

His familiar woodsy scent flows through me, and suddenly, I feel like me again. Like the past two years haven't existed.

"What the hell are you doing here?" Luca asks, a huge smile on his face when he pulls back and studies me.

His brows draw together when he runs his eyes down my body, and I know why. I've been working on it over the summer, but I know I'm still way skinnier than I ever have been in my life.

"I transferred," I admit, forcing the words out past the lump in my throat.

His smile widens more before he pulls me into his body again.

"It's so good to see you."

I relax into his hold, squeezing him tight, absorbing his strength. And that's one thing that Luca Dunn has in spades. He's a rock, always has been and I didn't realize how much I needed that right now.

Mom was right. I should have reached out.

"You too," I whisper honestly, trying to keep the tears at bay that are threatening just from seeing him—them.

"Hey, it's good to see you," Leon says, slightly more subdued than his twin brother as he hands me my discarded books.

"Thank you."

I look between the two of them, noticing all the things that have changed since I last saw them in person. I keep up with them on Instagram and TikTok, sure, but nothing is quite like standing before the two of them.

Both of them are bigger than I ever remember, showing just how hard their coach is working them now they're both first string for the Panthers. And if it's possible, they're both hotter than they were in high school, which is really saying something because they'd turn even the most confident of girls into quivering wrecks with one look back then. I can only imagine the kind of rep they have around here.

The sound of a door opening behind us and the shuffling of feet cuts off our little reunion.

"You in Professor Whitman's American lit class?" Luca asks, his eyes dropping from mine to the book in my hands.

"Yeah. Are you?"

"We are. Walk you to class?" A smirk appears on his lips that I remember all too well. A flutter of the butterflies he used to give me threaten to take flight as he watches me intently.

Luca was one of my best friends in high school, and I spent almost all our time together with the biggest crush on him. It seems that maybe the teenage girl inside me still thinks that he could be it for me.

"I'd love you to."

"Come on then, Princess," Leon says and my entire body jolts at hearing that pet name for me. He's never called me that before and I really hope he's not about to start now.

Clearly not noticing my reaction, he once again takes my books from me and threads his arm through mine as the pair of them lead me into the lecture hall.

I glance at both of them, a smile pulling at my lips and hope building inside me.

Maybe this was where I was meant to be this whole time.

Maybe Columbia and I were never meant to be.

More than a few heads turn our way as we climb the stairs to find some free seats. Mostly it's the females in the huge space and I can't help but inwardly laugh at their reaction.

I get it.

The Dunn twins are two of the Kings around here and I'm currently sandwiched between them. It's a place that nearly every female in this college, hell, this state, would kill to be in.

"Dude, shift the fuck over," Luca barks at another guy when he pulls to a stop a few rows from the back.

The guy who's got dark hair and even darker eyes immediately picks up his bag, books, and pen and moves over a space.

"This is Colt," Luca explains, nodding to the guy who's studying me with interest.

"Hey," I squeak, feeling a little intimidated.

"Hey." His low, deep voice licks over me. "Ow, what the fuck, man?" he barks, rubbing at the back of his head where Luca just slapped him.

"Letty's off-limits. Get your fucking eyes off her."

"Dude, I was just saying hi."

"Yeah, and we all know what that usually leads to," Leon growls behind me.

The three of us take our seats and just about manage to pull our books out before our professor begins explaining the syllabus for the semester.

"Sorry about the coffee," Luca whispers after a few minutes. "Here." He places a bottle of water on my desk. "I know it's not exactly a replacement, but it's the best I can do."

The reminder of the mess I left out in the hallway hits me.

"I should go and—"

"Chill," he says, placing his hand on my thigh. His touch instantly relaxes me as much as it sends a shock through my body. "I'll get you a replacement after class. Might even treat you to a cupcake."

I smile up at him, swooning at the fact he remembers my favorite treat.

Why did I ever think coming here was a bad idea?

Chapter Two
Letty

My hand aches by the time Professor Whitman finishes talking. It feels like a lifetime ago that I spent this long taking notes.

"You okay?" Luca asks me with a laugh as I stretch out my fingers.

"Yeah, it's been a while."

"I'm sure these boys can assist you with that, beautiful," bursts from Colt's lips, earning him another slap to the head.

"Ignore him. He's been hit in the head with a ball one too many times," Leon says from beside me but I'm too enthralled with the way Luca is looking at me right now to reply.

Our friendship wasn't a conventional one back in high school. He was the star quarterback, and I wasn't a cheerleader or ever really that sporty. But we were paired up as lab partners during my first week at Rosewood High and we kinda never separated.

I watched as he took the team to new heights, as he met with college scouts, I even went to a few places with him so he didn't have to go alone.

He was the one who allowed me to cry on his shoulder as I struggled to come to terms with the loss of another who left a huge hole in my heart and he never, not once, overstepped the mark while I clung to him and soaked up his support.

I was also there while he hooked up with every member of the cheer squad along with any other girl who looked at him just so. Each one stung a little more than the last as my poor teenage heart was getting battered left, right, and center.

With each day, week, month that passed, I craved him more but he never, not once, looked at me that way.

I was even his prom date, yet he ended up spending the night with someone else.

It hurt, of course it did. But it wasn't his fault and I refuse to hold it against him.

Maybe I should have told him. Been honest with him about my feelings and what I wanted. But I was so terrified I'd lose my best friend that I never confessed, and I took that secret all the way to Columbia with me.

As I stare at him now, those familiar butterflies still set flight in my belly, but they're not as strong as I remember. I'm not sure if that's because my feelings for him have lessened over time, or if I'm just so numb and broken right now that I don't feel anything but pain.

It really could go either way.

I smile at him, so grateful to have run into him this morning.

He always knew when I needed him and even without knowing of my presence here, there he was like some guardian fucking angel.

If guardian angels had sexy dark bed hair, mesmerizing green eyes and a body built for sin then yeah, that's what he is.

I laugh to myself, yeah, maybe that irritating crush has gone nowhere.

"What have you got next?" Leon asks, dragging my attention away from his twin.

Leon has always been the quieter, broodier one of the duo. He's as devastatingly handsome and as popular with the female population but he doesn't wear his heart on his sleeve like Luca. Leon takes a little time to warm to people, to let them in. It was hard work getting there, but I soon realized that once he dropped his walls a little for me, it was hella worth it.

He's more serious, more contemplative, he's deeper. I always suspected that there was a reason they were so different. I know twins don't have to be the same and like the same things, but there was always something niggling at me that there was a very good reason that Leon closed himself down. From listening to their mom talk over the years, they were so identical in their mannerisms, likes, and dislikes when they were growing up, that it seems hard to believe they became so different.

"Psychology but not for an hour. I'm—"

"I'm taking her for coffee," Luca butts in. A flicker of anger passes through Leon's eyes but it's gone so fast that I begin to wonder if I imagined it.

"I could use another coffee before econ," Leon chips in.

"Great. Let's go," Luca forces out through clenched teeth.

He wanted me alone. Interesting.

The reason I never told him about my mega crush is the fact he friend-zoned me in our first few weeks of friendship by telling me how refreshing it was to have a girl wanting to be his friend and not using it as a ploy to get more.

We were only sophomores at the time but even then, Luca was up to all sorts and the girls around us were all more than willing to bend to his needs.

From that moment on, I couldn't tell him how I really felt. It was bad enough I even felt it when he thought our friendship was just that.

I smile at both of them, hoping to shatter the sudden tension between the twins.

"Be careful with these two," Colt announces from behind us as we make our way out of the lecture hall with all the others. "The stories I've heard."

"Colt," Luca warns, turning to face him and walking backward for a few steps.

"Don't worry," I shoot over my shoulder. "I know how to handle the Dunn twins." I wink at him as he howls with laughter.

"You two are in so much trouble," he muses as he turns left out of the room and we go right.

Leon takes my books from me once more and Luca threads his fingers through mine. I still for a beat. While the move isn't unusual, Luca has always been very affectionate. It only takes a second for his warmth to race up my arm and to settle the last bit of unease that's still knotting my stomach.

"Two Americanos and a skinny vanilla latte with an extra shot. Three cupcakes with the sprinkles on top."

I swoon at the fact Luca remembers my order. "How'd you—"

He turns to me, his wide smile and the sparkle in his eyes making my words trail off. The familiarity of his face, the feeling of comfort and safety he brings me causes a lump to form in my throat.

"I didn't forget anything about my best girl." He throws his arm around my shoulder and pulls me close.

Burying my nose in his hard chest, I breathe him in. His woodsy scent mixes with his laundry detergent and it settles me in a way I didn't know I needed.

Leon's stare burns into my back as I snuggle with his brother and I force myself to pull away so he doesn't feel like the third wheel.

"Dunn," the server calls, and Leon rushes ahead to grab our order while Luca leads me to a booth at the back of the coffee shop.

As we walk past each table, I become more and more aware of the attention on the twins. I know their reps, they've had their football god status since before I moved to Rosewood and met them in high school, but I had forgotten just how hero-worshiped they were, and this right now is off the charts.

Girls openly stare, their eyes shamelessly dropping down the guys' bodies as they mentally strip them naked. Guys jealousy shines through their expressions, especially those who are here with their girlfriends who are now paying them zero attention. Then there are the girls whose attention is firmly on me. I can almost read their thoughts—hell, I heard enough of them back in high school.

What do they see in her?

She's not even that pretty.

They're too good for her.

The only difference here from high school is that no one knows I'm just trailer park trash seeing as I moved from the hellhole that is Harrow Creek before meeting the boys.

Tipping my chin up, I straighten my spine and plaster on as much confidence as I can find.

They can all think what they like about me, they can come up with whatever bitchy comments they want. It's no skin off my back.

"Good to see you've lost your appeal," I mutter, dropping into the bench opposite both of them and wrapping my hands around my warm mug when Leon passes it over.

"We walk around practically unnoticed," Luca deadpans.

"You thought high school was bad," Leon mutters, he was always the one who hated the attention whereas Luca used it to his advantage to get whatever he wanted. "It was nothing."

"So I see. So, how's things? Catch me up on everything," I say, needing to dive into their celebrity status lifestyles rather than thinking about my train wreck of a life.

"Really?" Luca asks, raising a brow and causing my stomach to drop into my feet. "I think the bigger question is how come you're here and why we had no idea about it?"

Releasing my mug, I wrap my arms around myself and drop my eyes to the table.

"T-things just didn't work out at Columbia," I mutter, really not wanting to talk about it.

"The last time we talked, you said it was everything you expected it to be and more. What happened?"

Kane fucking Legend happened.

I shake that thought from my head like I do every time he pops up.

He's had his time ruining my life. It's over.

"I just..." I sigh. "I lost my way a bit, ended up dropping out and finally had to fess up and come clean to Mom."

Leon laughs sadly. "I bet that went down well."

The Dunn twins are well aware of what it's like to live with a pushy parent. One of the things that bonded the three of us over the years.

"Like a lead balloon. Even worse because I dropped out months before I finally showed my face."

"Why hide?" Leon's brows draw together as Luca stares at me with concern darkening his eyes.

"I had some health issues. It's nothing."

"Shit, are you okay?"

Fucking hell, Letty. Stop making this worse for yourself.

"Yeah, yeah. Everything is good. Honestly. I'm here and I'm ready to start over and make the best of it."

They both smile at me, and I reach for my coffee once more, bringing the mug to my lips and taking a sip.

"Enough about me, tell me all about the lives of two of the hottest Kings of Maddison."

"O kay... how'd you do that?" Ella whispers after both Luca and Leon walk me to my psych class after our coffee break.

"Do what?" I ask, following her into the room and finding ourselves seats about halfway back.

"It's your first day and the Dunn twins just walked you to class. You got a diamond-encrusted vag or something?"

I snort a laugh as a few others pause on their way to their seats at her words.

"Shush," I chastise.

"Girl, if it's true, you know all these guys need to know about it."

I pull out my books and a couple of pens as Professor Collins sets up at the front before turning to her.

"No, I don't have diamonds anywhere but my necklace. I've been friends with them for years."

"Girl, I knew there was a reason we should be friends." She winks at me. "I've been trying to get West and Brax to hook me up but they're useless."

"You want to be friends so I can set you up with one of the Dunns?"

"Or both." She shrugs, her face deadly serious before she leans in. "I've heard that they tag team sometimes. Can you imagine? Both of their undivided attention." She fans herself as she obviously pictures herself in the middle of a Dunn sandwich. "Oh and, I think you're pretty cool too."

"Of course you do." I laugh.

It's weird, I might have only met her very briefly this morning but that was enough.

"We're all going out for dinner tonight to welcome you to the dorm. The others are dying to meet you." She smiles at me, proving that there's no bitterness behind her words.

"I'm sorry for ignoring you all."

"Girl, don't sweat it. We got ya back, don't worry."

"Thank you," I mouth as the professor demands everyone's attention to begin the class.

The time flies as I scribble my notes down as fast as I can, my hand aching all over again and before I know it, he's finished explaining our first assignment and bringing his class to a close.

"Jesus, this semester is going to be hard," Ella muses as we both pack up.

"At least we've got each other."

"I like the way you think. You done for the day?"

"Yep, I'm gonna head to the store, grab some supplies then get started on this assignment, I think."

"I've got a couple of hours. You want company?"

After dumping our stuff in our rooms, Ella takes me to her favorite store, and I stock up on everything I'm going to need before we head back so she can go to class.

I make myself some lunch before being brave and setting up my laptop at the kitchen table to get started on my assignments. My time for hiding is over, it's time to get back to life and once again become a fully immersed college student.

"Holy shit, she is alive. I thought Zayn was lying about his beautiful older sister," a deep rumbling voice says, dragging me from my research a few hours later.

I spin and look at the two guys who have joined me.

"Zayn would never have called me beautiful," I say as a greeting.

"That's true. I think his actual words were: messy, pain in the ass, and my personal favorite, I'm glad I don't have to live with her again," he says, mimicking my brother's voice.

"Now that is more like it. Hey, I'm Letty. Sorry about—"

"You're all good. We're just glad you emerged. I'm West, this ugly motherfucker is Braxton—"

"Brax, please," he begs. "Only my mother calls me by my full name and you are way too hot to be her."

My cheeks heat as he runs his eyes over my curves.

"T-thanks, I think."

"Ignore him. He hasn't gotten laid for weeeeks."

"Okay, do we really need to go there right now?"

"Always, bro. Our girl here needs to know you get pissy when you don't get the pussy."

I laugh at their easy banter, closing down my laptop and

resting forward on my elbows as they move toward the fridge.

"Ella says we're going out," Brax says, pulling out two bottles of water and throwing one to West.

"Apparently so."

"She'll be here in a bit. Violet and Micah too. They were all in the same class."

"So," West says, sliding into the chair next to me. "What do we need to know that your brother hasn't already told us about you?"

My heart races at all the things that not even my brother would share about my life before I drag my thoughts away from my past.

"Uhhh..."

"How about the Dunns love her," Ella announces as she appears in the doorway flanked by two others. Violet and Micah, I assume.

"Um... how didn't we know this?" Brax asks.

"Because you're not cool enough to spend any time with them, asshole," Violet barks, walking around Ella. "Ignore these assholes, they think they're something special because they're on the team but what they don't tell you is that they have no chance of making first string or talking to the likes of the Dunns."

"Vi, girl. That stings," West says, holding his hand over his heart.

"Yeah, get over it. Truth hurts." She smiles up at him as he pulls her into his chest and kisses the top of her head.

"Whatever, Titch."

"Right, well. Are we ready to go? I need tacos like... yesterday."

"Yes. Let's go."

"You've never had tacos like these, Letty. You are in for a world of pleasure," Brax says excitedly.

"More than she would be if she were in your bed, that's for sure," West deadpans.

"Lies and we all know it."

"Whatever." Violet pushes him toward the door.

"Hey, I'm Micah," the third guy says when I catch up to him.

"Hey, Letty."

"You need a sensible conversation, I'm your boy."

"Good to know."

Micah and I trail behind the others and with each step I take, my smile gets wider.

Things really are going to be okay.

DOWNLOAD NOW TO KEEP READING

www.ingramcontent.com/pod-product-compliance
Lightning Source LLC
Chambersburg PA
CBHW050755190726
48285CB00005B/1666